ORPHAN'S SONG

ORPHAN'S SONG

THE SONGKEEPER CHRONICLES — BOOK ONE

GILLIAN BRONTE ADAMS

an imprint of
GILEAD PUBLISHING

Orphan's Song by Gillian Bronte Adams
Published by Enclave, an imprint of Gilead Publishing, Wheaton, IL 60187
www.enclavepublishing.com

ISBN: 978-1-68370-028-9 (print)
ISBN: 978-1-68370-029-6 (eBook)

The Songkeeper Chronicles Book 1: *Orphan's Song*
© 2014 by Gillian Bronte Adams

Cover illustration and design by Darko Tomic

Printed in the United States of America

To the One who puts a new Song in my mouth

PROLOGUE

They were coming.

Gundhrold peered into the moonless dark, feathered wings ruffling in the breeze. Distant howls sounded to the beat of thundering hooves and clinking armor. Distant, but rapidly approaching.

Foul murderers. His claws dug into the bark of the limb, and dark sap bubbled out of the scratches. A fresh scent hovered around him, strange amidst the eerie screams borne upon the wind, and he studied the russet sap staining his claws like blood.

The limb groaned as he shifted his weight and clacked his beak impatiently, straining to pierce the heaviness of the woods with his gaze. Where was she?

A twig snapped in the depths of the forest. A branch rustled. He tensed, raising his wings for flight. Soft footsteps on damp leaves, a shuddering breath, then a whispered voice spoke from the shadows. "Gundhrold? Are you here?"

At last.

Dropping from the tree, Gundhrold spread his wings and glided to the forest floor. He landed without a noise, catlike on all four paws, before a woman hooded and cloaked. "Lady Auna, you are late."

The woman started, then breathed a sigh of relief. "Oh, it's you."

"Did you expect another, Songkeeper?"

"Do not call me that. Not when they are so close." She pushed

1

her hood back with a trembling hand, revealing eyes that sparked with urgency beneath a flood of gray hair. "There is no time. They have come for me."

A wild, undulating cry tore through the woods, nearer than before.

"Then I must see you safe from here." He stood and stretched, wincing at the tremor that ran from his shoulders to his wing tips. "It has been long since I have carried a grown human in sustained flight. Nonetheless, we will manage. There is a clearing west of here where we can be off—the upper canopy is too dense here to permit flight."

Auna shook her head. "No, friend, I am too old to flee. That is not why I summoned you."

"My lady?"

"Memory must not perish tonight, Gundhrold." She shrugged aside her dark gray cloak, revealing a bundle cradled in her arms. "We must not fail."

Gundhrold peered at the bundle. "Is this . . ."

"It is," Auna said, relinquishing the bundle to him. "This is your task, entrusted to your care and protection."

The bundle seemed to grow heavier as the weight of his responsibility settled upon him. "I will not fail, Songkeeper."

A soft, sad smile spread across Auna's face, smoothing the wrinkles crisscrossing her forehead. "The land of Leira owes a debt to you Protectors that she can never repay. And now, friend, you must—" She stiffened suddenly, listening.

An otherworldly howl shook the ground, and the harsh scream of a raven split the night air. Flickering orange lights appeared in the forest, bobbing toward them, cracking twigs and splintering branches keeping time with the quickening tramp of feet and hooves. Auna spun around, gripping the edges of her cloak to her neck so tightly that her knuckles turned white.

"They have come." Gundhrold clasped the bundle to his chest. Loosing his wings, he coiled to spring into the air, but his gaze strayed to Auna and he hesitated.

"Why do you delay?" she cried. "Go, before it is too late!" Clutching her cloak, she darted off through the trees, a glimmer of gray in the night.

Gundhrold launched from the ground and landed three-legged on the branch he had occupied minutes before. His fourth paw hugged the bundle, softening the jolt of his landing. Below, dozens of hounds raced up and skidded to a stop, snuffling and tearing at the loam where he and Auna had been standing. A howl of triumph burst from their throats, and they dashed away into the woods, following the path Auna had taken.

All but one. A massive beast lunged at the base of his tree, claws scrabbling at the bark, howl echoing through the woods. Even from a distance, he could smell the hound's rancid breath—like a battlefield, it reeked of death.

Though the hound could not reach him in the tree, it would be followed by the Khelari—soldiers with weapons, with axes, bows, and fire.

He scrambled along the branch, running awkwardly on three legs. The hound followed, its cries joined by the shouts of men drawn to the pursuit. At the end of the branch, Gundhrold dove, glided to the next, and ran again and again, ever westward toward the clearing and flight. He missed the craggy mountains and desert plains of his youth, where there were no trees to obscure flight and no Khelari to necessitate it.

The clearing came into sight just ahead, and he raced toward it, wings unfurled, heedless of the grasping branches on either side. A bough snagged his right wing, and he tore it free—releasing a cloud of feathers—and leapt into the air.

For a moment he hung suspended over the clearing. The hound burst from the trees below with a mass of armed men hard upon its heels, shouting and brandishing weapons. Torches blazed in their hands, lighting the clearing with an orange glow . . .

Wings beating, Gundhrold soared up out of the clearing and banked to the left. Something thrummed past his ear and vanished into the starless sky. An arrow. Another twang sounded and pain exploded in his right shoulder. His wing fell limp. A black feathered shaft stuck in his side, the steel point grating excruciatingly against bone. Gundhrold grasped vainly at the air and then dropped like a stone into the clearing.

He hit the ground with a dizzying thud, and immediately teeth sank into his neck. He lashed out with his claws and the hound yelped. It retreated across the clearing and stood staring at him, head hanging, bloody slobber dripping from its tongue.

Gundhrold flexed his wings and growled at the pain. Still clutching the bundle to his chest, he inched to his feet and slowly turned around. Black figures surrounded him, weapons aimed at his heart. Above, ravens swarmed to the tree tops, feathers glinting midnight blue in the torchlight, croaking calls rasping from their throats. And in the woods, chanting throbbed like the pulse of the ocean, drawing nearer like the incoming tide.

A mounted man broke through the circle of Khelari and dismounted, dropping his reins on the ground. Gundhrold's gaze darted to the slim bow in the man's hands and the black feathered arrow already on the string. His claws dug into the loam. Wounded as he was, he could not hope to dodge an arrow on the ground.

But the archer did not shoot. He lowered the bow and let the arrow slip from the string, then waved a dismissive hand at the Khelari. "We will let the Takhran deal with him."

The chanting grew louder and deeper, blending with the baying of the hounds. A dozen men marched out of the woods, followed by a pack of the beasts. They halted in front of the archer and shoved a gray-clad figure out of their midst. The figure stumbled to its knees in the middle of the clearing, head bowed, hands bound behind its back.

"Auna," Gundhrold whispered.

"Ah, the Songkeeper." The archer strode forward and towered over her, black armor melting into the darkness. His eyes, darker still, glared from beneath a sharp brow set above a curved nose. The ringing of a drawn blade filled the clearing and a sword flashed dully in the man's hand as he raised it to Auna's neck. "We searched long for you, Songkeeper, after slaying your sons. I had almost given up hope of finding you, but now at long last, here you are. You have failed."

Auna's shoulders sagged and her face grayed with weariness. She looked suddenly like a frail old woman. "I may have failed," she said, "but you have not won yet. Emhran will not be forgotten."

The archer lashed out with a mailed fist, and Auna fell back beneath the force of his blow.

With a shriek, Gundhrold leapt forward, only to feel the sharp prick of the sword point at his throat.

"Not dead yet, eh griffin?" The man's snarl broadened into an amused sneer. "We have been watching for you. Do you think the Takhran does not know the role you and your kind have played these many years? Protectors?" His eyes flashed. "Traitors all." His gaze dropped to the bundle in Gundhrold's forearm and his expression hardened. "What have you there?"

Gundhrold clutched the bundle and clamped his beak shut as he shuffled backwards.

"You will not answer? Then I shall have to see for myself." The sword point lowered and the archer stooped over the bundle, lifting his hand to draw back the cloth.

An opening.

Jaws agape, Gundhrold reared back his head and struck. The cold steel of the metal gauntlet filled his beak and he clamped down on the archer's wrist. A sharp crack, an agonized scream, and the man fell to the ground, clutching the bleeding stump of his right wrist to his chest. Gundhrold spat out the iron-clad hand and spun to face the rest of the Khelari.

The hounds bayed as they rushed in to attack. Gundhrold leapt to meet them, ignoring the pain in his side. He pounced on the first hound and dispatched it with flashing claws. The second fell victim to his beak. On the third pounce, he caught a soldier, and the man fell beneath him, vainly slashing with a dagger, screaming in terror as his paw descended. Arrows whistled on all sides, and the Khelari yelled as they hemmed him in.

Gundhrold bared his teeth. This was death. This was the end. And he would meet it with all the fury in his soul and wake in Emhran's land to greet the dawn.

A faint cry like the first note of a song stilled the fury beating in his breast. He glanced down at the bundle—torn open in the midst of the fight—and halted, transfixed by a pair of blue eyes. An infant stared up him, head crowned with a thatch of soft dark hair, tiny fingers curled into a fist against white cheeks.

A woman's scream tore his attention back to the fight. Auna lay on the ground at his feet, an arrow protruding from her side. Her mouth opened and she struggled to speak.

"Protector . . ."

The word recalled him to his duty. Barreling over two Khelari who stood in his path, he launched into the air. Agonizing pain tore through his shoulder, but his wing held. He labored to fly up, up, through the clearing and then out over the trees where the thick canopy would grant some protection.

Wind and weapons whistled past his head. An arrow bit deep into his side, and a roar burst from his throat.

Cawing raucously, the ravens in the treetops took flight, diving toward his head to peck at his eyes. He lashed out with his left forepaw, swiping a cluster of black birds out of the sky. Then wheeling to the right, he soared past the clearing and sped toward the south, leaving the ravens behind.

For a brief instant, he caught a glimpse of the Songkeeper below, struggling to stand as the raging horde closed in around her, then she disappeared from sight in the broiling throng. "Emhran, guard her," he croaked.

He had no strength left but for the next stroke and the one after that. But though he flew a straight course, the sounds of pursuit grew gradually fainter.

Darkness fluttered at the edge of his vision. Each beat of his wings drew a ragged gasp from his lungs. He faltered and dropped nearly twenty feet before catching himself and struggling to maintain momentum.

A sharp crack sounded; Gundhrold's wing failed. A shudder seized his body, and he hugged the bundle as he plummeted through the forest. Branches rushed at his head, thwacking and tossing him this way and that. A shower of leaves drifted down around him as a rocky plateau appeared below.

Gundhrold screeched, flashing his left wing wildly, desperately trying to pull back, but to no avail. He crashed, and a dizzying blast of lights burst across his vision. His talons flew open with the impact, and the bundle slipped from his grasp and fell over the edge of the plateau.

Unable to move, Gundhrold watched the bundle drift down. A soft cry echoed below. Then a roar like the rush of a mighty river filled his ears, and darkness engulfed him.

PART ONE

1

"Wretched girl! What are you doing?"

Madame's voice jolted Birdie to her senses, away from the world of light and beauty woven by the melody that still sang in her ears and back to the damp stone of the kitchen. She lurched to her feet, cringing at the sight of Madame's upraised hand.

"Please, Madame—"

Madame's hand landed on her ear, and the last floating notes of the melody were lost in an explosion of stinging pain. Birdie stumbled. Her feet tangled in the squat three-legged stool, tumbling her down onto the warm stone of the hearth. The flames licked at her long hair, and she scrambled away from the fire.

"Daydreamin' again? When there's work t' be done?" Madame loomed over her, hands propped on her angular hips. "Worthless! That's what you are. Worthless!"

Birdie stared numbly from the dripping wooden spoon in her hand to the pot of blackened porridge bubbling over the fire. The smell of burnt food stung her nostrils.

Madame yanked her to her feet. "What were you doing?"

Birdie opened her mouth to speak, but the words withered on her tongue. It would never do to mention the melody. Perhaps it was best to say nothing.

Madame took a step forward, bony hand held out in front of her, finger jabbing toward Birdie's face like a spear. "Mad as a night

11

moth," she declared. "A lazy, useless, worthless child! That's what you are! Useless since the day Dalton picked you up off the road! Twelve years now, I've put up with this nonsense. And what have you done in return? Lolled around like a daisy. Spouted insane nonsense and caused endless trouble for my poor sons!"

Birdie caught sight of Kurt and Miles, the "poor sons" in question, peering at her around the door frame. Poor sons? More like two terrors. Miles stuck his tongue out before Kurt jerked him out of sight.

"Well, I've no use for a half-wit or a mad girl! A girl whose own parents didn't care enough to bother with and abandoned to the kindness of strangers . . ."

The words stung more than Madame's blows, but Birdie had heard them all before. Worthless. Half-wit. Mad girl. On and on Madame's rant continued, until she could no longer distinguish the individual words.

She studied the stone floor beneath her toes, clenching her fists to hold back her rising anger. She had to get out of here . . . had to get away. Without a word, she spun on her heels, pushed past the startled woman, and tore through the common room out into the clear light of day. She slammed the front door, enclosing Madame's furious shouts within the walls of the inn.

Birdie ran. Past the barn, across the dusty inn yard, and out over the hills surrounding the Sylvan Swan Inn. Autumn grass crinkled beneath her feet. Blazing orange fire flowers burst as she brushed past, exploding into wild puffs of floating petals that drifted away on the wind. She ran until she gasped for breath and stumbled to her knees in a wide open space. Sobs rose in her throat, smothering her anger, and she flung herself flat against the cool brown earth and cried into her arms.

Deep below, a sepulchral rumbling from the depths of the earth— a distant melody— rose to greet her. Warm as a summer sunrise, the song caught her up in its embrace. The tears dried on her face. Her sorrow eased. The song was familiar—she had known it all her life—and yet new and wondrous, something too great to be fully known or understood. It spiraled upward, carrying her soul to reach for the sky. Then it stopped abruptly and the melody faded away.

She sat alone on the hillside, the only noise the ordinary sounds of an autumn afternoon: the whispering of windswept grasses, the trilling whistles of the Karnoth birds winging northward to the ice and snow ere Winter Turning, and the peaceful munching of herds of sheep grazing in the troughs between one hill and the next.

Disappointment settled over Birdie. Always it was the same, every time she heard the song. Five notes without resolution. A beginning, constantly repeating, without an end. And yet the five notes were so beautiful that her heart ached at the sound, and every fiber of her being yearned to hear more.

She closed her eyes and strained to listen.

"Agh, ye tummy-grubbin' bit o' crab meat!"

Birdie bolted upright at the voice.

"Will ye not move on?"

It seemed to be coming from just over the next rise. The speaker—a man—sighed heavily. "Ye won't, eh? Then, by Turning, I'll make ye . . ." There was a dull thwack followed by a yelp. When the man spoke again, his voice sounded pained. "Well fine then, have it yer own way. Here's as good a place as any t' break fer an afternoon snack. An' ye can wipe that silly grin off'n yer silly donkey face, ye pitiful blatherin' slewstop!"

A smile spread across Birdie's face. There was only one man who could invent an insult like that—traveling peddler, Amos McElhenny. "Amos!"

She broke into a run, raced to the top of the rise, and stopped, overlooking the little valley on the other side. At the bottom of the slope a tall, pack-laden donkey stood knee-deep in the grass at the base of a hallorm tree. The donkey's legs were splayed and his head bent down—an image of defiance—but of the speaker, Amos, she could see no sign.

"Amos? Where are you?"

"Birdie, lass? Is that you?" Amos appeared, sitting up out of the grass beside the donkey. He struggled to his feet and waded uphill toward her, tugging his plumed cap down over his wild red hair. He dusted the dirt off his overcoat and breeches and readjusted his belt around his stout girth. Birdie ran down the hill toward him and, a moment later, found herself engulfed in his strong hug.

"Perfect timin', lass. Couldn't be better. Just in time to join me an' old Balaam here fer a wee afternoon snack."

He released her and hustled back to the donkey, Balaam. Birdie followed as Amos undid the straps holding the packsaddle in place and let it drop to the ground. He dug through the packs and pulled out a skillet and a string of sausages.

"Gather some wood, lass, an' hurry. I'm starved."

Birdie collected fallen limbs from beneath the hallorm tree and tossed them to Amos. Then she scrambled up the tree and perched in a comfortable crook where she could look down on the peddler at work.

"But aren't you coming to the Sylvan Swan tonight, Amos?" she asked as the peddler employed his tinderbox.

"Oh, aye. O' course I am. Don't I always? Just got hungry, that's all. Decided 'twas high time fer a snack."

"With the Sylvan Swan less than a mile away?"

"Aye, lass, I've got t' eat my fill before I arrive. Ye know Madame— none too fond o' me an' my lack o' coin. Besides, who could enjoy a meal with that bollywag breathin' fire down his neck? Whew. Gives me the shivers, just thinkin' about it."

The way he said it made Birdie shiver up in the tree, and a little shower of dark green leaves sprinkled Amos's head. Whatever a *bollywag* was, *fire-breathing* certainly seemed to describe Madame. There would be flames aplenty awaiting Birdie when she returned to the inn.

She sank back against the obliging tree trunk, hugging her arms as a chill breeze snuck through the threadbare cloth of her dress and blew her dark hair back from her face, twisting it around a cluster of branches.

From his flint and steel, Amos got a spark that he slowly blew into flame, then he settled back on his heels and dropped sausages into a skillet. "Actually lass, truth is I only stopped here because old grumpy-guts-Balaam decided 'twas time fer a break. I've learned after fifteen years with that fool beast: when he makes up his mind t' somethin', there's no gettin' around it. Best t' sit back, break out the food, an' wait 'til he's ready t' move again." He chuckled to himself, and then peered at her. "Ye're quiet today, lass. What's botherin' ye?"

Birdie studied her hands. Black smudges from the hearth covered her palms. She could still hear Madame's angry tirade ringing in her ears.

Worthless. Half-wit. Mad girl.

Dare she tell Amos the truth? She only saw the traveling peddler every few weeks when he passed through the village of Hardale on his circuit. But he had always been a friend.

"Are you sure you want to know?"

"Course I want t' know."

He was the only one she could tell, and she *had* to tell someone. Mind made up, she peered down at him through the overlapping branches. "You don't think I'm . . . insane . . . do you, Amos?"

"Whatever put such an idea in yer head?" He stirred the sausage sizzling over the flames. The tantalizing aroma of cooking meat rose in the cloud of smoke, and Birdie's stomach rumbled.

"Everyone else does."

"Why d' ye say that? I mean"—Amos shifted on his heels and wiped the sweat from his brow with a red-spotted handkerchief—"why d' ye say that everyone thinks ye're insane?"

"I've heard them talking about it. They say I'm not right in the head. That something's wrong with me. And I . . . well . . ."

"Go ahead, lassie, spit it out."

"Well, I'm starting to wonder if they might be right. I hear things all the time, but now more than ever before. I hear . . . music."

"D' ye now?" A smile creased Amos's bronze, weathered face. "Well, that's not so bad. Naught like a cheerful song t' help pass the time o' day."

"No, it's not like that." She sighed. How could she explain it to the peddler? It wasn't like the ordinary working songs farmers' wives sang in the fields, or the bawdy sea shanties drunken sailors belted out at the top of their lungs, or even the magnificent ballads traveling bards occasionally sang at the Sylvan Swan.

"It's always the same. Well," she hastened to clarify, "not exactly the same. It's the same five notes, but it always sounds different, like a different voice is singing it."

Even as she spoke, the notes echoed in her ears. The voice, a deep throaty hum like the droning of a dragonfly's wings, was joined by another, a jouncing baritone. Five notes repeated, lowest, high, middle, low, low.

Haunting, echoing, reminding.

"Do you hear it, Amos?"

The peddler solemnly shook his head.

Birdie's breath, pent up in her excitement, exhaled from her lips in an audible sigh. She dropped to the ground and sprawled on her back in the soft grass. She shouldn't be surprised at Amos's response. No one else ever heard the music.

As a child of five, she had first heard the ethereal melody floating through the summer grasses and ran inside, bursting with excitement to tell Madame. Her joy had earned a cuff to the ear. The Song returned several times as she grew up, each more real and beautiful than before, yet never remaining for long. A short spell, a breath, and then it was gone again and she knew not when it would return.

But now she heard it almost constantly. Madame scoffed at her "fantasies," and the two terrors never wearied of teasing her about it. She couldn't summon the courage to question Master Dalton on the subject, and now surely Amos too would think her insane. She must be. Why else would she hear a song that no one else could?

Amos cleared his throat, signaling the end of the conversation, stabbed a sausage link with his knife and bit into it. His face melted into a satisfied grin as he chewed slowly, soaking in the pleasure of the moment.

"Good?" Birdie sniffed appreciatively. The conversation might not have turned out as she'd hoped, but it hadn't been as bad as she'd expected either.

Amos speared another sausage and offered it to her. Her stomach rumbled—a reminder that Madame had deprived her of her last two meals. She took a bite and forced herself to chew slowly, ignoring the urge to gulp it down at once.

"Have some more, lass. There's naught t' satisfy like a belly full o' meat an' laughter, as me mother used t' say!"

After they finished eating, Amos clambered to his feet and stuffed his supplies into the packsaddle while Birdie put out the fire. The peddler tossed the packsaddle onto the donkey's high-withered back and cinched it tightly. Balaam peered over his shoulder at the mountain of packs, and an expression of resigned misery darkened his brown eyes.

Amos smacked the donkey's neck. "Reckon we're both due fer a rest. Only a few more days an' then we'll be headed home to my mother in Bryllhyn. Visit's long overdue."

Bryllhyn. Somehow the name filled her with an incredible longing. It sounded like a quaint, homey sort of place, like she always dreamed of.

Birdie rested her chin on her knees and gazed at the western horizon. It taunted and beckoned to her at the same time, whispering of lands beyond the Midlands and the narrow confines of the inn, of a place beyond Madame's reach and the two terrors' mockery.

And somewhere out there, before the sky touched the sea, was the little village of Bryllhyn where Amos's mother lived.

The place Amos called *home*.

"How is life at the Sylvan Swan?" Amos squatted beside her, wrinkles crinkling his forehead. "Are they treatin' ye well? What about those two terrors?"

Birdie studied the ground. Somehow Amos always knew when something was wrong.

"Ah, so I've struck on it. Been gettin' ye in trouble again have they?"

Her cheeks burned. "No, it was my fault. I can't ever seem to get anything right."

She was about to say more, but the music drifted over her and she felt silent, spellbound by the beauty of the five repeated notes. Then a second voice joined in with a different melody. Dark and terrible, a hideous distortion of the first song. It wrapped around her like a plume of smoke, draining the air from her lungs.

"Lassie? What's wrong?"

"Did . . . did you just hear that?"

He shook his head.

"The song," she insisted. "Didn't you hear it?"

"Lassie, I—"

A thought leapt into her mind. "Perhaps if I sing it for you!" She jumped up and opened her mouth to sing. For the first time the melody poured from her lips, pure and golden like drops of liquid sunlight. The effect was startling, even to her.

Silence fell upon the hillside. The crisp autumn breeze stilled. The swaying grasses froze. High above, birds halted amid flight, hanging motionless in the vast blue sea. She shuddered under the sudden weight, as if everything was pressing in around her, drawing near to watch and listen. Even the trees seemed to have bent over, dipping their gnarled boughs in silent but rapt attention.

A hand clapped over her mouth. "Stop it, lassie," Amos hissed in her ear. "Stop it now!" He removed his hand slowly, eyes darting to scan the horizon. Worry and fear marred his white face, and his hands trembled as he let them fall to his side.

Birdie stared in astonishment. Amos frightened?

"What was that?" he demanded. "Some kind o' witchery?" Sweat beaded his forehead.

She shook her head but could find no words.

He grasped her by the shoulders, searching her face with his eyes. "Where did ye hear that song? Who taught it t' ye? Does Dalton know about this?"

"Nobody taught it to me." She swallowed to moisten her dry throat. "I just heard it."

"Well, ye mustn't sing it again."

"I don't understand."

He released her and sank heavily to the ground. "That song. 'Tis unnatural. 'Tisn't right. There's somethin' about it that reeks o' . . . I don't know! Ye just mustn't sing it, d' ye understand? Never again."

The deep-throated whinny of a horse broke into the conversation. Birdie spun around. Beside her, Amos stood, fumbling for a weapon, finding nothing but the knife at his belt.

A mounted stranger reined his horse to a stop before them. He was clad in black armor and wore a long silver cape that hung down to his booted feet. The visor of his helmet was raised, revealing a swarthy face shadowed by a black beard. A thin-bladed sword rested in an ornamented scabbard at his side. His left hand flashed in movement, and the sword sprang forth, red-stained tip pointing toward Amos and Birdie.

Hand on Birdie's arm, Amos slowly sidestepped toward Balaam, pulling her with him.

The stranger's voice halted any further movement. "Drop your weapon." His horse—a massive, armored creature with an odd, reddish-black mane and tail—danced in place, but he scarcely seemed to notice, moving with the horse like a tree swaying in the wind.

Amos growled and his gaze flickered from side to side. The stranger's horse screamed—such a wild, harsh sound Birdie had never heard before—and reared, pawing at the sky. Amos threw down his knife and yanked Birdie behind the protective shield of the donkey's protruding belly. Balaam hee-hawed nervously but did not move.

"Send the girl over here," the stranger commanded in a cool, distant voice. "I want to talk to her."

"Stay still," Amos mouthed at Birdie. His right hand inched toward the packsaddle. "No need," he called out to the stranger. "She can talk just fine from here."

Birdie rose on her toes to peer over the tall donkey's back. The gray horse snorted and pawed the ground. A leather skirt, patchworked with metal plates, covered the horse's chest and rump, while a metal mask concealed its face from view—for protection probably—but it made the steed look sinister, like a statue rather than a living beast.

"Don't try my patience, old man."

"An' don't try mine." Amos's arm jerked, dipping into the pack and out again. A strange black tube appeared in his hand and extended until it matched the length of his forearm. Birdie watched in bewilderment as he slipped a red-tufted shaft into the tube and raised it to his lips.

"If ye an' that horse o' yers have a mind t' dance, I could blow a fair sort o' tune on this, don't ye think?" Amos said. "Or have ye never heard o' the spear pipe o' the Vituain Desert? Solid cane shaft with an iron tip coated in poisonous Vrimgor sap leaves a nasty wound, so I'm told."

"I've heard of it," the stranger spat. "Put it away. You have nothing to fear from me. I only wish to ask the girl a few questions."

"Aye, we've naught t' fear from you, Khelari. But ye've quite a bit t' fear from me if ye don't turn yer prancin' pony around and get out o' the Midlands an' back t' the North where ye belong."

The stranger's dark eyes flickered with some expression or thought that Birdie could not identify. He seemed to be almost chuckling as he sheathed his sword and twitched his cape aside to reveal a large medallion hanging around his neck beside a teardrop shaped red jewel. He lifted the chain holding the medallion, and Birdie recognized the engraved symbol—a shepherd's crook entwined with a crown—as that of the ruling family of the Midlands.

"My name is Carhartan, the Second Marshal of the Khelari," the stranger said. "I travel as the Takhran's representative, under the protection of your King Earnhult. You dare not touch me."

"I don't care who or what ye are. If ye try t' harm any o' mine, I'll see that ye rue the day ye did it."

"How old are you, child?"

The sudden question startled Birdie into answering, "Twelve." She forced her chin up and stared at Carhartan's eyes—so dark and terrible they seemed, now that his gaze was bent upon her.

The lines across his forehead deepened. "And where do you live? Is this man your father?"

"Enough," Amos said. "No more questions. Lass, it's time we were goin'." He grabbed Balaam's lead rope, ignoring the donkey's snort of refusal—and tugged, forcing the stubborn beast to move through sheer strength.

Birdie followed. She glanced back at Carhartan and just caught sight of a hideous expression of wrath and hatred on his face before it smoothed away and the strange coldness returned. He dipped his head in salute and smiled. His steed danced in place, then spun around and galloped southward.

Amos kept the strange weapon in his hand until the pounding hooves faded in the distance and the gray shape of horse and rider disappeared over the top of the next rise. Then he shakily mopped his face with his kerchief, and removing the shaft from the spear pipe, tucked it away in the packsaddle.

He was frightened, Birdie realized. Really, truly frightened. For some reason, that thought scared her even more than the stranger. "What just happened, Amos? Who was that?"

He must have heard the worry in her voice, for his face brightened visibly and he winked. "Bah, a bit o' nonsense that's all. Naught t' trouble yer pretty little head. Now, isn't it about time ye were gettin' back t' the inn?"

2

By the time Birdie and Amos neared the Sylvan Swan, the sun—Tauros—was fast approaching the westerly horizon. Birdie chafed at Balaam's lumbering pace. Despite Amos's prodding and pulling, the big donkey waddled along at a snail-like tempo, snatching mouthfuls of pricknettle weeds as he went.

"Can't he go any faster, Amos?"

The peddler whacked Balaam's hindquarters with the rope. "Not unless I carry him—which I'm not goin' t' do. The slobgollomly grub-belly. He's stubborner 'n a gadfly an' more obstinate 'n a toothache."

Birdie bit her lip and followed in silence, trying to ignore the swift, downward trajectory of the sun. She had never been so late before. Every second that passed was fuel for Madame's wrath. Of course she could run ahead of Amos, but when it came to facing Madame, having a stout friend at her side might mean the difference between merely losing a meal and gaining a beating.

Finally, they rounded the curve of the last hill and beheld the Sylvan Swan at the bottom of the trough before them. The inn, a long, low, stone building, whitewashed, and thatched with rushes weighed by hanging rocks against inclement winds, stood in the center of a wide yard. The double doors of the barn opposite the inn yawned open, reminding Birdie of a dozen chores already overdue.

"No sign o' Madame, eh?" Amos chuckled. "Quick. Let's go while the goin's good. I'll help with yer chores."

Birdie hurried down the hill into the yard with Amos and the donkey at her heels. She had nearly reached the barn when the inn door swung open, and Madame stepped out onto the threshold.

"So, the runaway returns."

Birdie stumbled to a halt, took a deep breath, and turned to face the innkeeper's wife. Madame's face was flushed from afternoon baking, and flour speckled her apron and dusted the tip of her pointed nose.

Madame folded her arms across her chest. "I had begun to hope you were gone for good."

Birdie dropped her gaze to her toes and clasped her hands before her, presenting the submissive posture she knew would please the innkeeper's wife. Given the choice, she would have been gone for good long ago, but without even a name to call her own, she had no hope outside of the inn.

"Now, now, don't be hard on the wee lassie," Amos said. "'Twas my fault. I detained her—"

"Mind your place, peddler. This is none of your business. Come here, girl."

Slowly Birdie stepped away from the refuge of the barn and the protection of Amos's shadow and halted just beyond Madame's reach.

"Don't think you can fool me! I know what you've been about—lollygagging and fantasizing in the hills while I do all the work. If you don't work, you don't eat, so there'll be no supper for you tonight. Now get on with your chores."

"Yes . . . Madame." She dipped her head toward the innkeeper's wife and pressed her lips together to keep from saying anything more. At least Madame had not beaten her—that was something to be grateful for—and Amos had been kind enough to share his sausages, so she would not go to bed completely hungry.

Madame turned to Amos. "As for you, peddler, if you can't pay in coin you'll eat and sleep in the barn as usual till you've exchanged wares with Master Dalton. I won't have nonpaying customers in the inn. It's bad for business. If it were up to me, I'd make you pay for the use of our haystack too."

Amos ruefully shook his head, pulling out the empty linings of his trouser pockets for Madame's inspection. "No coin, I'm afraid."

Madame's glare could have singed a fire flower, but it had no effect on the hardy peddler. "Off with you to the barn then, before the smell of you and that wicked beast drives away my payin' guests!"

"Yer wish is my command." Amos pulled the feathered cap from his head with an elaborate flourish and shuffled to the barn, bowing dramatically as he went.

The inn door slammed behind Madame.

Birdie sighed and followed Amos into the barn, threading her way through clucking chickens scratching in the dust and pecking at flies. Her thoughts turned to the stranger on the wild horse. She shuddered at the memory of his dark eyes and the cold detachment of his gaze. The terrible melody she had heard just before his arrival filled her ears. Shadows swirled across her vision, and she blinked away the frightening images.

Amos was right. This song business had to stop. It might not be insanity—Amos's reaction to the melody had proven that there was *something* to the song she heard—but it would bring nothing but trouble. It *had* brought nothing but trouble.

But if Amos knew enough about the song to know that it was "unnatural," then surely he could tell her more. Maybe explain why she heard it and what it was.

"Whew, lassie, ye've got a face on ye almost as sour as the look Madame gave me a moment ago." Amos's cheery voice broke into her dismal contemplation.

Lost in the pathless wanderings of thought, Birdie looked up and found herself already standing before the row of battered stalls at the far end of the barn.

Amos grinned over the dividing wall. "What's troublin' ye? Is it because ye're t' have no supper? Och, don't ye know that's pure poddboggle? My lassie won't go hungry s' long as Amos McElhenny is around."

She smiled halfheartedly, caught up a pitchfork from its resting place against the wall, and waded into the first stall to clean out the muck left by its latest occupant, Madame's star-spotted cow. For a moment, there was no sound but the scrape of her pitchfork and the dull thud of the wet forkfuls she threw over the stall's half door. Then the door creaked open, and Amos's concerned face appeared beside her.

"All right then." He plucked the pitchfork from her hands and tossed it aside. "What's worryin' ye?" He led her out of the stall and sat down on a pile of fresh hay. "Tell yer old friend Amos."

Birdie took a seat beside him and studied her clasped hands. "Amos . . . I . . ."

"Go ahead."

She *had* to find out what Amos knew about the song. "That man we met earlier. He frightened me. Why did he ask so many questions? What did he want? Is it because of what I sang? I didn't know there was anything wrong with the song, Amos. Honestly I didn't."

"Whoa there, lassie. Not so fast." Amos stroked his bristling beard. "I'll tell it t' ye plain. The song is dangerous. Ye can't sing it again. Ever."

"How is it dangerous?" What was different about her song that set it apart from all others?

"I can't explain it all. But there are those who would try t' use ye t' get at that cursed song. Ye have t' trust me an' never sing it again. Do I have yer word?"

Birdie gnawed her lip. Why couldn't Amos give her a straight answer? Simply telling her that the song was dangerous didn't help when she wanted to know why. "But Amos . . ."

"Never again."

The peddler's jaw was iron and determination filled his eyes.

She sighed. "I promise." Now perhaps he would tell her more— later, once he was sure that she would keep her word. Besides, if the song *was* dangerous, then perhaps it would be best to leave it alone, at least until she knew more. She had trouble enough as it was.

"Good. Good." A heavy breath puffed from Amos's lips. "Now, there's naught t' worry about. Supposin' that is, ye get yer chores done an' I get me wares t' Master Dalton afore Madame decides t' have both our hides fer tannin'!" He winked and strode to his donkey, whistling a merry tune.

Birdie sat for a moment in silence, with Amos's warning running through her mind. Then she stood and picked up the pitchfork to finish cleaning out the stall. One thing she knew for certain: the song could be very dangerous for her if thinking about it kept her from finishing her chores tonight.

Night hung over the Sylvan Swan before Birdie at last finished her chores and crept into the inn. A few guests still clustered around the fire in the common room, while hearty snores proceeding from the back rooms attested to the sleeping presence of others. The kitchen door was closed, but firelight shone through the cracks, and she could hear Amos's deep brogue blending with Master Dalton's softer rumble within.

"Good night, my lambs."

Birdie jumped at the voice and spun around in search of the speaker. A door stood open at the end of the hall—the door to Kurt and Miles's bedroom—and just within, silhouetted against the lamp in her hand, was Madame.

"Sleep well."

So altered was Madame's voice, so kind and loving, that Birdie could scarcely believe that it was she who had spoken. Such a gentle tone had never before passed her lips when Birdie was within earshot.

A lump swelled in Birdie's throat as Madame bent forward and kissed her sons on their foreheads. Kurt wrinkled his face in disgust, and Miles swiped a hand across his forehead before burrowing beneath his quilt.

Madame closed the door softly behind her and strode down the hall, pausing as she came abreast of Birdie. Her face tightened into a scowl, sharp cheekbones highlighted by the lamp in her hand. "What do you want?"

The lump gnawed at the back of Birdie's throat. She gazed up at Madame's unyielding face through a blur of tears. "Nothing, Madame."

"Chores done?"

She nodded.

"Off to bed then."

Madame swept away into the common room, and Birdie stood alone in the dark hallway. Blinded by tears, she stumbled to the storeroom and curled up on her straw mattress beneath her worn blanket. Though her mattress was squeezed into a corner of the crowded room, when night shadows descended, the walls seemed to retreat and the barrels and sacks fell back, 'til there was nothing but her and the night and the wide empty space beyond.

Raucous laughter burst from the common room. The rumble of Master Dalton and Amos's voices drifted toward her from the kitchen. But she was alone, and the darkness crouched above her like a monster waiting to smother her in its grasp. She could almost hear the beast's rasping breath hovering beside her ear.

Then soft as a whisper, the melody crept toward her, banishing the midnight fears and easing the ache of loneliness. It wrapped around her, the comforting embrace of a friend.

Dangerous, Amos had said. Unnatural.

But dangerous or not, it was all she had. Birdie slipped into the mysterious melody and allowed it to carry her to sleep at last.

"Ah, Dalton." Amos sighed, tipping his chair back to rest his stockinged feet on the kitchen hearth. His abandoned boots sprawled before the fire to dry, steam already rising from the worn leather soles. He had tucked his burlap pack under his seat. There would be time enough later to bring out his wares.

"I've traveled many a mile an' visited many an inn, but there's nary a one with a brew so fine as this." He tipped the earthenware mug and took a long sip. The brew trickled down his parched throat like refreshing rain.

Over the rim of the mug, he caught sight of Dalton sneaking a peek around the door jamb into the common room. "Dalton?" The front legs of Amos's chair settled with a thud. "I didn't come in here t' drink by myself."

Dalton jerked at the noise and spun around. "Eh, what was that?"

"I was complimentin' yer brew. What's come over ye? Ye're actin' like a scared rabbit."

"My brew? Oh yes." Dalton shuffled over to his rocking chair. "Actually, it's not mine. Madame would probably kill me if she knew, but I can't stomach her recipe, so I bought my own private stock from Brog at the Waterfly."

Amos chuckled. "I thought it tasted familiar. Good old Brog. I just may have t' visit the Waterfly tomorrow when I go into town t' peddle my wares. Sample some o' Ma's cookin'."

"And Brog's brew."

"O' course."

Dalton rocked in silence, the warped runners creaking across the uneven stone floor. "Amos," he spoke suddenly in a hushed voice. "I saw one today . . ."

Amos plunked his mug down on the hearth and sat up straight in his chair. "A Khelari?" No doubt it was the same fly-swoggled villain he had seen earlier with Birdie, but to have him show up at the inn as well was disconcerting to say the least.

"Yes." Dalton shuddered. "I haven't seen one of the black armors in over twenty years. It brings back terrible memories."

Amos grunted. No matter how many times he encountered the death-hued armor, the sight never failed to carry him back to that horrible night so long ago.

"He came by just before you arrived, traveling under the protection of King Earnhult. What do you think? That's . . . that's bad news isn't it? Do you think the Takhran means to move south now? What if . . . what if King Earnhult is working with the Takhran?"

Amos stroked his beard, carefully choosing his next words. That a Midland king would dare consult with the Khelari, the murderous dogs of the Takhran, set his blood boiling. He swallowed hard. "I'd say it'd be a safe wager that the Midlands are the next tribe the Takhran intends t' *subject*. What did the Khelari want here?"

"Information. Asked a lot of questions. He looked . . . familiar. I could have sworn I've seen him—"

"Huh, the Khelari are all alike—black-hearted murderin' scumgullions. What sort o' questions was he askin' ye? Anythin' about Birdie?"

"Birdie? Why would he care about her?"

Amos blinked. Was the man deaf? True, he'd just discovered Birdie's ability himself. But he supposed that Dalton—living with the lass as he did—must have known long before and refrained from mentioning it, knowing Amos's thoughts on the matter. "D' ye mean ye don't know?"

"Don't know what?"

"That the lassie . . ." He stopped, unable to speak a word so long buried beneath the ashes of regret and shattered hopes.

Dalton didn't seem to notice his pause. "The Khelari was *here*, Amos. Here! The Takhran must have discovered who I am ... *was*. This could be the end of everything."

So that was what ailed the man. "Dalton, that was nearly thirty years ago. The Takhran is not interested in ye anymore."

"But why else would—"

"Don't be blind, man! There's bigger game involved. The Takhran has already taken the northern tribes. Up there, just beyond Dunfaen Forest, his soldiers patrol the streets, his hounds haunt the woods, his dark spies cover the skies. He's goin' t' come south soon. We've always known that. It's only a matter o' time before all of Leira is in his grasp. We must be ready—"

"Ready for what? War?" Dalton cast an anxious glance over his shoulder and lowered his voice to a hissing whisper. "You are a fool,

Amos. If what you say is true, then the Takhran *will* become the arch-ruler of Leira. There's nothing we or any of the tribes can do to stop him."

Nothing we can do . . .

It was because of men like Dalton that the Takhran's power had grown so much in recent memory. Because of men who sat idle, refusing to act, while the Takhran ventured forth from his city-kingdom in Serrin Vroi where he had ruled for ages past, and the northern tribes fell.

It was because of men like Dalton . . .

Men like Amos . . .

Men who had fought and failed and forgotten that the Takhran marched across a land of ashes—a broken people at his feet, the united banners of Serrin Vroi and the northlands at his back.

While the Midland king sought to curry favor and sued for peace.

"Arch-ruler?" Amos stood so quickly that his chair flipped over. He paced back and forth across the hearth stone. "Self-proclaimed tyrant ye mean! Which o' the tribes has ever acknowledged his rule? He has no right t' demand our allegiance."

"What cares he for rights? He will demand our blood if we do not give it."

"Aye! Our blood. An' what if he does? Ye were there, Dalton. Ye've seen what he can do! Fer years now, we've tried t' forget. S' long as he didn't interfere with our measly lives, what did it matter what he did elsewhere? Now, we will pay the price fer our selfishness. The Takhran's tyranny will be felt in the Midlands, an' there is *no one* left t' fight it."

"No." Dalton rose, fists clenched even though his head only reached Amos's chin. "You are *mad* to talk about fighting the Takhran after what happened! If you want to bring danger on your own head, then do it and welcome. But you shan't drag me or my family into trouble! I won't have such talk in my house."

Anger boiled in Amos's veins. "Very well," he said through clenched teeth. "While I'm a guest in yer house, I'll say naught o' the matter. But if ye in truth mean it, ye're not the Dalton I knew."

Dalton swallowed visibly. "Time changes many things, Amos . . . even men."

"I've heard it said. But there are some things that don't change, even with time. Amos McElhenny won't change. The Takhran can bet his life on it."

"Shh!" Dalton held a shaking finger to his lips and darted back to the door. "We are fools to talk so! Someone may be listening."

Amos set his toppled chair back on its feet. A grin tweaked the corners of his mouth. "D' ye have rats in the walls, or are ye worried about Madame?"

"Oh!" Dalton jumped as if he expected his wife to burst in. "It's getting late. She'll be wondering what's taking so long. It's time we settled our affairs."

"Aye, pleasantries aside." Amos tugged his heavy burlap pack into his lap and twitched loose the straps. "To business."

3

A bead of sweat trickled down Birdie's face. She raised a grimy hand to swipe her forehead. After her escapade the previous afternoon, Madame had kept her busy with chores since sunup, and now the shadows were beginning to lengthen once more.

From the milking rack, the star-spotted cow let loose a mournful bellow. Birdie sighed, scooped up an armful of hay, and dumped it in the feed bin. She was reaching for the stool and a pail when the calm of the hazy afternoon was shattered by a terrible yowl.

"Who's there?"

Another screech.

The pail slipped from her hand. She darted out of the cow's stall and slammed the gate shut. Balaam's stall was still empty. The peddler had left around noon, donkey in tow, to peddle his wares in Hardale

The cry rang out again.

This time, Birdie thought she heard something else as well—stifled giggles accompanied by an odd creaking. The blood rose hot in her veins and she clenched her fists. The two terrors were up to their old game—torturing innocent creatures. Villains!

The sound seemed to come from the direction of the hay loft. Birdie darted to the ladder and scrambled up. The sweet, prickly scent of hay filled her nose, and she crawled forward into a world of golden brown. Old chains rattled and groaned. A yowl of distress, smothered laughter, then two voices spoke beyond the haystack.

"Shh! Not so loud, Kurt! What if Papa hears?"

"Aw, leave it be, Miles. Papa's busy in the inn."

Birdie wriggled through the itchy mountain of hay to peer cautiously over the top. Dust clouds stirred by her movement hung in the air, visible in the squares of light spilling through bare patches in the thatched roof. The two boys crouched on the floor of the loft next to the pulley. A crumpled bundle of something yellowish-orange and furry hung from the bottom of the rope that Kurt held in his hands. He bent over and straightened again in a jerking rhythm of raising and lowering, accompanied by the shattering groans of the pulley's chains.

Miles stood at Kurt's side, tongue sticking out in concentration, a pointed stick in his hand. "Hold it still, Kurt!" He jabbed at the dangling bundle and the creature yowled.

Both Kurt and Miles tumbled to the ground with laughter.

Birdie charged over the haystack, skidding to a stop before the two bullies. "Kurt and Miles, you let it go right now!"

The two boys looked up. A fleeting expression of panic flashed across their faces, and they crowded away from the pulley. Kurt released the rope as if it had caught fire in his hands. The yellow bundle plummeted toward the barn floor, screeching in terror. A knot ran up the rope and lodged in the pulley wheel, snapping the creature to a painful halt. It hung swaying on the end of the line a few feet above the floor.

Kurt laughed, but it sounded hollow. "Let go of it?" he repeated in a mocking falsetto. "Fine. I let go. Does that make you happy?" He paused and then continued when she didn't speak. "No? Well, guess what? I don't care. And I'm not going to stop either. What are you going to do about it?" His eyes flickered tauntingly. Miles peeked around his older brother's shoulder, and Birdie caught a glimpse of his red tongue sticking out at her before he ducked to safety.

"What am I going to do about it?" Birdie snatched a broom off the floor. "I'll show you what I'm going to do!"

Thwack. A well-aimed thrust rapped Kurt across the head. *Thwop.* Miles staggered back, clutching his belly and gasping for air.

Their courage shattered by her ferocity, Kurt and Miles fled before the strokes of a broom wielded with skill acquired through many hours acquaintance. Birdie's ire rose with each furious swing.

"You miserable torturin' scoundrels!" she shouted, giving vent to a store of insults supplied by the master, Amos McElhenny. "Out of here, you flea-gathering breath-moldering tummy-aching bullfrogs!" It sounded silly, but she didn't care.

Kurt turned and shouted a reply and received a mouthful of bristles. The two boys scrambled backward, slipping and sliding through the haystack to gain the ladder and escape. Kurt won, trampling his brother in his haste, Miles tumbling after. They burst through the barn door and landed in a cloud of dust as Birdie scrambled down, clutching her broom at the ready.

Kurt lurched to his feet, reeling like a drunkard. "You just wait, Birdie!" he rasped. "Wait until we tell Mama. Then you'll get what's comin' to you."

"Yeah," Miles said. "Just *wait*."

Kurt yanked his brother up, and the two boys staggered toward the inn.

"Do it!" Birdie shouted. "See if I care!" She spun on her heel and slammed the door behind her.

The dust cloud slowly settled. She took a deep breath and the broom fell from her shaking fingers. Her brazen words echoed in her ears. *See if I care!* Unfortunately, she did care a great deal. She had endured Madame's rod far too many times for the threat of her displeasure to be taken lightly.

She suddenly remembered the captive and darted back up to the hayloft. The yellow-orange bundle of fur lay so still that, for a moment, Birdie was afraid it had died—whatever *it* was. Then the beast wailed and startled wriggling again, jerking on the end of the rope. She hauled it up and set it down in the hay.

It was a large cat, paws trussed together and suspended from a hook. The cat's wide yellow eyes followed her hands as she untied the knots. The moment it was free the cat sprang away, bounding into the farthest corner of the hayloft to perch on an overturned crate.

It eyed her suspiciously, tail twitching. Birdie took a step forward, extending her hand palm upward. The cat hissed and arched its back, fur puffed out like a loaded fire flower.

"It's all right," she said, crooning like a mother to a frightened child. "I won't hurt you." Another step. The hay rustled beneath her feet. "You needn't be afraid."

"Afraid? A Waltham? Preposterous."

Birdie spun around in search of the speaker. She peered over the edge of the hay loft. In the milking rack the cow still worked methodically through the pile of hay, tufted tail swishing back and forth across her star-spotted hide. The remaining four stalls were vacant. Other than the shifting groups of fowl, the barn stood silent and empty as always.

Except for . . .

Birdie tilted her head at the yellow cat. "Did . . . did you just say something?"

As soon as the words passed her lips, she realized how absurd they sounded. This was the last straw. The final proof. She *had* gone mad as a night moth. At least Kurt and Miles had left and Amos was gone. None but the voiceless cat would stand witness to the cracking of her sanity.

The cat considered her with unblinking eyes the color of desert sand. Daintily, it lifted a forepaw for cleaning, long pink tongue scraping through thick fur. The voice of a lazy tenor wafted through the barn, uttering five repeated notes.

"No, I'm just imagining things." Somehow saying it out loud made it seem more plausible, though no less frightening.

"Perhaps you are. I wouldn't know," the voice said. There could be no mistaking it this time. The yellow cat simply opened its mouth and spoke . . . spoke words.

Birdie raised trembling hands to her head and sank into the haystack. "What's happening? Are you really talking?"

The cat glared—the sort of smoldering look of utter disdain that only a feline can deliver effectively. "Of course I'm talking. We always are. You humans are simply too dense to understand."

"But . . . this can't be happening!"

"Since it is, that would seem to prove the fallacy of your statement. Ah, forgive me," the cat broke off and bent his head in an elegant bow. The action revealed a leather collar peeking through his neck fur, adorned with a single red-glass bead. "Allow me to introduce myself. George Eregius Waltham the third, traveler extraordinaire, at your service. And you are?"

She shook her head to clear her dazed mind. "Birdie," she said.

"A pleasure to meet you, I'm sure. What is the name of this homely domicile? And who were those two fiends? Not any relation of yours, I hope?"

Birdie struggled to wade through his strange language and merely succeeded in latching onto the concept of the fiends. "Kurt and Miles? No, thank goodness."

"Personally, I'd sooner be eaten by a hound than be related to one of them." George stood and shook until his fur stood wildly on end again. "Speaking of eating, I haven't in quite a while. Since you've already proven your compassionate nature by rescuing me from those foul tormentors, perhaps . . . might I beg you . . . that is to say, might I have something to eat?"

"Oh . . ." Birdie cast an anxious glance toward the barn door. The two terrors were certain to carry out their threat, and Madame was predisposed to regard her with little favor. She could just picture trying to explain the situation to Madame. *There's a talking cat in the barn* . . . It already seemed likely to prove yet another unpleasant evening. "I can't. Madame would be furious with me. I'm in enough trouble as is."

George's whiskers drooped, and his legs sagged as if he lacked the strength to stand. "It's all right. I'll manage . . . somehow."

Birdie sighed. "I'll do what I can."

"Birdie—" Madame's shriek made Birdie jump. The barn walls muffled the rest of Madame's sentence, but there was no mistaking the tone or the message.

George cocked his whiskers at her. "And that would be?"

"Madame. I have to go. Stay out of sight until I get back." She scrambled down the ladder, nearly falling in her haste, and shoved the barn door open.

Madame stood in front of the inn door, hands on her hips, lines standing out on her forehead like furrows in a newly plowed field. "Come here." Her eyes blazed with fire, but her voice made Birdie shiver. This was not the usual railing Madame, switch in hand to "whip some sense into her."

This was something far more frightening.

Birdie slowed to a walk. A white face peered at her around the side of Madame's voluminous skirts, red tongue sticking from a wide mouth—Miles. Kurt lurked in the background, leering smugly at her beneath a purpling black eye. Birdie forced her gaze from the pointed toes of Madame's shoes, up past her woven gray skirts, pinched mouth, nose, and into her shadowed eyes.

"Inside." Madame stood back and Birdie slipped past her. She followed Madame's directing arm into the common room, her bare feet thudding against the cold, stone floor. The long trestle table gleamed in the firelight. Its lone occupant sat at the far end like a lurking shadow. A pipe in his mouth, meal untouched, studying Birdie with his strange dark eyes.

Carhartan.

Birdie jerked to a halt and bit her lip to keep from crying out. What was he doing here? And why had Madame brought her to see him?

Carhartan's mouth twisted into a thin-lipped smile, but he did not speak. On the far side of the room, just visible over Carhartan's shoulder, Master Dalton bent over the fireplace, his back to the door as he restocked the wood box. The fire sparked and popped, the sound loud in the heavy silence.

"Dalton!"

At his wife's voice, Master Dalton jumped back from the fire, clutching a log like a weapon. "What is it?"

"There!" Madame rustled past Birdie to stand at his elbow. "There you have it." She pointed at Birdie.

The terrified expression on Dalton's face eased into one of pure bafflement. He glanced at Carhartan and dropped the log onto the hearth. "Have what?"

"What I've been warning you about. For years I've said this would happen. You can't pick a baby up from beside the road like a stray beast! It's bound to end in trouble."

This was an old argument. Birdie had heard it nearly every day since she could remember. Maybe this had nothing to do with Carhartan after all. Squaring her shoulders, she took a deep breath, steeling herself to face whatever else might come

"Twelve years I've warned you and you've refused to listen!"

Master Dalton waved his hands before his face as if to ward off the stinging barbs of her tongue. "Easy, woman. What has she done?"

"Only attacked your poor sons and beaten them with a stick. Mad—that's what she is. Vicious. Wicked! She should be handed over to the magistrate and locked up!"

As if on cue, Kurt moaned from the doorway, and Miles sniffed, wiping his eyes on his sleeve. Master Dalton's gaze bounced to his sons and a look of disgust crossed his face.

"I tell you, Dalton, I've borne too much for too long. I won't have it anymore. It's time for her to leave."

The words filled Birdie with a strange sense of relief, quelling the fear that threatened to grip her. To finally leave the inn, Madame, the two terrors. To be free. It was worth all the doubts and uncertainty in the world, wasn't it?

"I want her out of my house—the lazy, worthless wretch—and if she isn't gone by morning, I'll fetch the magistrate myself!"

Birdie turned to Master Dalton, half hoping he would speak, half fearing he would. He stood with his head bowed, one hand ruffling through his hair. He had always stood up for her in the past. Would he just stand by now and allow Madame to send her away?

Dimly, Birdie was aware of the crushing burden of Carhartan's gaze resting on her still. Then his chair scraped back and he rose to his feet, armor clinking, the red jewel around his neck flashing in the light of the fire.

"I will take the girl off your hands."

Birdie stared at Carhartan, her mouth hanging open, mind struggling to comprehend the words he had just spoken and determine the reasoning behind them. The answer struck like a blow, and she staggered before it.

It was because of the Song.

It had to be.

"Yes!" Madame cried. "Take her."

"No." Master Dalton brought his fist against the heavy oak mantel in emphasis, then danced back, clutching his hand to his chest. Soot dropped from the chimney into the groping flames and a cloud of smoke arose.

Carhartan chuckled tonelessly. "You mistook me. That wasn't an offer."

Birdie barely had time to see his hand move before the red blade hovered at Dalton's throat. Carhartan snarled at the trembling innkeeper. "I am Carhartan, Second Marshal of the Khelari and a servant of the Takhran. You dare not refuse me."

Dalton's mouth moved, but no sound came out.

"What are you waiting for?" Madame shrieked. She rushed over and seized Birdie by the arm, dragging her toward Carhartan. "Give him the girl and we'll be rid of her."

Birdie's head erupted with a thousand pleas, but all she managed was a strangled, "No. Don't!" She tried to wrench free, but Madame's fingers tightened, nails digging into her skin.

Carhartan pressed forward, forcing Master Dalton against the wall. "Need we revisit Drengreth?"

Master Dalton's face turned the color of porridge at that word, as if it were a curse and its mere utterance had doomed him to unending torment. "You! I . . . uh . . ." His eyes darted from side to side, trapped, like an animal in a snare. Then he bowed his head. "So be it."

"No," Birdie cried. "Please—"

Madame slapped her across the face, and she stumbled back, tears rising in her eyes, struggling to comprehend what was happening through the cloud of horror that surrounded her.

A smile stretched across Carhartan's face. He stepped back and pulled the sword away from Master Dalton. The innkeeper relaxed. Then Carhartan drove the blade into Master Dalton's chest.

Birdie's cry melded with Master Dalton's agonized scream.

"That is for Drengreth," Carhartan said.

The innkeeper collapsed, blood staining his white apron and pooling on the stone floor. Madame stood speechless. Carhartan took a step toward Birdie, blood dripping from his sword. The clanking of his armor, the thudding of his boots, even the licking flames of the fire became a confused roar in Birdie's ears. She snapped out of her terrified daze and bolted, past the stunned Kurt and Miles, past the orange cat peeking around the doorframe, and out of the inn.

A single thought drummed through her mind, impervious to the shouted curses Carhartan called after her or the quickening tattoo of his feet. She had to find Amos. Amos would know what to do.

"Amos!" Birdie burst through the double barn doors and stumbled to a stop. Balaam's stall was still empty. Amos was gone.

A heavy hand fell on her shoulder and spun her around. "No more tricks," Carhartan snarled. His left fist smashed against her head and she fell.

4

"Well, if it isn't Amos McElhenny!" Brog's voice boomed out over the clamor and hubbub of the Whistlin' Waterfly Tavern—a hundred merry voices raised in loud conversation, raucous song, and all manner of noisy eating. "Welcome back to Hardale."

Amos plucked the feathered cap from his head, and—gripping the proffered hand—shook it heartily. "Aye, 'tis good t' see ye again!" He stared at his friend's broad girth. "Whist now, Ma's been feedin' ye well."

"Finest cook in these parts. Tell me." Brog's face wrinkled in disgust. "How can you bear it up at the Sylvan Swan? Madame's tongue could sour the finest brew—which hers certainly isn't!"

"T'is good then that I stay for Birdie's sake, an' not fer Madame's cookin'. But now that ye mention it, I'm reminded o' how parched me throat is . . . I can scarce talk. Bring me a mug o' yer finest brew an' a plate o' stew."

"Certainly. Certainly." Brog started toward the kitchen and then stopped. "Ah, Amos . . . much as I hate to mention it, you do have coin with you, don't you?"

"Innkeepers." Amos snorted. "All alike." He jangled the new coins in his pocket, an unusual weight, and smiled. "Just finished peddlin' a pack load off t' the general store. Sweet music t' me ears!"

"Music to mine as well." Brog paused halfway through the kitchen doorway. "As I recall, you still owe me from your last visit." The door swung closed behind him, sending a wave of heat and the savory aroma of roasting meat and vegetables wafting through the room.

"Trust a tavern keeper t' remember." Amos shuffled to a small, round table on the far side of the room. He shrugged aside his heavy overcoat and tossed it on the back of his chair, dropped his cap on the table, and settled back to wait.

A few locals clad in drab homespun lounged near the door, gulping down huge quantities of Ma's stew and even larger amounts of Brog's brew. Whether their ruddy faces came from long hours spent in the sun or at the bottle, Amos could not say.

Others, more strangely clothed, filled nearly every available seat in the tavern. Loose cotton shirts, wide legged trousers, salt battered boots, and colorful headscarves proclaimed the sailors, Waveryders from the West coast. Three curly-headed dwarves from the Whyndburg mountains, clad in flowing tunics and robes ornamented with bronze brooches, huddled at a stumpy table beside the fire, large mugs overflowing in their hands. In a far corner, wearing fringed shirts and leggings made from various combinations of lion, tiger, and leopard skin, armed with light throwing spears, sat the Saari, the people of the Vituain desert.

Amos grunted. Nearly all the tribes of Leira were represented in this one room and those that weren't present, like the Khelari, certainly wouldn't be missed.

"Here you are, Amos." Brog plunked a steaming earthenware bowl and large mug on the table before him.

Amos sniffed appreciatively. "Hoo-whee, Brog! I do believe yer wife has done herself proud tonight."

The chair across from Amos groaned as Brog sat, laboriously folding his long legs under the table. "Aye, nobody's found reason to complain. With this crowd, that's quite a compliment. We're full up tonight. A passel of Waveryders came in this morning seeking lodging. There's been a constant stream passin' through over the past few weeks, with new tales of horror every day."

"Langorians?"

"Aye, the pirates've been marauding along the west coast. Night attacks. Villages burned. People starving 'cause the fishing boats and merchant ships daren't put to sea."

Amos curled his lip in disgust. Accursed foreign devils. "Ye haven't heard any news o' Bryllhyn, have ye?"

Brog shook his head. "Thinkin' of your mother? No, no news of Bryllhyn. Doubt the Langorians will go that far north. Though I wish pirates were all we had to deal with."

Amos shot him a quizzical look.

"There've been other travelers on the road lately. Unwholesome folk. Won't say where they're coming from or where they're goin'." His voice dropped. "Even seen some dark soldiers."

"Khelari?"

"Aye, travelin' secretive like. Didn't come near me, and you can be sure I kept my distance."

Amos scraped the last traces of stew from his bowl, then tugged his long-stemmed pipe from his belt, lighting it with the aid of the sputtering candle. He mulled over his words before he spoke. "I met one today."

Brog's eyes widened into an unspoken question behind his spectacles.

"The Second Marshal o' the Takhran's forces was riding through the hills out near the Sylvan Swan. But that's not all." Amos hitched his chair closer to the tavern keeper. In return, Brog leaned forward across the table, so intent upon the conversation that he ignored the candle flame licking at his beard. "He travels under the protection o' King Earnhult."

Brog shook his head. He looked like a man struck unaware by an arrow. "A Khelari bearing the pledge of the Midland king? By Turning, what evil days are these?"

"Evil enough, I'm—"

The tavern door burst open, slapping against the opposite wall with a noise like thunder. In staggered a bloodstained man. He croaked, a piteous plea for aid, and collapsed on the threshold. Amos nearly overthrew the table in his haste to reach the fallen stranger. Brog followed at his heels, rumbling commands that few heard or cared to heed.

Amos placed a hand beneath the corner of the man's jaw. A pulse. He lived. "Quick, get him over t' the fire. Bring water an' bandages." He shouldered the limp form. The crowd scattered, cleaving an open path to the fireplace, while the three dwarves grumblingly shifted to a vacant corner.

Amos lowered the dead weight onto the hearth and relinquished his position to Brog, who barreled past with a wet cloth in his hands. He watched the tavern keeper tend the man's wounds. Despite copious amounts of blood, the wounds did not appear serious. The man's face was pale, and his light hair was plastered to his scalp by congealed blood from a gash on his forehead. He was clad in plate mail, and a sheath hung empty at his side.

Amos's breath caught in his throat. Beneath the layer of mud and smirch, the dark color of the armor was visible. Black. A Khelari. He stared at his hands as if they might be contaminated.

"Amos? Are you listening?" Brog's voice startled him out of his daze.

"What? O' course," Amos said.

"I asked you to pass me the bandages." Brog glared at him over the rims of his spectacles. "Would you see the man bleed to death? We're not at war. Not yet. Any wounded man has the right to claim my help, regardless of the color of his armor."

Biting back a reply, Amos forced his wooden hands to work. In a moment, Brog completed his task, and wiping his bloodied hands on his apron—sat back on his heels to survey his handiwork.

The soldier moaned. His eyes shot open. Wide staring eyes, enormous in his haunted face. Lashing out with his fists, he curled up into a defensive ball, whimpering. "No! No . . . don't hurt me!"

The fires in Amos's stomach wilted. The soldier seemed so . . . young. No more than two or three years past twenty.

But a Khelari none the less.

A fist whistled past his nose. Amos caught the arm. "Enough o' that. Take it easy."

The soldier stared at him, face wrinkled in concentration. "Where . . . am I?"

"The Whistlin' Waterfly, in the village of Hardale," Brog said. "Can you stand?"

"Yes . . . I think so."

"Let me give you a hand. Amos?"

Amos stared stupidly at Brog, then—swallowing his distaste, helped heave the soldier to his feet, set his broad shoulder under the man's arm, and half carried him to the spare chair at his own table. Once more the crowd parted before him—this time stumbling back as though he bore death in his arms.

Brog disappeared into the kitchen, returning a moment later with his favorite remedy: a mug and a bowl of stew. The soldier raised the mug with trembling hands and took a long gulp before sinking back into his chair, leaving the stew untouched.

Gradually, the tavern hum resumed, interrupted conversations and half-sung songs starting midsentence as though the stranger's arrival had never occurred. Though from the black glances cast their way, Amos knew what was foremost in every mind.

At length Brog gave utterance to the shapeless thought. "We're none too fond of the Khelari here," he said.

Defiance steeled the soldier's gaze. "Perhaps you *farmers* should get accustomed to us. Might be you'll see a lot more of us in the future, once the road's finished."

"What road would that be?" Amos asked.

"The Takhran's new expansion project. A road from Serrin Vroi straight through Dunfaen Forest to the Midlands, bypasses the River, Shallow Pass, everything." The soldier shrugged. "We'll be here before you know it."

"What was wrong with the old one?" Brog demanded.

The answer was obvious. At least to Amos. The old road was too long. Too long and too roundabout to provision and reinforce an army on the road to war. "The Takhran needs a clear route southward."

"The Takhran's purposes are his own. I simply obey orders."

"Don't take offense, lad," Brog said. "Do you mind tellin' us what happened to you, er, Mister . . ."

The wild look crept back into the soldier's eyes. "Hendryk. My name's Hendryk."

"So, Hendryk," Amos said, a grin tweaking his face. "What happened? Did ye run afoul o' a farmer with a pitchfork?"

A red flush suffused Hendryk's pale cheeks and his lips trembled. "Don't mock me, old man. I have seen things you cannot imagine. A monster! Enormous. Screeching like a hawk on the wing. Four of us were scouting ahead of the main party, and we didn't stand a chance against it. We tried to run, but it was everywhere we turned. Bredger fell. Zerek and Fullers attacked it with spears. I saw Zerek crash against a rock, and then the thing dove at Fullers. And I ran, as hard and fast as I could, my head splitting with the screams of my comrades and the roars of the beast. Got lost in the forest for a day . . . maybe two. Finally stumbled out on a hillside and have been wandering ever since."

For a moment, Amos said nothing. A fly buzzed past his head, and he swiped irritably at it. He realized how quiet the inn seemed. Strange. He looked up into the incredulous glares of tavern-goers gathered in a semicircle around his table.

Bilgewater! That didn't look good.

"Well," one drawled, "ye don't say." The man's tattooed arms and bright head scarf proclaimed him a Waveryder. He spat into a large brass spittoon several yards away, a perfect hit. "That's quite a tale, Khelari."

"It's true."

"What d' ye take us for, babes? Nightmare—that's all it was. Afeard of the dark, are ye?"

"I tell you I saw a monster! As clear as I see you now. He haunts Dwimdor Pass in Dunfaen Forest."

"D' ye hear that, mates?" the sailor bellowed. "Now he'd have us believin' in ghosts and fairy tales! Whoo-hee, did the big bad beastie scare ye laddie?"

Brog stood. "Come now, Corrd. That's enough. He's a customer, same as you."

"Customer? He's a blaggardly Khelari." Corrd stooped to stare Hendryk in the eye. "I tell ye soldier, the only monster in Leira lurks in the heart of Serrin Vroi—your master, the Takhran."

"That's a filthy lie!" Hendryk fumbled for his missing sword.

"Enough!" Brog's fist descended like a sledgehammer on the table. Hendryk's bowl of stew bounced off and shattered on the floor. "I won't have any brawlin' in my tavern. Take your disputes outside."

Corrd grinned and folded his brawny arms across his chest. "With pleasure. How's that Khelari? Are ye man enough to come out and fight me?"

The soldier licked his dry lips. His face seemed even paler than before. "I . . . will fight."

The room erupted in a roar of approval, and the crowd surged toward the door. Amos stifled a groan. Pity tugged at his heart, combating the hatred stirred by the whispered name of the Takhran. What did he care? The man was a Khelari. A plague. He deserved death. No matter how young and frightened he looked, he could never change that.

"Belay there!" A voice split the exulting tumult, and Amos was surprised to discover that it had come from his own throat. The crowd's questioning eyes gazed into his own. He fought to speak. "The man . . . is injured. Corrd, ye're no Waveryder if ye'd fight a wounded man."

Corrd squared off with Amos, the muscles standing out like ropes on his neck. His boulder-like fists tightened.

Amos set his teeth. His hand moved to the knife at his belt. Pity he had sold the spear pipe to the general store. It would have come in handy . . . to save a Khelari? What was he thinking?

Corrd spat. "Keep yer friend, peddler. I won't dishonor my hands with his blood." He stormed away and the crowd dispersed.

"I would have fought him, but thank you."

Amos spun around. The soldier stood at his elbow, clutching a chair for support, right hand extended. "I didn't do it for ye, Khelari." Amos brushed past and snatched his overcoat and cap from the table. "T'wasn't a fair fight."

Brog's voice stopped him halfway to the door. "Amos, haven't you forgotten something?"

Amos filled his lungs with air and slowly turned around. "No, I don't think I have."

"A small matter of four coins . . ."

Amos dug around in his pouch as he stumped over to Brog, and then dropped the coins into the tavern keeper's hand. He swept his cap from his head, bowed to the tavern and its inmates, and stalked out into the night, thoroughly disgusted with himself and the whole evening.

"Bloodwuthering blodknockers!"

Master Dalton was dead, and it was all her fault.

A shuddering breath escaped Birdie's lips, and she blinked away the tears streaming down her cheeks. Again and again she saw him fall, heard his cry, smelled the sickening tang of blood.

She sat behind Carhartan on the leather, skirt-like armor that covered the gray horse's rump, her legs chaffing against the back of the saddle. Forced to cling to Carhartan's waist to keep from falling, though the very thought of his touch repulsed her.

The pounding ache in her head drummed in time to the horse's beating hooves. A relentless, jarring trot. The rocky red road dragged past underhoof, while heather-crowned hills and sheep-sheared troughs fell away on either side.

At last, she summoned the courage to venture a question. "Please . . . Sir . . ."

He gave no sign that he had heard her.

She forged ahead, louder. "Where are you tak—"

"Be silent," Carhartan snarled.

She shrank away from him. Back into silence. Her head throbbed, and her back ached, and exhaustion crept over her, weakening her grip and weighing down her eyelids.

On and on they rode. Now walking . . . now trotting . . . now slowing to a walk once more. Until night settled over Leira and darkness hid the road from view. Overhead the moon, Mindolyn, drifted across the sky while the stars stirred and came alive, glowing like pearls in the blue, black sea.

Birdie gazed at the dancing constellations, reveling in their beauty. For a moment, peace washed over her. High and far away, the melody echoed in her mind. Pure and glowing, yet strong and cold as steel, achingly, hauntingly beautiful. A tear slipped from her eyes.

The stars. Were they singing? The melody swelled inside her like a wave, threatening to burst from her lips in triumphant refrain.

Then the dark music crashed into her mind. Black, ominous, foreboding. She flinched and clasped her hands to her ears in a vain attempt to block the noise. Her head spun and she swayed. Carhartan's left hand shot out, steadying her.

"Careful." A single word barked beneath his breath, then he faced forward again, urging the horse back into a trot. Once more, Birdie found herself staring at the armor on his back.

How long would the night last?

She lifted her gaze to the stars, as though expecting some answer to her unvoiced question, but the stars made no reply. Even the airy enchanting melody faded from her mind. She was alone in the dark, a captive with her captor.

Birdie bowed her head and longed for the night to end.

5

"C'mon ye fly-swoggled lollygaggin' worthless lump o' dragon bait! 'Tis only a wee bit further!" Amos yanked at Balaam's lead rope, forcing the donkey to stumble after him into the yard of the Sylvan Swan.

It had been a fine pair of days. What with the Khelari turning up at the inn on the same day Amos discovered Birdie's curse, then Brog's news of pirates pillaging the coast, and now word of a new road through the forest—a road that could only be the prelude to war.

Aye, 'twas grand. Boggswogglingly grand.

Amos stumbled to a halt in front of the barn and scrubbed at his bleary eyes with the back of his hand. There would be time enough to worry come morning. For now, he planned on getting some sleep. Thanks to the new coins in his pouch, he'd be able to sleep *inside* the inn for once, instead of roughing it in the barn.

He tugged the barn door open and fought with Balaam's girth until the packsaddle slid off, and the donkey was free.

"Gerroff with ye." Amos slapped the donkey's hindquarters.

Balaam grunted but stood still, head swaying between his knees, asleep on his feet before the opening.

"Suit yerself." Amos slung the packs over his shoulder and trudged toward the inn. The lazy donkey would never consider running away. It required too much effort with too little reward, especially when there was fresh hay waiting in his stall.

The inn door slid open on oiled hinges, and Amos tiptoed inside, noting his muddy footprints with a touch of satisfaction. He'd have to pay for it in the morning, but for the moment, revenge—however pointless—was sweet.

A voice stopped him just before he reached the guest quarters. "Back here to gloat?"

He whirled around and froze at the sight of Madame standing, arms crossed, in front of the kitchen door. Bother the woman! Why wasn't she asleep like any sensible person ought to be at this hour of the night?

He tugged the feathered cap from his head and plodded over to her. "Madame—"

Smack.

He blinked, cheek stinging from her slap.

"Don't speak to me, you brute," Madame said. "If it wasn't for you none of this would have happened!"

"None o' what?" He dodged another strike, stumbled through the kitchen door, and halted in shock.

"Stay out of there! You can't go in!" Madame's frantic cries buzzed around his ears like a swarm of flies. He swatted her away.

Dalton, swathed in blood-soaked bandages, lay on a bedroll beside the sputtering fire. The orange glow highlighted his hollow cheeks and the dark circles beneath his eyes. Breath rasped in his throat, and his fingers clutched feebly at the covering.

"Dalton?"

The innkeeper moaned, and his head rolled to one side. Madame pushed past Amos and knelt beside the cot. For a moment, as she bent over her husband, the sharp lines of her face smoothed to tenderness. Then Amos shuffled closer, and the fire returned to her eyes.

"That cursed Khelari stabbed him. All to get that wretched girl!"

"Birdie?" A twinge of pain in Amos's chest sent the blood roaring to his head. He grasped the startled woman by the elbow. "Where is she? Is she safe?"

Madame wrenched herself away. "I don't know, and I couldn't care less. The fiend took her away. Good riddance."

"When? Where did they go?"

A cold hand clutched his wrist. "Amos?" Dalton struggled to rise and fell back, gasping for breath, his face the color of bread dough.

Amos dropped to his knees and clasped the innkeeper's hand in both of his own. "Dalton. Listen t' me. Ye have t' listen. What happened t' Birdie? Where did he take her?"

Dalton's eyes dulled. "It's over, Amos," he rasped. "He's taken her." He choked and hacking coughs shook his frame. "She's gone. Like Artair and the others, and not even Hawkness could have saved her."

Artair.

Amos jerked back and fell over his own feet. The name pounded in his head, and he spat to rid his mouth of the horrible taste rising in his throat. He gritted his teeth. "Just tell me about Birdie. When did they leave?"

"Rode out north two hours ago—"

Two hours . . . then there was still time!

Amos did not wait to find out more. Thrusting Madame aside, he yanked his cap onto his head and barreled out of the inn into the starlit dark of the night. He paused just outside the door, flung his packs open, and rummaged through them. Bolts of cloth, pots, an empty brew skin, odds and ends—all that he had not yet sold—went flying. He growled and dumped out the contents of the first bag, then started on the next.

There, at the bottom of the pack, he felt it, and a chill ran up his arm.

He withdrew the oilcloth packet, yanked the string off, and tore open the wrappings. The dirk fell into his hands—battle-scarred leather sheath, blade miraculously free of rust, and the bronze hawk's head pommel crowning the carved wooden handle. Amos fastened the dirk to his belt and started back to his feet, leaving his wares scattered in the inn yard.

Balaam startled awake, eyes bulging in terror, as Amos bore down upon him. Amos forced a ragged breath into his lungs and leapt astride the donkey. Grasping the lead rope in both hands, he drove his heels into Balaam's flanks.

Hard.

The donkey stood still. Ears quivering, tail twitching, he flipped his head around to stare at Amos through eyes steeled with rebellion.

"Amos!" The innkeeper stood on quivering legs in the doorway, clutching the doorframe for support. "What do you mean to do?"

Madame appeared at his side, trying to pull him back inside.

Amos kicked and the donkey jumped but refused to move. Fury rose in his throat and burst forth in a strangled cry. "I'll tell ye what I'm not goin' t' do. I'm not goin' t' sit around like some stuffed goose an' allow 'em t' harm my wee little girl! I'm goin' t' get her back." He punctuated each of his last words with a sharp kick. "An' . . . no . . . fool . . . donkey . . . is goin' t' stand in my way!"

Balaam heaved a deep, donkeyish sigh and continued chewing the wad of hay in his mouth. Blackness swept across Amos's vision, a hideous cloud fueled by wrath. He fingered the end of the rope, and his limbs sprang to action. Kicking again and again in a frenzy. Whipping the fat donkey with the rope.

Amos heard his own voice as though it belonged to another, screaming like a mad man. "Come on. Come on. Come on!"

From the stoop, Dalton implored him to be silent, to calm down, and be careful. Be careful! Amos's ire rose at the thought.

Balaam lurched forward, submitting to the barrage of blows first with a staggering walk, accelerating to a drunken trot, and then a bone-jarring lope. Amos whooped, swiping the feathered cap from his head and fanning it in the air. His heels brushed the knee-high grass with each wobbling step the donkey took, but he traveled on Birdie's trail and that was enough.

"Amos." Dalton's choked voice reached him as he turned out onto the main roadway. "It was . . . he . . . knows . . ." Then the innkeeper collapsed, and Madame's screams burned Amos's ears.

He brushed all thought of Dalton from his mind. There was naught he could do to help, and Birdie needed him. He had to save her.

Reason spoke against it. It wasn't his responsibility. She was just a wee lass he'd befriended—a special lass, to be sure, but no duty of his. And now that he'd learned who she was—*what* she was—he ought to be riding as fast as he could in the opposite direction.

"No," he whispered. "I have t' get t' her. I have to."

He had to save her from Artair's fate. At least he knew where Carhartan was taking her. North, to Serrin Vroi. He had passed within a league of the great stone city several times. Even ventured inside once—a horrible experience that still haunted his darkest nights.

The rumors were enough to keep any sane man away, and his own memories were more than convincing. Once taken within those walls, no one ever returned. And that was where Carhartan would take her, as the Takhran had taken all the others.

As he had taken Artair.

The name rose unbidden in his mind, and he shoved it away.

Curse Dalton for dredging up the past.

He drew in a ragged breath. "Birdie lass, don't worry. I'm comin' fer ye."

PART TWO

6

"Catch the little thieves!"

Ky gritted his teeth and lunged forward, bare feet pounding against Kerby's cobblestone streets. His extra burst of speed brought him even with Dizzier. The older boy glanced at him, and a grin flashed across his face, sweaty beneath a tangle of thick black hair that flopped over his eyes.

"Keep up, little brother," he gasped. "Cause I ain't stoppin' for you."

Inwardly railing against Dizzier's longer legs, Ky strained to run faster. His jacket flapped awkwardly against his ribs, pockets weighed down by the afternoon's take.

There were three simple rules in the Underground: be invisible, look out for yourself, and no going back. Ever. They all added up to the same thing:

Keep up or get left behind.

Dizzier had drilled those rules into him with knuckle and fist. His ears still rang with Dizzier's recitation after each muffed run, each rule punctuated with a punch, repetition broken by repeated outbursts of "You got it yet, Shorty?" and "Can't nobody be *that* stupid!"

Until he *did* get it and could recognize the rules playing out a dozen times over every day among the other runners. It was the way of the streets, of the Underground. The young fell behind and were caught, while the older and stronger escaped.

Ky grunted and pushed up beside Dizzier. *Not this time!*

Angry shouts split the air.

He risked a glance over his shoulder, and the dark figures of armored men filled his vision. Instinctively, he reached for the leather sling looped like a belt around his waist, then pulled his hand away. It was a good enough weapon as far as it went, but hardly a match against an armed man.

The shouts grew louder. Ky knew without having to look that *more* soldiers had joined the chase. Fresh soldiers.

No time . . . we'll be run down in no time!

An idea blazed in his head, and he acted upon it, spinning to the left and darting down a side alley. "Come on, this way!"

Dizzier stopped hard. "Naw, don't do that."

"Come *on*." Ky raced down the alley, dodging puddles of dark water and leaping over piles of refuse, jacket tails slapping against his hips

Dizzier easily caught up to run alongside. "*Idjit*, this leads to the marketplace."

"I know." Ky grinned. "Keep up." His grin widened at the look of frustration that passed over Dizzier's face.

Behind, the pounding feet grew louder. Dizzier glanced back and his face turned white. He picked up speed until he passed Ky and disappeared around the corner of the alley into the marketplace.

No! Ky forced his aching legs to churn faster. Wind tore at his throat, and he could hardly find enough air to fill his lungs. He put forth his final reserves of strength, and tucking his head, he sprinted forward and dove into the market day crowd.

Startled cries rang out above. Crawling on all fours like a wild cat, he darted through the milling river of trailing skirts and leather boots. At last, an opening appeared before him, and he scrambled toward it. Just then, a man wrapped in a billowing cloak stepped into the gap. The sea of heavy fabric engulfed Ky. He kicked to free himself, knowing the man's indignant shouts would attract the attention of the dark soldiers.

Whack.

Ky clutched his head, blinking to see through the tears in his eyes. *Should have known he'd be carrying a cane.* He tumbled free of the cloak and slipped back into the crowd, steering clear of a glimpse of black armor to his left.

At least the crowd impeded the soldiers' progress as much as it did his.

A grin tweaked his lips. A fellow had to appreciate the small gifts in life, or he'd wind up just like Dizzier. Bitter. Rude. Foul-mouthed. Ready to pounce on anyone who got in his way.

"Psst . . ."

Ky spun around.

"Pssst . . ."

He studied the churning sea parading past. A stout farmer narrowed his gaze and gave Ky a wide berth, a basket of apples hugged to his chest. A few fashionable ladies glared down at him, contempt marring their powdered faces. But there was no sign of the speaker.

"Hey! *Slowpoke.* Over here." Dizzier's grimy face poked out beneath the crooked sign of an empty seller's stall. His head jerked in a sharp gesture and then dropped out of sight.

Dizzier *never* waited on him. Had he hung back this time to ensure Ky's silence about another muffed run? *He knows I wouldn't blab.* Ky forced himself to maneuver casually over to the stall, then ducked under when he was certain no one was watching.

Dizzier pressed to one side to make room for him. "Where ya been, Shorty?"

"Hiding. Where were you?"

"Watching." Dizzier grinned. "Come on. Time we disappeared." He yanked on a rope that stuck out of the boards lining the floor of the stall, and Ky jerked back as a two-foot-square hole opened between them.

A wide-armed V-shaped mark was carved into one of the boards. The hawk winging its way to freedom—the Underground symbol marking an entrance. After three years out on the streets, Ky had come to know the hidden passages fairly well. This must be a new one.

He traced the symbol with a finger. "Risky place to put a tunnel, isn't it?"

Dizzer cocked a quizzical eyebrow at him and slipped into the hole. "What d' you mean?"

"What if someone moves the stall? Or starts using it again?"

Dizzier's head and shoulders reappeared as he pulled himself back up. "Who's goin' to mess with an old wreck like this? You worry too much. C'mon."

Ky rolled his eyes and dropped down. *Now who's the idjit?* There was a difference between worrying and actually thinking things through. He'd never dare say it aloud though. Dizzier was too unpredictable. One moment, he'd be grinning ear to ear. The next, you'd be flat on your back in the mud.

As Dizzier pulled the trap door shut, Ky closed his eyes and counted to thirty, knowing it would take that long for them to adjust to the dark. Then he and Dizzier set off at a shuffling run, arms outstretched to keep from bashing into the walls.

"This is a new tunnel." Dizzier spoke over his shoulder. "Cade wants you to learn it. Provides the perfect in and out for the marketplace. Hidden but close to the action."

Perfect, right. So long as no one spots it.

For a long time, the only sounds were their measured breathing, the soft thud of their bare feet on the packed dirt floor, and the jingle of newly acquired coins lining the hidden pockets of their coats. Then Ky heard a creak and a light flared.

In that brief moment of visibility, a boy—Paddy—dove into the tunnel. He wore a heavy cloak tucked around him, but there was no mistaking that mess of red hair. From the odd lumps and bulges beneath the cloak, Ky guessed that he had been out apple bobbin'. Looked like he'd brought in a good haul, too.

The trap door thudded shut and the light blinked out. After his eyes readjusted, Ky could make out the dim form of Paddy running ahead.

A short time later, the tunnel joined a familiar larger passage and began sloping down underfoot. A gradual change, but unmistakable. They were nearing the Underground.

Five more times trap doors opened high above and runners clambered down the entrance shafts, hastening home with their spoils. Then a dim light appeared ahead, casting flickering figures dancing on the walls. The chatter of voices filled Ky's ears and brought a smile to his face. Silence might be a good rule of thumb in the tunnels—so shallow and close to the city streets—but in the heart of the Underground, secreted far below the earth in caverns where brave men once fought, laughter and loud conversations reigned.

Here, they were free from fear.

The tunnel bent to the left and then spilled out into a cavernous room lit by dozens of torches and a large fire blazing in the central ring. Runners flooded from the tunnels pockmarking the walls and collected around the storage room to add their contributions. Apples, bread loaves, and cheese wheels dropped from sleeves and coat pockets into the food bins. Kerchiefs, belts, hats, articles of clothing, and other miscellaneous items were packed in barrels for later sorting by the storeroom keepers. Coins and other objects of value useful for bribery were taken to a large chest at the far end of the store room.

Ky pushed through the swarming children, casting an appraising eye over the quantity and quality of the crop.

"Good harvest today." Rab, one of the older Underground runners—leaned against a barrel, elbows resting on the top, a half-eaten apple in his hand. He grinned, and his blue eyes twinkled behind unruly strands of curly brown hair. "Reckon Emhran's been good to us."

Ky grunted. He wasn't sure what Emhran had to do with it, but the harvest *had* been plentiful yet again.

"Oi, Ky," a voice called from his left.

"Oi, Paddy."

Something whooshed through the air toward him. He flung up his hands and caught the apple just before it smashed into his nose. The sudden reaction threw him off balance, and he bumped into the girl behind him, knocking her to the ground.

"Sorry, Aliyah." He helped her to her feet and retrieved her crutch from where it had skidded when she fell. "You all right?"

A wispy smile parted Aliyah's lip. "Fine, thank you, Ky." Tucking the crutch under one arm, she hobbled over to help at the food bins.

"Well done, laddy-boyo!" Paddy bobbed toward him, a grin wrinkling his freckled face. "Wait 'til Cade hears you knocked his sister over."

Ky chucked the apple back at Paddy. "Case you didn't notice, that was all your fault."

"How was harvestin' this morning?"

"Wait an' see." Ky winked and led Paddy over to the chest. He pulled his coat open and upended the large pouch sewn inside. Coins spilled into the chest, along with a lady's necklace, a brooch, and two rings. Paddy whistled his admiration.

"That's not all." Ky reached for the treasure stowed in his belt, but a voice from behind arrested the action.

"Not bad."

Ky spun around. A tall boy stood before him, clad in a ragged white blouse and tattered breeches, with a fine leather vest on top and a sword belted at his side. His arms were folded across his chest and his chin lowered so that his eyes seemed to look straight through Ky. Cade, the leader of the Underground.

Dizzier peered over Cade's shoulder. "Eh, I got more 'n him. Guess that means I'm still your second in command." He guffawed.

The laughter rankled Ky. Wasn't it Dizzier's fault their run had been cut short? If he hadn't insisted on sneaking into the fine goods shop, Ky might have had more to show for the day.

He tugged the dagger from his belt and shoved it toward Cade.

Dizzier's jaw dropped. "I never saw you take that."

"Guess I'm better 'n you give me credit for."

Cade's eyes lit up, and he snatched the dagger from Ky's hand. Slowly, almost reverently, he drew the weapon and held it up so the torchlight played on the blade. "It's well crafted. Couldn't ask for better. How did you get it?"

"Slipped it off a soldier's belt." Disbelief registered on their faces, and Ky crossed his arms. "It's *true*." Sure, the soldier *might* have been occupied talking to a lady at the time, but he saw no need to mention that.

Cade grunted and studied the dagger, massaging the grip with his fingers, then his eyes flickered back to Ky for a moment. "Good work." He jerked his head at Dizzier and strode off toward the armory.

Paddy whistled, doubling over in an elaborate bow. "Allow me t' congratulate you on those rare words of approbation from our worthy chief! You're a master runner, laddy-boyo! Care t' share a few trade secrets? Given a few years, you might even become as good as . . . as *Hawkness* himself, and *he* had the Takhran's price on his head."

Unlikely.

Ky shrugged and turned away. When it came to Cade, "good work" was high praise. So why wasn't he satisfied? What else had he expected? A clap on the back, maybe an independent thieving run without his assigned older brother watching his every move? No, that was asking too much. Gratitude wasn't Cade's way.

Or the way of the Underground.

7

"Uh oh," Paddy said around a mouthful of bread. "Trouble's comin' and it's staring straight at you."

Ky didn't bother looking. He scrubbed the last traces of mud from his sling and tied it around his waist. "Who is it?"

"Cade and Dizzier."

Ky popped the last of his bread and cheese into his mouth and finally glanced up. He and Paddy sat with the rest of the forty or so children in the Underground around the central fire ring to eat supper. Already, those who had finished were drifting away to complete their assigned tasks.

Several of the older boys had been working in the armory through supper, trying to coax bows and arrows and sling stones from the raw material gathered during the day. Cade and Dizzier had detached themselves from this group and were coming toward him.

"So long, pal. 'Twas nice knowin' you." Paddy slipped away.

Ky squelched a tremor of anxiety as Cade and Dizzier sat down on either side.

But Cade simply reached inside his vest and pulled out the dagger Ky had stolen, turning it over in his hands. "This cavern used to be the hideout of a band of outlaws led by Hawkness. Did you know that? My father told me about them, about him. Back then, Hawkness was the only one strong enough to stand against the Takhran and his soldiers. They were brave men, those outlaws, all of them heroes who fought against tyranny and died because of it. Like my father." He raised the dagger so firelight played across the blade. "Do you know what this means to us, Ky?"

Ky nodded. Real weapons were scarcer than one of Dizzier's good moods. Cade had his father's sword, and there were a few other blades scattered about—most in the possession of the biggest boys and girls. He glanced over at the armory where a dozen open barrels and crates lined the wall, filled with makeshift bows, arrows, clubs, and the other simple weapons they had been able to fashion themselves.

"It means more than you think." Cade rested his elbows on his knees. "It means hope. Freedom. Vengeance. You're ready to know the truth about us, about the Underground. We're not just collecting weapons to make thieving easier. We're building an arsenal for war."

"With who?" Even as the question left his lips, he realized what Cade would say. The dark soldiers were hated by all the Underground, but by none so much as Cade. "That's insane. We can't fight the dark soldiers—there's too many of them."

"It *is* insane. For now." Cade's eyes glittered in the firelight. "Now it's just a dream, but one day it will be a reality. Even now, every dagger we steal, every purse, every coin is a step toward breaking the soldiers' hold on Kerby. And when we're ready, we'll fall upon them and drive them from the city. Then we'll be free again."

The energy pulsing through Ky brought him to his feet. "The soldiers have been here for five years, Cade. They won't just leave."

"Yes, five years. And that's how long I've been here. The soldiers are responsible for all of this, for all of us." Cade's gaze darted to Aliyah limping across the room, her crutch tapping on the stone floor.

Cade avoided talk of his past with the same skill that had brought him through a hundred harvesting runs without getting caught, but Ky knew the dark soldiers were somehow responsible for Aliyah's injuries. Still, just knowing the soldiers were evil didn't give the Underground the means to fight back.

He turned to Dizzier. "You in on this too?"

Dizzier settled back against the fire ring, reclining with his arms behind his head. "Eh, the dark soldiers aren't any friends of mine, Shorty. Sooner they're gone, the better."

"Are you with us?" Cade asked.

Ky's shoulders drooped. No one said *no* to Cade, however hopeless the proposition. "Yeah, I'm with you."

Dizzier shot up and pounded him on the back. "Got good news for ya, Shorty. You've just earned your first independent command."

The coveted words fell flat on his ears. He blinked and turned to Cade for confirmation.

The older boy nodded and stood, clasping his hands behind his back. "Tomorrow. Apple bobbing. You've been assigned a new little sister."

"Quick! Get down." Ky shoved Meli behind the barrel and threw himself flat in the shelter of an overturned crate. Two black-armored soldiers stalked past the alleyway, boots rat-tatting on the cobblestones.

Once it was clear, he pushed up onto his knees, muck clinging to his clothes and hands. The crate looked like it had once housed chickens. Smelled like it too. He wrinkled his nose at the stench and checked to make sure his sling was still tied around his waist and hadn't been loosened by the fall.

Meli crept over to him, lifting her rust-red cloak clear of the mud. Wisps of brown hair clung to her face and she pushed them aside. "What're we s'posed to do, Ky?"

"Apple bobbin'." He turned back to study the street. What was Cade *thinking*, sending a seven year old out on the streets with him on his first independent run? She wasn't ready for this.

He could only hope he was.

"When we get out there, remember the rules. Be invisible, look out for yourself, and no going back. Ever." It was odd to hear his own voice saying the familiar words, now that he was in charge of a thieving run and not just one of the runners.

"Time to go. Just do what I do." Ky scurried to the end of the alley. A cluster of well-dressed city dwellers passed by, followed by an old man leading a mule laden with kindling. Ky spotted his objective across the square—a fruiter's cart—and slipped into the stream, motioning for Meli to follow.

The trick to being invisible was all a matter of timing. His gaze darted around the marketplace, and the necessary moves ran through his mind as he performed them. *Pause for a count of two. Take three paces and duck. Turn around and study the bakery window. Four steps to the left and stop.* All with the assumed casual air of an ordinary market-goer. It was simple, once you got the hang of it.

He crouched behind the fruiter's cart, eyeing the wares. Apples, plums, pears, grapes, and cranberries, all bursting with juice and color, teetered on the lips of the baskets stacked inside the cart. Ripe for the taking.

"You ready, Meli?"

There was no answer. Ky spun around. A glimpse of red caught his eye, and he spied her standing in the middle of the square as the tide of traffic parted around her like a river skirting a rock. The oversized cloak dwarfed her small form so that only her head peeked out, staring wide-eyed around her.

"Psst, Meli. Over here." The market-day symphony of tramping feet, noisy chatter, and sellers hawking their wares swallowed the hushed words as they left his lips. Ky ground his teeth together and let out a hiss of frustration.

Why can't she pay attention?

The clatter of iron-shod hooves and rattling wheels jerked his attention away. A large wagon drawn by four horses jolted toward him, piled high with soldiers, tools, and equipment—shovels, ropes, and the like.

In his mind, Ky darted through the city, marking off the gates and troop placements. This route through the market meant the soldiers were headed toward the west gate. There had been a steady stream of soldiers coming and going through there lately, though what they found to do beside the River Adayn or out on the wild moors of the Westmark beyond was a mystery to Ky.

But wouldn't Cade give anything to find out what they were up to?

The thought scarce crossed his mind when he spied a familiar, tall, cloaked figure gliding behind the wagon, following the same odd pattern of progression that he had used. The figure lifted its head and their eyes met, then Cade faded into the crowd.

"Hoi, get out o' the way, girl!"

The shout sent Ky's heart plunging to the cobblestones. Meli stood frozen in the middle of the square as the wagon bore down upon her.

"Look out!" Ky raced forward. His feet left the ground and he dove, knocking her out of the way. The wagon barreled past, wheels churning inches from their toes. Startled gasps rippled above their heads, but Ky knew from experience that the citizens of Kerby wouldn't dare display any greater sign of disapproval toward the dark soldiers.

He picked himself up, careful not to step on the girl laying at his feet, a shapeless lump drowning beneath the folds of her enormous cloak. He gently prodded her with his finger. "You in there?"

Her head peeped out. "Is it safe?"

"Yeah, it's safe."

She scrambled up and threw her arms around his waist.

Ky pulled back and then gingerly patted the top of her head. "Don't forget, we still have a job to do. Can't go back to the Underground empty handed, now can we?"

She shook her head.

"Good. Keep your mind on the task. See that stall over there?" He pointed to a fruit and vegetable stand across the street. An apron-clad farmer slept on a stool in front of the stand, feet propped up on a basket, head lolling to one side with his mouth hanging open. "That's your target."

Meli nodded and scurried off. Ky waited until the fruiter's back was turned and then squirmed under the cart to watch Meli through the spokes of the wheels. She bobbed through the crowd, ducking, twisting, standing stock still, then creeping forward on silent feet as Ky had taught her. As she tiptoed past the sleeping farmer, her arm shot out, snagging an apple from the stall and concealing it in the folds of her cloak. She dropped behind a barrel of pears.

The tension eased from Ky's forehead. He smiled when her head peeped up over the barrel and gave her a thumbs-up. *Not too bad for a first timer. Little slow maybe, but not sloppy.*

Boots crunched into his line of vision, and he jerked, nearly hitting his head on the underside of the cart. Through the slatted wood above, he saw the bulbous nose and pockmarked face of the fruiter. There was a great deal of thumping as the fruiter fumbled through the baskets, and then he turned back to his customer. "There you go, ma'am. Prime of the crop, just for you."

Ky rolled to the far side of the cart and snaked his hand up over the side. Three apples and a pear dropped down his sleeve and into the pockets sewn in his jacket before the customer left. Circling the cart on hands and knees to avoid the fruiter, Ky pocketed another four apples before moving on to the next stand where he followed the same drill.

At last his jacket bulged around his waist like the fruiter's barrel-shaped belly. He spied Meli hunkered down against the wall of the bakery shop. Digging through his pouch, he selected a small, round stone and lobbed it through the crowd. *Ping.* It bounced off the wall above her head. She jumped and her eyes met his.

Ky twitched his head over his shoulder, and she stumbled toward him, head bowed and eyes down to avoid tripping on the dragging ends of her cloak.

The pent up air whooshed from Ky's lungs as he retreated toward the alley. Soon they would be safe in the Underground. From the looks of her cloak, Meli had done well for her first time out on the streets. Cade would be pleased.

A dark figure wandered into his line of vision, and Ky dropped behind the corner of a fishmonger's stall. He bent down and pretended to be examining his dusty foot while the dark soldier passed by, leading a sweat-soaked horse. The soldier studied a scrap of parchment in his hand, pausing here and there to push his light hair out of his eyes and peer up and down the street as if he were unsure of his direction.

Beyond the soldier, Meli toiled on, struggling beneath the weight of her morning's take. A warning cry rose in Ky's throat and dashed against his teeth without any sound coming out. *Meli's small. She won't be noticed.*

Not if she kept her wits about her.

The soldier approached the little girl without appearing to see her. In a moment, he would pass by and she would be safe. Just then, Meli tripped on her cloak, smacked into the soldier's arms, and fell backward to the ground.

An apple rolled from beneath her cloak and bumped against the soldier's feet.

8

Ky caught his breath as the soldier bent over—to pick up the apple, he thought. Instead, the man's hand settled on Meli's arm. "Are you all right?" he asked.

She scrambled back. There was a ripping sound and her cloak tore off, trapped under the soldier's foot. Half a dozen apples spilled out, thumping on the cobblestones.

The soldier's face crinkled. He stooped and lifted a red apple to the sunlight.

"Run," Ky muttered. "Can't bluff this one. You have to *run*!"

Comprehension flooded the soldier's face. He stepped forward, pointing a finger at Meli. "Thief!"

She bolted and his hand descended on empty air. His shouts chased her across the square, awakening the farmer she had robbed, alerting the crowd. Terror painted on her face, Meli flew past Ky's hiding place, eyes darting, searching for escape. Searching for him. The farmer and soldier lurched after her, followed a moment later by two more soldiers drawn by the shouts.

Ky's hand drifted to his sling. He had to help her. Had to . . . But the rules of the Underground pounded through his brain, arresting the action. *Look out for yourself.* Cade would say the rules came before everything. They were the only way to survive on the streets. Dizzier would pound him on the back and encourage him to slip away. Say he was *finally* getting it.

It was the way of the Underground.

Hang the Underground! Ky burst from the shadow of the fishmonger's stall, fingers flying to load his sling. He barreled through the onlookers, seeking a clear shot.

"Hey! Over here!"

The rearmost soldier twisted around just in time to catch the sling-stone on his forehead beneath the beak of his helmet. He fell flat, as if he had run smack against a wall. The clatter of his armor on the cobblestone brought the other soldiers and the farmer to a halt.

"That's right!" Ky loosed another stone, and it cracked off the light-haired soldier's breastplate. "You can't catch me, you foul-smelling, bumble-headed, thick-nosed cave bats!"

A thrill of excitement coursed through his veins as the soldiers turned from Meli and charged him, weapons drawn. He continued slinging. One soldier dropped his spear and clutched a hand to his chest. Two more stones felled the farmer with a double blow to the stomach. Then the peril of Ky's position settled in his chest, and he took off at a sprint.

No chance of disappearing now. The patterns of invisibility required stealth and precision—things hard to achieve on the run. So he led the soldiers on a merry chase. Up and down the square, in and out of shop doors, brushing past begrimed laborers and pushing through forests of bustled skirts and dapper trousers.

But the light-haired soldier refused to be shaken. Ky could hear the breath grunting in the man's throat. Time for a change in tactics.

A wine merchant's shop with a mountain of barrels stacked out front was just ahead. Ky veered toward it, scaled the stack like a sailor in the rigging, and hopped down the other side, knocking over a whole row behind him. He dropped to his knees and slid under the belly of an old cart horse. A chorus of furious shouts and clanging armor split the air as his pursuers tripped over the barrels and crashed.

He nipped into a side street, racing as fast as his legs would carry him through the maze of alleys and byways. Three lefts brought him back into the square, and he crouched beside the fishmonger's stall, watching the soldiers hurtle into the side street he had just vacated, calling curses down on his head.

He slipped into the crowd. By now, Meli should be safe on her way to the Underground.

At the far end of the alley, Ky halted in front of a stone etched with the hawk symbol and scanned the horizon to make sure no one was in sight. He slipped inside the concealed trap door, lowered it back into place, and was instantly enveloped in a tight hug.

"Ky!" Meli squealed.

Warmth crept through his chilled limbs. He gulped and strove to steady his voice. "Shh, not so loud. We're too close to the streets. C'mon, we need to get back."

As they neared the heart of the Underground and he felt the heat of the fire on his face, he dug four apples out of his pockets and slipped them into her cloak.

Cade met them at the storeroom entrance, arms folded across his chest, still clad in the cloak he had worn aboveground. Black mud stained the cloak hem, his trouser knees, and covered his boots.

That sort of muddiness didn't come from harvesting in the city.

Ky simply nodded at Cade in passing, concealing his curiosity, and proceeded to empty his and Meli's pockets into the proper baskets. At the sight of the four apples he pulled from her cloak, Meli's eyes grew round, but Ky pressed his lips together and shook his head, and she kept quiet.

Eleven apples and five pears. Not bad considering they were the fruits of his solo labor. Not good either, since Cade would suppose it was his and Meli's combined work.

He turned from the basket to find Cade staring at him. Swallowing hard, Ky walked over to him. Better to face the lion and get it over with. "Oi, Cade."

"Ky." Cade nodded. "So, how did he do?"

Ky felt his forehead wrinkling. Cade must have made a mistake. He had been assigned a little sister. *She* had done fine. More or less. Then he realized that Cade was looking past him, at someone behind. He twisted around and met Dizzier's mocking gaze.

"Eh, not too bad," Dizzier drawled. "If only he could remember to *look out for himself,* like I been tryin' to drill into that thick skull of his for the past three years."

Cade's eyes narrowed. "If you're talking about what happened with the wagon, I already know about it. It was stupid, but excusable. Aside from drawing a little attention to himself, he caused no harm."

Cade standing up for him—that was a rare thing. Ky stood straighter, thrusting his shoulders back, until he realized what Dizzier's words meant. "You were spying on me?"

Dizzier waved the accusation aside. "Naw, as if that wasn't bad enough, the fool jumped out of a perfectly safe hiding place to draw the dark soldiers away from the little girl."

"Aw, c'mon! It wasn't *exactly* like that." Ky stopped as a scowl spread across Cade's face. "Well, what did you expect me to do, walk away?"

Cade's hands tightened into fists. "To the Ring."

Ky swung the short sword in an experimental slash. It whooshed through the air as he brought it around to guard his head, then his lower legs. The sword felt dull and clumsy in his hand. Lifeless. Like every other sword he had ever fought with.

Scarce five minutes had elapsed since Cade announced that Ky was to meet him in combat, and the Underground had already set up the rope barriers that formed the Ring around the central fire pit, provided Ky with a borrowed weapon, and gathered all the runners to witness the spectacle.

Paddy squeezed Ky's hand. "Good luck. You're going t' need it, laddy-boyo." He retreated into the crowd of runners lining the Ring.

Ky sighted down the sword at Cade limbering up within arm's reach and gulped down a ragged breath. The son of a swordsmith, Cade insisted all the Underground runners learn to handle weapons. He held a weekly training session in the Ring where he and the older boys assisted the younger runners with mastering basic fighting techniques.

Cade was also fond of using the Ring as a form of punishment. Anyone caught disobeying the rules or endangering the Underground was sure to be summoned to face him in the Ring. It was a good deterrent.

No one wanted to fight Cade.

Clang.

Cade's blade hammered into the crossguard of Ky's sword.

He started and nearly dropped his blade.

An unnerving twinkle danced in Cade's eyes. He fell back into position, sword in his left hand, right arm raised. "You ready?" Without waiting for a reply, he turned to Dizzier and said, "Five minutes."

Ky stifled a groan. Thirty seconds—let alone five minutes—in the Ring with Cade meant bruised shins, cut and broken fingers, and wounded pride to boot. Still, he would give it the best shot he could. He fell into the middle-guard position, content to let Cade take the offensive. Mindful of the children on the edge of the Ring, and equally careful to avoid the fire ring in the middle, Ky circled to the left.

Cade lunged.

Ky deflected the blade to the right with a twist of his arm, and followed it up with a downward cut at Cade's shins. Not fast enough. Cade easily evaded the stroke. Ky barely had time to recover before Cade slashed at his exposed right shoulder. He stumbled back, blocking a dizzying combination of cuts and thrusts.

How did Cade move so fast?

Out of the corner of his eye, he caught a glimpse of movement as Dizzier pushed through the runners. For a brief moment, their eyes met, and Dizzier's mouth stretched into a derisive grin. He winked and shoved the little girl next to him to the ground.

Ky broke away from Cade. The little girl looked up, tears showing in her eyes beneath her tangled brown hair. "Meli!" He darted toward her.

Something hard hit him in the back of the knees, and he pitched forward onto his face. His right elbow smashed against the ground, and the sword fell from his numb fingers, sliding to rest a few feet away. Clutching his arm to his chest, he rolled up onto his knees, but was kept from rising by the tip of Cade's sword against his throat.

"Pay attention," Cade said with exaggerated patience. "If this was a real fight, you'd be dead by now."

"Huh." Dizzier tugged Meli to her feet and dusted her off. "If this was a real fight, Shorty wouldn't have lasted ten seconds. Stop going easy on him, Cade."

Ky glowered at his older brother as he massaged the feeling back into his right arm. He wouldn't mind facing Dizzier for five minutes, even five seconds. Just long enough for one solid punch to wipe away that sneer. His hands clenched into fists.

Cade whacked him with the flat of his sword. "Wake up. You still have three minutes left. Retrieve your weapon."

Dizzier's chuckle filled Ky's ears as he stalked over to his sword and snatched it up from the ground. His neck and cheeks burned with contained wrath. What kind of no-good pushed a little girl for no other reason than to distract him?

Across the Ring, Paddy's sympathetic grin drew his eye. Then Paddy's face contorted, eyes winking, cheeks wrinkling, mouth stretching abnormally wide. He looked to be mouthing *something*, but Ky couldn't figure out what. *Look out . . .*

Was Cade sneaking up on him?

He cast a glance over his shoulder, but Cade was a good five paces away.

Paddy rolled his eyes, repeating the message in a harsh whisper. "Look out for yourself, laddy-boyo."

Paddy's meaning settled as a lump in Ky's throat. This wasn't just a punishment, it was a test. To see if he could follow the rules when it mattered most. Cade planned it this way, for Dizzier to distract him, for Meli to fall.

"Any day now." Cade's blade swooshed past his head, carving a figure eight in the air.

Anger rushed through Ky's veins and into his sword arm. Gritting his teeth, he stood with legs slightly bent, sword at an upward angle, awaiting Cade's attack. It came without warning. One moment, Cade stood before him, sword poised motionless in his hand. The next, he transformed into a wild eyed beast, hurtling toward him like a stone from a sling.

Ky jumped to the side, batting away the hungry blade. It returned a moment later, licking at his throat. He fought the urge to fixate on the gleaming steel, and focused instead on the man behind the sword. His target. *Swing from the left, block lower left, upward cut.* He mentally recited the moves, limbs obeying the silent commands. *Parry and forward thrust.*

Cade swept Ky's blade aside just before it reached his vest. They stood, swords locked, metal grating against metal. Drops of sweat glided across Cade's forehead, and a brief grin flickered across his face.

"Let's make it more challenging, shall we?"

More challenging?

Ky pulled back as Dizzier and several older boys spilled into the Ring carrying rope, crates, and barrels. Within seconds, an intricate maze of obstacles littered the ground.

Cade toed a trip line. "This should keep us from getting bored."

Sure! Ky huffed a long breath. *Wouldn't want it to be too easy.*

He waited for Cade to raise his sword and then charged. The two swords met with a clash. Ky felt a momentary tremor of fear as he ducked and parried and slashed in return. Cade may have been holding back before, but he was going all out now, fighting at a blinding speed. Now the rhythmic clanging of their swords was punctuated by the thud of feet, leaping, jumping, and climbing in a deadly dance to avoid the obstacles.

Cade's sword grazed Ky's shin, and blood trickled down his leg. *Twang.* A trip line snagged his ankle, and he tumbled head over heels to the ground, knocking over a bucket. Cade charged, and Ky grabbed the bucket and sent it skidding at the older boy, giving him just enough time to regain his feet.

Then he saw his chance. As Cade lunged, he hurtled into a roll, allowing his momentum to carry him back up onto his feet inside

Cade's guard. Leg crossed behind Cade's knee, he threw all his weight onto the older boy's shoulder, toppling him to the ground. He scrambled to his knees atop Cade's chest and pressed his sword to his windpipe. "Do you yield?"

Sweat dripped from his hair into his eyes. He could feel the heat of the fire radiating across his back and suddenly became aware of the stunned silence filling the cavern.

Then Cade erupted.

His left hand dashed Ky's sword from his throat at the same time as his right fist crashed into Ky's jaw. Lights blared across Ky's vision. He toppled back into the coals at the edge of the fire ring. His hands landed on the glowing embers, and searing cramps shot up his arms. Half blinded, he scrambled away, slapping at the orange tongues of flame licking his hair and sizzling against his dripping skin.

Hands grasped his arms and pulled him to his feet. Through bleary eyes, he made out Paddy's concerned face peering at him. "Whew, laddy-boyo! You're insane, did you know that?"

Ky shook free of Paddy and blinked to restore his vision. Across the Ring, Cade sheathed his sword and stood with his arms crossed in blatant disregard of the blood dripping from the cut on his neck.

"Insane," Cade said. "But creative. Reckless and creative." He turned to Dizzier. "Do you think he is ready?"

Dizzier shrugged. "Dunno. Mebbe you should ask him."

Cade's gaze swept back to Ky, and he forced himself to stand tall under the scrutiny.

"Yes," Cade said after a long pause. "I do believe he is."

Paddy whooped next to Ky's ear, and Dizzier threw an arm across his shoulder. He flinched from the touch. "Cade, what's this all about?"

"A new mission." Cade's eyes glinted, cold and hard like steel. "A dangerous one. Are you in?" He stuck the tip of his toe beneath Ky's short sword and kicked the blade up into the air.

Ky caught it by the hilt, sending shivers of pain through his blistered palms. "I'm in."

"Come with me." Cade strode away, followed by Dizzier and Paddy. Ky hefted the short sword in his hand and hurried after them, stepping just a little bit taller than normal.

9

Mud seeped through Ky's jacket and slithered up the holes in the knees of his trousers as he belly-crawled up the slope after Cade. The cool mud soothed his burned hands, though he probably should have bandaged them before setting out. He jerked his head back as Dizzier's heels almost slammed into his nose for the third time.

Behind him, Paddy grunted and spat. "Bleh. Stuff tastes awful."

"Quiet," Cade growled. "You want an entire company of soldiers after you?"

Ky lifted his gaze and could just make out the dark edge of the slope against the bluer night sky beyond. There was an odd black lump in the middle . . . Dizzier's head. A second lump arose next to the first and yanked it down.

He stifled a chuckle.

Digging his toes and elbows in, Ky made his way to the crest of the slope and lay flat with his chin resting on the wet grass and the pommel of his new short sword pressing into his side.

He closed his eyes and took a deep breath. It had been a long time since he had been outside the city gates, away from the noise of the market and the stench of the streets and the bustle of the Underground.

The deep whisper of the River Adayn below filled his ears, recalling his attention to their purpose. His gaze swept down the slope, drawn to the cluster of red torches and bonfires at the base, and the dark hulk of the bridge spanning the water a little ways to his left.

Black figures, their movements exaggerated and jerky in the firelight, moved to and fro along the bank and across the bridge. Boats fitted with tiny flickering lights drifted across the surface of the river. Voices drifted up the slope, words and their meaning distorted by the wind, but one name burned in Ky's ears: the Takhran.

Looked like this was what kept the dark soldiers busy beside the river, though Ky still didn't know what *this* was, or what it had to do with the Underground. "This is what you wanted to show me?"

"No, Shorty." Dizzier's voice dripped condescension. "We thought a midnight roll in the mud would improve your looks."

"What're the soldiers doin' down there?" Paddy asked.

"That's what we'd like to find out," Cade said. "Whatever it is, it must be important. They've been working here for months. Searching for something. And for months before that, they were working farther up the River."

"So, what's that got to do with us?" The words were out before Ky could stop them. "I mean, why're we here?" He felt Cade's steely gaze on him, though he couldn't see it in the darkness.

"This is our new mission. We're going to watch them, day and night, until they find it—whatever it is. Then we'll strike and steal their prize."

"I like it," Dizzier said.

"Shure," Paddy said. "Seems simple enough."

Didn't *anybody* have any sense? Bobbing apples and nicking coin purses in the marketplace was one thing, but stealing from the Khelari was something entirely different and a thousand times more dangerous. Ky searched for the argument that would have the most impact. "Didn't you say they've been searching for months? They could be looking for months more!"

"No," Cade said. "They're close."

"How do you know that?"

"The number of soldiers has increased. They're stepping up their efforts. They know they're almost there—that or they're getting desperate. Either way, we have to be ready. If we want to win this war, we'll have to strike first."

Ky bit his tongue to keep from speaking. Anything more was sure to earn him the title *idjit*.

"What? No other objections from our newest recruit?" Dizzier chuckled. "I'll take first watch then."

"Good. Paddy, replace him in four hours. Ky, you're after Paddy. I'll get the rest of the runners on rotation after you."

Ky followed Cade and Paddy down the slope and back toward the city, pondering Cade's last words. How many others knew of Cade's war plans, and how long had *he* been kept in the dark? Only yesterday he had thought they were just ordinary kids banded together against hard times, but now Cade seemed to think they were some sort of an army. What could they hope to accomplish against trained soldiers?

"Somethin' wrong, laddy-boyo?"

Ky blinked away his thoughts and realized that he was standing at the base of the city wall. Cade was already scaling it above him, and Paddy waited at his side. "Nah, sorry," he muttered, and started climbing. The rough stone scraped his burned hands, and he wished again that he had taken time to bandage them before starting this midnight expedition.

Sneaking in and out of the city wasn't especially difficult at night. The dark soldiers enforced curfew and patrolled the gates, but there were at least a dozen low places in the walls where a decent climber could pass over. Still, caution was necessary lest a sentry find strangers on the wall-top. Once in the streets, they could fade into the night and disappear beneath the cobblestones without a trace.

Ky paused just below the wall-top until he was sure there was no one in sight, then dropped to the walkway and scurried down the steps. A hand gripped his collar, yanked him into the shadows beneath the stairway, and threw him up against the wall. The air burst from his lungs in an audible puff. He looked up into Cade's narrowed eyes.

"You passed the test today, Ky, but I have to know I can trust you." Cade gripped the front of Ky's shirt with one hand, pressing his forearm against Ky's neck, pinning him in place.

"You can," Ky choked out.

"Is everythin' good here, lads?" Paddy's anxious face appeared over Cade's shoulder. "All gettin' along, are we, like good mothers' sons?"

"It's fine. Stay out of it." Cade glared at Paddy and then turned back to Ky. "The Underground has rules for a reason. It's the only way we've survived this long. If you're going to ignore the rules or endanger our mission in any way, then I need to know now."

"I won't endanger your mission. But Cade, have you thought about what'll happen when you pit your army against the soldiers? We'll all be killed—"

"And if you keep questioning me," Cade's voice lowered to a growl, "then you'll have to face the consequences. I need you all behind me. This is our chance to get revenge on the dark soldiers for everything they've done. To avenge the lives they've stolen. To reclaim what's rightfully ours."

"I'm with you, I already told you." The words tasted like a lie, but what else could he say? He *was* with Cade, by necessity, if not by heart.

"You'd better be." Cade released him and stood back. "The time is coming, Ky. I can feel it. Soon, very soon, we'll be rid of the soldiers. And this mission is at the heart of it all." Ky could almost hear Cade's smile in his words. "This will be our best run yet."

With a rustle of his cloak, the older boy vanished into the darkness. Ky pushed away from the wall and bent over, hands on his knees, breathing hard.

Paddy chuckled softly. "You're such a fool, y' know that, Ky?"

He snorted. "Thanks, friend."

"Just tellin' the truth. Are you tryin' to aggravate Cade, or somethin'?"

"Of course I'm not."

"Well, I hate t' tell you this, but you couldn't do a better job if you set your mind to it, laddy-boyo." Paddy sat down with his back against the wall.

Ky followed suit, wincing as he stretched his legs out in front.

Thanks to his tussle with Cade in the Ring, his body ached all over. "I just can't understand him. Why does he want to fight the dark soldiers so much?"

"I s'pose not havin' been here from the beginning, you wouldn't understand. It's not much talked of now. Cade discourages it. You know Cade's father, Lucas Peregrine, was a swordsmith?"

Ky nodded.

"Well, when the soldiers first came to Kerby, they sought 'im out. Wanted 'im to do somethin' fer them—I don't know *what*. When he refused, they slew 'im and 'is wife, locked Cade and Aliyah inside the smithy, and set the place afire. But Cade's father had told 'im about these caves that the outlaws used in the old days, and showed 'im the trap door. Cade managed to get inside with Aliyah, but not before a burnin' timber fell on her leg and broke it."

"That's why she limps?"

"Aye. Not long after, Cade's uncle and aunt were taken, and his cousin, Dizzier, turned up in the tunnels. There were a lot of folks bein' killed and taken in those days—more so than now—and no one dared ask any questions of the dark soldiers. People just disappeared and more often 'n not the orphans were left behind. That's when Cade started the Underground. He figured if all the orphans banded together, we'd be able to survive, maybe even become family."

"Family?" Ky shook his head, thinking of Dizzier. Cade's system of assigning older brothers and sisters to new arrivals wasn't the best. "The soldiers killed my parents too, Paddy."

"And mine."

Ky ran his fingers over the pommel of the short sword. "They're evil and someone should stop them. But we can't."

Heavy silence draped over them. Ky studied the raw wounds on his hands. Like the others, he had been offered a new home in the Underground, hope after despair. And now, "Everything Cade's worked to accomplish . . . everyone he's tried to help . . . he's going to risk it, just to get back at the soldiers." Just to prove himself a hero, like the outlaws he idolized. Like his father. Like Hawkness.

Ky traced a flaring V in the grime coating the cobblestones

and embellished it, adding thicker wings, a tail, the hint of a beak. Hawkness would never have endangered the innocent to fight a pointless war for vengeance.

"Think of the young ones in the Underground, Paddy. Aliyah. Meli. Cade's going to get them all killed."

Paddy slapped his hands against his knees. "You take it too serious, Ky! Cade's been full of talk of war and revenge ever since the beginning. That's all it is. Talk!" He broke off and lowered his voice. "We'll do this mission, steal whatever it is, and it'll settle back down again. You'll see."

Ky stared his friend in the eyes. "If you think this is just talk, then you're the fool, Paddy."

PART THREE

10

Something hard drove into Birdie's side. She startled awake, curling in on herself to protect from the blows. Her breath came in short gasps. Over the crook of her arm she saw him—Carhartan, Master Dalton's murderer.

A lump swelled in her throat.

"On your feet," Carhartan said.

She staggered up, wincing at her aching muscles. They had ridden long into the night, halting at last as the stars faded in the eastern sky. Tauros's golden orb now hung above the horizon. She could scarce have slept for more than a couple of hours.

Carhartan saddled the gray horse, his back toward her, posture as rigid as an iron pole. He moved with precision, each action measured to a clipped rhythm of strict efficiency. Fleeting thoughts of escape while Carhartan was preoccupied drifted through her mind, but she could not get far on foot, nor was there anywhere to go if she did.

Carhartan gave the girth a final yank and then turned toward her, spurs jingling. "Eat. We leave soon." His hand jerked, and Birdie barely had time to catch the hunk of bread he tossed her before he clanked away.

When she finished, Carhartan led the gray horse over. She shrank from his touch as he hoisted her up and then mounted in front, the saddle shifting under his weight. Carhartan spurred the horse forward, and the jostling began once more in her precarious position on the beast's hindquarters.

Cool dawn shriveled into the glaring heat of the afternoon and then melted into the brilliant orange of sunset, distant mountains silhouetted black against the horizon. Green hills and grassy downs slept beneath the cover of a dark forest. The dusty road vanished into the trackless wilderness where leaf-laden branches blotted out Tauros's setting light and intertwining pricknettles barred the way.

Carhartan proceeded without faltering.

On all sides, mist-shrouded trees rose to support the dark canopy above, limp foliage dangling from wrinkled branches adorned with graybeard moss. A sweet, musty scent permeated the air. Rotting leaves squelched beneath the iron-shod weight of the horse's hooves.

A splatter of color drew Birdie's gaze to the ground. Dragon's tongue sprawled in the loam, pale-green, heart-shaped leaves with blood-red centers slouching at the ends of crawling vines as thick as her wrist.

The dense quiet gnawed at her. She had to do something—anything—to break the silence. "Where are we?"

"Dunfaen Forest."

Carhartan had actually answered—that was something. Perhaps he would tell her more. The forest's name sounded familiar. At the inn she had often snuck away to listen to the travelers spin wild yarns around the common room fire. Hidden in a corner, she'd dreamt of distant lands and adventures until Madame's hand descended on her ear, dragging her back to work.

From what she remembered, few travelers passed through Dunfaen Forest, preferring to take the long road around rather than the uncertain route over the mountains and through the pathless woods. But of what lay beyond the forest, she had only heard vague rumors. Of the northlands, of tribes enslaved, of fear and the whispered name of the Takhran.

"Sir …" She forced her voice to be steady. "Where are you taking me?"

But he did not answer and silence engulfed her once more, leaving her to the torture of her own imagination. Her head throbbed from the repetitive assault of questions. But no matter how far her thoughts took her, somehow they always turned back to the Song in the end. The cursed melody was to blame for what had happened—her capture and Master Dalton's death.

She saw again the innkeeper slumped against the wall, blood soaking his white apron, and a tear trickled down her cheeks.

Dangerous, that's what the Song was. Amos was right. It *was* a curse.

The horse lurched up a steep incline, forcing Birdie to cling to Carhartan's waist to keep from slipping backward. Exhaustion folded its arms around her. Her eyelids drooped.

"G'on, ye stubborn bit o' lettuce-mouthed, dredged-up pond scum." Amos brought the end of the rope across Balaam's hindquarters and threw in another kick just for good measure. The donkey grunted and responded with a jarring burst of speed.

By Turning, it was working! He *would* catch them. Amos knew it in his heart, believed it in his soul. Nothing could keep him from rescuing Birdie from Artair's fate.

"Hyah! Get on—"

The world flipped upside down.

He shot forward off the donkey's back and hurtled toward the ground. He tried to twist around, to bring an arm or shoulder up to break his fall, but there was no time before he crashed and the air bust from his lungs.

A crushing weight landed on top of him, driving him into the ground, squeezing the life from his body. Balaam. Amos fought to breathe, to move, to stay awake, but his vision blurred, and the world slipped away.

• • •

Amos groaned and dug his fingers into the ground, straining against the weight of the fallen donkey on his right leg. Grunting with exertion, he managed to crawl forward a few inches, transferring the pressure from his knee to his calf. He kicked at Balaam with his free foot. "C'mon! Get up, ye earth-shatterin' lump o' charbottle."

Balaam struggled to rise but fell back before Amos could free his leg. Pain blazed through his knee. He had . . . to get . . . free. Shoving his elbows into the ground, he dragged himself forward, inch by inch, biting his lip until he tasted blood. At last, only his ankle lay beneath the donkey.

One final effort and he dragged himself free.

Amos lay on his back, gasping, searching for the strength to rise. A few feet away, he saw the small petra burrow that had been the cause of their fall. He shuddered—nasty little creatures, petras, with their bright green eyes, leathery wings, tiny sharp teeth, and inconveniently placed burrows.

Tugging his feathered cap down on his head, he forced himself to sit. A searing burst of pain speared his knee, and he swallowed a cry. He tugged the broad sash from his waist and wound it around the already swollen joint, tying it off with a skillful knot.

He cast a baleful eye at the donkey thrashing about on the ground with the rope twisted about his legs. "Easy there, lad. I'll get ye out." Amos yanked the rope free, and Balaam staggered to his feet.

Now it was *his* turn. Amos levered upward with the assistance of a cooperative tree near at hand and took an experimental step. A stab of pain warned him to be careful, but the wounded limb supported his weight. Setting his teeth to endure, he limped over to Balaam and ran his hands down the donkey's legs, searching for injuries. The donkey's right foreleg bent at an unnatural angle at the knee. It was hot to the touch and already so swollen that the skin felt stretched and hard.

"Blithering barnacles." No way the beast could travel now. He removed Balaam's rope halter and tucked it under one arm. "Sorry, laddie. Afraid 'twas just a wee bit too much fer ye."

The donkey nuzzled Amos's sleeve. He jerked his arm away. "G'on with ye. Get out o' here!" He brought his hand down on Balaam's rump, and the donkey lumbered off into the night.

Poor beastie deserved a better fate. Amos watched as the gray figure dwindled in the distance. "Mind ye don't get eaten by wolves!" He turned away. "Daft—that's what I am. Talkin' to a donkey? Simply daft. Forget it, Amos. Ye've got t' find Birdie, so stop standin' around like a mournin' duck an' get on with it."

Stirred to action by his own words, Amos tucked the rope in his belt, hoping it would prove useful when he caught up with Carhartan.

And he *would* catch up.

Even if he had to walk all the way to Serrin Vroi.

His hand struck his sheath in passing, and it bounced against his leg. Empty. A shimmer in the soil drew his gaze, and he shuffled over to snatch the dirk up. The blade gleamed like moonlight reflecting off the surface of a woodland pool.

He returned the dirk to his scabbard, blade whispering against the leather as he did so. Setting his jaw, Amos faced north, into the darkness of Dunfaen Forest, and took a deep breath. "I'm comin', Birdie."

11

Birdie jolted awake, gasping for breath. She lay still, gazing upward, listening to the night. Tauros still slumbered. Stars blinked softly through shredded wisps of cloud. Her gaze plunged through the forest to the horse, hobbled and staked to a tree, coat shining pale blue in the moonlight. The saddle and leather armor were perched on a rock beside the horse, bridle laid across the seat.

There was no sign of Carhartan.

Birdie inched to her feet, peering into shadows beneath the eclipsing tree limbs. Still nothing. She scarce dared believe her good fortune. Was he really gone? She tiptoed forward a few steps and then froze in place.

Sibilant whispers drifted toward her from the shadows beneath the trees to her left—two voices. The louder voice sounded like Carhartan, though she couldn't discern what was said nor identify the second speaker. Had another Khelari arrived during the night?

She took a deep breath, hoping to calm her trembling limbs. She could not hope to escape two of them. It would be better to wait for Amos to—

No! She clenched her fists. It was high time she admit the truth. Amos would not come. If she wished to be free, she would have to escape on her own.

She crept forward another step.

The horse's head sprang up, and the beast snorted.

A shout split the sleepy silence, followed by heavy footsteps and a ragged voice cursing. Birdie fled, clutching her skirts to her knees to grant her legs free movement.

The horse was not yet saddled—should give her a few minutes head start.

A root snagged her foot, sending her sprawling into a patch of dragon's tongue at the base of a tall, black cliff. She scrambled upright on the squelching, swaying bed, slapping aside the wet leaves that clung to her arms and legs, and then tore off through the woods away from the cliff.

She didn't know where she was going, and she didn't care. Her only thought was to put as much distance between herself and Carhartan as she could. So long as her back was set to Madame and Hardale and the two terrors, it didn't matter where she wound up. She had nowhere to go, nothing to do, but run.

So she ran.

Until her lungs ached with each heaving breath, and her legs trembled with each step, and she was forced to skid to a halt, doubled over, hands resting on her knees as she fought to breathe. Her hair hung in damp cords about her face. Sweat dripped into her eyes. She dashed it away, and as soon as her gasping breaths slowed to manageable puffs, she began to walk.

She picked her way along the clearest path she could find through the thick underbrush, while the night marched past in rhythm with the measured tread of her feet.

Then she saw it.

And all hope vanished.

Silhouetted in a gap through the trees, a tall, black cliff stabbed toward the sky.

No . . .

Birdie's legs quivered, threatening to give way beneath her. She clutched a nearby zoar tree for support, resting her forehead against the smooth trunk. It was the same cliff she had seen earlier, after slipping on the patch of dragon's tongue. Somehow . . . someway . . .

she had run in a circle. She was no farther from Carhartan than when she started.

The woods seemed to press in about her. Dark trunks stood like sentinels stationed on either side to keep her from escaping. Grasping boughs snagged her hair and limbs, as if the forest itself conspired with Carhartan.

Iron-shod hooves rattled somewhere to her left.

Carhartan screamed her name.

Birdie tore away from the trees and dashed parallel to the hindering cliff, ducking branches and scrabbling over fallen boulders. Ahead, a broad gash carved down the cliff face. She sprinted toward it and stumbled to a stop, skree shifting beneath her feet, at the entrance to a yawning gorge that melted into blackness.

Drumming hooves behind.

Birdie sucked in a deep breath and dashed headlong into the gorge. Splintered rocks snagged her bare toes. Pricknettles stabbed her feet. Her lungs ached and a stitch burned her side.

Hoofbeats jerked to a stop at the gorge entrance.

She froze midstride. A long moment of agonized waiting, stifling shuddering breaths, then the hooves clattered down the gorge.

Down the rough path she raced, arms and legs flying. Silence was no longer an issue. All that mattered was speed. Already the hooves drew nearer. The horse's heavy breathing puffed on her heels, and she could hear the bit clanking against its teeth as its head moved in stride.

Her gaze darted around the gorge. Scrubby bushes armed with thorns crawled up the side of the cliffs. Jagged walls of rock stretched toward the stars on either side.

The horse skidded to a stop, cutting her off. A hand caught her arm and yanked her from the ground.

"No!" Birdie shrieked. She planted a solid kick in the horse's belly and it shied away from her attack. An oath broke from Carhartan's lips as he lurched to stay in the saddle. One of his gauntlets came loose in her grasp and she fell, landing on her back with an aching thud.

Carhartan clutched his right arm to his chest, the hand missing at the wrist. His gauntlet clanked to the ground beside Birdie's head, and she screamed as it rolled toward her, stopping with the open end facing her.

Empty.

Carhartan swung down from the saddle. Gasping for breath, Birdie scrambled away. Her back struck something hard, and she felt the cold rock of the gorge wall against her palms. She rose, pressing herself against the cliff, as he strode toward her.

Distorted as a mountain crumbling to dust, the black melody burst into her mind. Hopeless it seemed, despairing, yet filled with malice. Then soaring above the darkness, the five notes arose in her heart. The Song quelled the misshapen tune with beauty. Surging higher and higher until it filled the gorge, shielding her with light.

Trapped without hope, Birdie did the only thing she could. She lifted her head, closed her eyes, and sang the cursed melody.

Loud and clear, her song rose like the first drop of spring sunlight after a long gray winter. Carhartan, before so tall and terrible, seemed to shrink. She was suddenly aware that she did not sing alone. Hundreds of voices harmonized with her. Some deep and slow, a hollow echo from the depths of the earth; others light and airy like the whisper of butterfly wings fluttering through crystal skies.

While the other voices repeated the same five notes, her own lips breathed forth a complete melody of pure and radiant light. She reveled in the beauty of the Song and the rippling dance of the undulating notes that poured from her heart.

A hideous metallic *shiiinnngg* broke through her reverie, and she glanced down to find herself staring at the crimson tip of Carhartan's sword. The melody faltered on her tongue and faded away.

Carhartan's face twisted in hatred, but there was fear in his eyes. "Silence, little Songkeeper."

The warmth fled from her cheeks, but anger burned within, heating her tongue to action. "You are afraid. That's why you threaten me. You're afraid of the song I sing—"

A stinging blow landed on her mouth. Her head snapped back, striking the gorge wall.

"Filthy little vermin!" Carhartan spat at her feet and struck again.

Specks of light flared across her vision through the tears swimming in her eyes. Carhartan drew his fist back a third time, and she raised her arms to protect her head.

A horrible screech rang out, bouncing off the walls of the gorge to sound forth again and again. Carhartan stumbled back, and Birdie slumped to the ground, her head spinning. Through blurred eyes, she saw Carhartan assume a defensive posture as he circled, gazing into the night sky.

All was silent.

At last, Carhartan relaxed and lowered his blade. He took a step toward her.

Birdie struggled to rise.

The screech tore through the gorge again, then a massive shadow plummeted from the sky and tore the helmet from Carhartan's head.

Carhartan yelled and stabbed over his shoulder. With a roar, the creature snatched the sword from Carhartan's hand, snapped the steel like a dry twig, and flung the broken pieces aside. Carhartan launched himself at the beast, and the two tumbled to the ground.

Birdie forced herself to rise on trembling limbs and circled the fighting pair until she was in the middle of the gorge again. Scarcely daring to breathe, she backed away. She watched as the creature fought its way to the top. Pinning Carhartan with dagger-like claws, the creature loosed a ferocious roar and drew its head back to strike.

Birdie's heel struck a rock and she fell. The creature looked up and met her gaze. In an instant she sprang to her feet and raced away, but it was already too late. She knew that. The creature had seen her.

The dull throb of beating wings overwhelmed the thudding of her feet. She staggered on, weaving from side to side. Something swiped her legs out from beneath her, and she fell onto a muscled body covered in feathers. She managed to twist around and throw her arms about the creature's neck before it shot into the air.

A scream rose in her throat, but the burst of speed forced her to bury her face in the beast's feathers and hold on with all her might lest she fall. Maybe that was the creature's plan—to drop her from a height and feast on her remains.

Thump. The creature landed, and the jolt threw her from its back. She scrambled to her feet atop a cliff with a drop-off behind her. Trapped again, with nowhere to run.

The creature stalked toward her. It was a massive beast, built like an enormous cat with a face that was somehow both bird-like and cat-like at the same time. Reddish-brown feathers covered its head, chest, and wings, while the rest of the beast's body was clad in tawny fur.

Slowly, she stretched out her hands, palms toward the beast. "Please . . . please don't hurt me."

The creature lowered its head. A voice, like a rumbling growl, came from its open beak. "Quiet, little Songkeeper."

12

Plunging farther into the woods with each painful step, Amos pressed onward, eyes fixed on the ground. A line of disturbed leaves was the only trail he had to follow—he could only hope it was Carhartan's. He had heard tales of the legendary hunters of the Vituain Desert who could track their quarry across the shifting sands for weeks without losing either the trail or the scent. Pity he'd never learned the trick.

A screech rang out.

Amos halted, arms and back prickling. Halfway between a scream and a roar, the sound reverberated through the forest. Twisting spirals of leaves tumbled from shaking limbs. A large black bird burst from its perch in a tree a few yards away and winged skyward.

The words of the Khelari from the Whistlin' Waterfly filled his mind. *A monster in Dwimdor Pass.*

The scream came again. He held his breath. Such a terrible rasping noise could never come from a human throat. It was followed by a cry of terror—this time distinctly human. And close.

"Birdie!" Amos barreled through the underbrush, following the echoing cry. Thorns tore at his legs, and his knee throbbed at every step. He whipped the dirk from its scabbard and clenched it in his fist.

He *must* reach Birdie. The thought propelled him past the limits of endurance. Then the last repetitions of the scream trailed away into nothingness, and Amos staggered to a halt in a narrow rift between two cliff faces.

Too late?

"Birdie!" His voice bounced back at him from the surrounding cliffs, mocking, scornful, hopeless. "Where are ye, lass?"

There was no reply.

"Bloodwuthering blodknockers!"

The patch of sky visible through the open ceiling of the gorge grew pale. A faint tinge of pink trickled across the gray expanse as night fled before the coming dawn. Amos threw his head back and filled his lungs with crisp air, then started walking once more.

He would not rest until he found her, even if it meant wearing his feet to shreds and walking until his legs gave way beneath him.

Clang.

His booted foot struck something metal, and he looked down. His hand flew to his belt and ripped his dirk from its sheath. The Khelari Marshal, Carhartan, sprawled at his feet, legs crumpled beneath him, arms shielding his face. A puddle of blood, still glistening wet, pooled around his body.

Amos studied the fallen man in silence, then seeing no sign of life, knelt over the still form of his enemy. A bleeding gash traversed the man's face from his scalp, diagonally across his nose, to his right ear. Below his ear, a puckered brown scar, half hidden by his mail, marred the flesh of his neck.

Amos traced the flaring lines with a finger. Looked almost like an old burn scar . . .

The world suddenly shifted.

He could still feel the roughness of the gorge beneath his feet and the cool morning breeze puffing against his cheek, but he beheld a distant place. Veiled in darkness, spattered with the dim light of torches, marred by the bodies of the fallen. He had not seen in it in many long years, but it haunted his dreams nonetheless.

He could almost taste the smoke in the air.

Rough wood scraped his palms. Flames licked at his fingertips.

Distant shouts and screams—dying screams—filled his ears. A roar ripped from his throat. "Traitor!"

Dark eyes opened wide, a cry frozen on his lips, the man scrambled away as Amos thrust the torch in his face.

Oran Hamner.

The Khelari groaned.

Amos fell back, lungs heaving. Fury settled in his throat like a noose about his neck, threatening to strangle him. "Still alive? After all these years?" He dropped his dirk, snatched the limp form up, and shook him by the shoulders. "What of Birdie? What have ye done with her ye sneaking, treacherous ormahound?"

Warm blood seeped onto his hands. With a jerk, he released the body and staggered to his feet. His boot clanked against his dirk. Slowly he picked it up, staring in fascination at the red stain his fingers left on the gleaming blade. His hand shook as he raised the dirk over the Khelari soldier at his feet.

"Twice accursed traitor, ye deserve t' die." He tensed to strike, breath hissing through clenched teeth. Death would be best. Not murder—merely an execution long delayed. He'd failed to kill Oran once, and it had resulted in sorrow. He couldn't fail again.

But his arm wouldn't move. Looking down at the fallen soldier, he saw not the bearded Khelari nor the traitor of that terrible night, but the young man he'd once called brother. He clenched his fist and thrust the image from his mind. "Ye deserve t' die!"

Still he could not strike. Even now, so many years later, he could not do the deed. Even now, he proved a failure.

The dirk slipped from his quivering hand and clattered on the ground. Amos spun away, stomping about aimlessly, shouting incoherent words to the sky. Then he made his way back to Oran's side.

"By rights ye should have died long ago. I couldn't slay ye then, an' I can't do it now, not in cold blood. But know this: if ye cause any more trouble fer my lass, I swear I'll cut yer throat an' rest easy doin' it."

He collected his dirk and inspected the ground step by painstaking step. Red blood splattered the cliff face behind Oran . . . Carhartan. A twisted iron horseshoe peeked out from beneath a flat rock. Large brownish-red feathers scattered before a puff of wind.

He caught one of the feathers and held it up to his eye. The markings were unfamiliar, but at least it was not the black feather of one of the Takhran's spies. He released the feather and the wind blew it away.

Flapping like a night moth with a broken wing, the feather rose and then dropped, landing atop a crimson mark on a distant boulder. It fluttered where it lay, like a hand beckoning him. Amos scoffed at the idea—flibbersticks and roughnash—still, he followed and bent over the stone to examine the mark.

The air turned cold, and the earth seemed to tilt beneath his feet. He clutched at the boulder to keep from falling. A bloodstain in the shape of a four-toed clawed print marred the surface of the rock. He placed his hand inside the pad of the print and fingered the deep gouges left by the claws. Similar cuts scored the rock in several other places. And pressed into the bottom of one of the cuts was a tattered scrap of light-blue material.

Amos dug it out of the scratch and clenched it in his fist. Birdie's dress. He spun around, searching the gorge. "Birdie. Birdie!" He shouted her name again and again, until the cliffs took up the cry and carried it ahead of him. Then he began to run, staggering down the gorge.

Always, he arrived too late.

"Quiet, little Songkeeper."

Birdie pressed her palms to her aching head. Would the nightmare never end? The creature could talk, just like that strange cat back at the Sylvan Swan.

Somehow, it was all bound to the melody.

The creature must have heard her sing. Something about the song had led Carhartan to kidnap her. Whatever it was, it must have also driven the beast to attack Carhartan and take her captive. It was the only connection she could make. The only thing that made sense—as much sense as something so utterly insane could make. Assuming, of course, that the beast wasn't just planning on having her for supper.

"What do you want from me?" Her voice quavered despite her efforts to keep it steady.

"Want from you?" The creature made an odd hissing sound. It took Birdie a moment to realize that it was laughing. "I have been searching for you for years, little Songkeeper."

Little Songkeeper—Carhartan had called her that. A chill crawled up her arms and questions tumbled from her lips. "What? Why search for me? Who are you? Why do you call me that?"

"Because that is what you are. That is your gift."

"Gift?" Birdie set her jaw. "What do you know of it?" The melody had brought nothing but sorrow. It was no gift. It was a curse.

A strain of music caught her ear. Fierce, wild, and free, the voice seemed to be coming from . . . the creature.

She grasped at the thought. "Can *you* hear it?"

The creature's head drooped. "Nay, little Songkeeper, I cannot."

The melody vanished, and the last spark of energy seemed to drain from her limbs. Her legs sagged beneath her. The creature caught her with a wing before she could fall. At the beast's touch, terror coursed through her veins, and she scrambled beyond the reach of its beak and claws.

"Please . . . please just let me go." It didn't matter where she went. So long as it was far beyond the reach of strange creatures and cursed melodies and fearsome Khelari soldiers.

The creature folded its wings across its back. "I am not going to hurt you."

"Then let me leave."

"I cannot."

Birdie fought against the panic rising in her chest. To have escaped Carhartan only to be captured by a monster. Would she never be free?

"Birdie!"

The familiar voice sent a burst of hope through her. "Amos?" She spun around and knelt on the cliff's edge, peering down into the gorge. The peddler staggered into view around the bend, half running, half limping, hair streaming back from his face.

Birdie dug her fingers into the ground, clenching a handful of earth in each fist. He *had* come. "Amos! Up here."

Amos stumbled to a stop and cast about in a circle, finally locating her on the cliff top. "Birdie? Are ye—blitherin' barnacles!" Faster than Birdie could have imagined possible, he drew his dirk and brandished it aloft. "What d' ye want, monster? Let the lass go free, or I swear by the Turnings, I'll carve yer hide from yer bones an' leave yer carcass fer the carrion birds."

The creature muttered something. It clacked its beak together, turned a piercing eye on Birdie, and motioned her forward with a sweep of its wing. "Is he your Protector?"

Birdie nodded slowly. The title certainly seemed to fit Amos.

"Then I must take you to him," the creature said. "Come."

It's a trick, a voice inside her screamed. The beast meant to lure her within reach and kill her . . .

She dismissed the thought. The creature was so much faster and stronger than her, it did not need to resort to trickery.

Swallowing her fear, Birdie climbed onto the creature's back, and the beast launched into the air and spiraled down into the gorge. As soon as the creature's paws scraped earth, she jumped off, raced over to Amos, and flung her arms around his middle.

His hands settled around her shoulders. Safe. Secure. Comforting.

"You came," she whispered. Everyone else had abandoned her, but Amos came.

"O' course I came. Couldn't let anything happen t' my wee lass, now could I?" He brushed the hair off her forehead and smiled, then his gaze flickered past her, and his expression hardened.

Birdie twisted around and saw the creature seated behind her, wings furled at its sides. Not a threatening pose, but alert, every muscle taut and ready for action. "What *is* it, Amos?" she whispered.

"A griffin—foul monster. Not t' be trusted. Thought the Takhran had hunted them all down over twenty years ago."

"Is it so strange to you that one should have escaped the Takhran's wrath? You of all people should know that is possible." The griffin inclined his head. "My name is Gundhrold. I may be the last of my kindred, but that I yet draw breath is a living defiance against the Takhran, and in that I am satisfied. *I* will never stop fighting him."

Amos's hand tightened on Birdie's shoulder. "Look . . . I don't know who exactly ye think I am, but ye've got the wrong man. I'm just a peddler, an' we need t' be on our—"

"Do you think to keep your true identity hidden when any beast of sense can recognize that blade from half a league away?"

"This *blade* was a gift from an old friend, an' I don't know what ye're talkin' about—"

"Are you the Songkeeper's Protector?" Gundhrold's feather-tufted tail swished. "How came she to be in the hands of that villain?"

"Look, *beast*." Amos emphasized each word as if speaking to a dimwitted child. "There is no Songkeeper here. An' I won't waste any more o' my time listenin' t' yer superstitious podboggle. Come lass, 'tis time we left."

He tugged at Birdie's arm to draw her after him, but she resisted his pull, bewildered by what she had heard.

"C'mon," Amos said.

"No, no. I don't understand. Is this about that song?"

"Not now, lass. 'Tis not safe—"

"You are the Songkeeper," Gundhrold said. "And I am sworn to protect you."

"Aye, ye've done a grand job o' that so far, haven't ye?" Amos jabbed a finger toward the griffin's face. "She's my lass, not yer precious Songkeeper, an' I intend t' keep her safe. From the Takhran, an' ye, an' all the rest o' yer foolish friends!"

They were in each other's faces now, nose to beak, neither yielding an inch. Birdie shoved between them. "I don't understand. Tell me what's going on."

The peddler gripped her shoulders in both hands, bending over so that his face was level with hers. "I'm tryin' t' keep ye safe. Ye have t' trust me. We have t' get out o' here. Get ye home."

Home. The word had a hollow sound. Birdie wrenched free of Amos's grip. "What home? I don't have one. I'm not going back to the Sylvan Swan. You can't make me."

For a moment, Amos stood as if dumbstruck, mouth hanging open, head tilted to one side. "But what . . . o' course not, lassie. I won't take ye back t' that wretched woman, ye have my word on it. I'll take ye home. My home. My mother can look after ye."

Birdie searched his eyes for any hint of falsehood, scarce daring to believe he meant it.

"On my honor, lass." He clapped a hand over his chest. "I'll take ye t' my mother, and ye'll have a home—a true home—at last."

The griffin clacked his beak in disapproval. "You cannot take the Songkeeper away. She was entrusted to my care and instruction. I am duty bound to—"

"The last place I want her is under yer tutelage, ye fraudlin' codger-headed beast! Ye would see her destroyed for yer petty song."

"And you would see the Song destroyed by your blindness!" Wings trailing along the ground, Gundhrold paced a circle around Amos. "You have become a far greater fool than I supposed. You have turned your back on the truth, denying all you once were, all that you once knew, willfully blinding yourself in the Takhran's greatest delusion."

"I'm no dupe o' the Takhran. He's no friend o' mine. Anyone who claims t' know Amos McElhenny knows that."

Birdie's hands tightened into fists. "Look!" She had to shout before the two stopped bickering and turned toward her. "What is this all about?" She faced Gundhrold. "Who entrusted me to your care? When? What do you know about me?"

"Can't ye see that he's trying' t' manipulate ye?" Amos spun her back toward him. "Offerin' ye information t' draw ye in, so he can use ye. Just like Carhartan wanted to. Just like all o' 'em will, once they find out. They won't care about ye—just who they think ye are an' what they think they can make ye. I warned ye, lass. Ye can't trust anyone with yer secret."

His words struck home. She had been manipulated, used, forced to become what others expected of her for her entire life. But she had to understand what was going on. "Them? What *them*, Amos?"

"*Them.* Him. The Takhran. Carhartan. Everyone. Ye can't believe a word they say, an' ye certainly can't trust him—the lyin' snake-tongued slumgullion!"

"You realize I could slay you in an instant, peddler." Gundhrold spoke behind Birdie. The echoes of his voice ran along the gorge walls, and Birdie's skin tingled.

It was the voice of a killer. Cold, hard, and deadly.

She slowly turned around.

"Aye, beast, ye could try." Amos said. "But ye'd wind up with the point o' me dirk protrudin' from the back o' yer empty skull."

The griffin growled and tensed to spring, his head hunched between his shoulder blades.

"Stop. Please stop!" Birdie cried.

Neither Amos nor Gundhrold acknowledged her. Another moment and it would come to blows, and Birdie had no doubt that Amos would be killed. Even with the protection of his armor, Carhartan had been unable to defeat the griffin, and Amos had none.

She had to stop them. But what could she do?

She could sing. The answer brought a shiver of fear. She recalled the effect the melody had on Carhartan. Cursed it might be, but it was the only chance she saw to prevent bloodshed, to at least buy a few moments . . .

She searched within for the fountain of melody and began to sing.

The first note struck the two belligerents dumb. By the time she had sung through the five notes twice, the atmosphere of anger had melted away. Amos moaned—the sort of sound a man might make if a blow knocked all the air from his lungs, but the griffin sat in silence as firm and unyielding as the gorge walls.

Birdie opened her mouth to speak, but a horn call blazed through the gorge from the south, stifling her words. The echoes skittered around them, leaping off the cliffs, before continuing north down the gorge.

Gundhrold surged to his feet. "The Khelari!"

"Aye, by Turning, that cursed brute Carhartan must have awakened." Amos glared at the griffin. "Pity ye didn't slay him when ye had the chance, beastie."

The griffin snorted. "I noticed you didn't kill him either, peddler. Lost your nerve?"

Birdie clutched a hand to her throat. If Carhartan was still alive and had heard her singing, then it could only be a matter of time before he followed the sound and found her again. "What do we do?"

The griffin shook out his wings. "He will know we are close."

"Aye," Amos said. "But that horn call will do him no good 'less there are reinforcements nearby."

"Near enough. There is a company of Khelari working on the Takhran's road just north of the gorge, scarce ten minutes away."

"Hounds?"

"Yes." The griffin sighed, and his neck feathers rustled as he shook his head. "There is no time for talk. You will protect the Songkeeper?"

"Better than ye would, beast."

"Then go. Just beyond the next curve, there is a crack that leads into a separate gully. It will take you past the soldiers. I will hold them off here."

Amos nodded. "Do me a favor, beastie. Kill that brute Carhartan for me."

The griffin's features hardened—even beneath his fur, Birdie could see that—and a cold fire burned behind his eyes. The muscles tightened in his shoulders, deep cut lines accentuated by his tawny coat. "I intend to. But beware, *peddler*, if any harm befalls the Songkeeper, I will hold you responsible. And I will find you."

He turned to Birdie. "Farewell, little Songkeeper, until we meet again. May Emhran protect you." In a flurry of beating wings, he launched into the air and soared over their heads.

Amos grabbed Birdie's arm and pulled her after him around the bend to a narrow crack in the cliff wall.

Rumbling hooves approached. Hounds bayed. The griffin screeched.

Then Birdie squeezed into the crack behind Amos, and all she could hear was the clatter of loose stones underfoot and the puff of her breath rebounding from the rock face.

13

"Get back. Stay down!" Amos hissed.

Birdie pressed her back against the cliff wall, wishing that she could melt into the stone itself. They stood at the far end of the crack Gundhrold had instructed them to follow. No sounds of pursuit came from behind. It appeared the griffin had saved them.

Or sent them into a trap.

"Bearded pikes and mottlegurds," Amos said.

Birdie craned her neck to see around the peddler's shoulder, anxious to find what had caused his exclamation. About a hundred yards away, a broad gash carved through the musty green of the woodlands that covered the mountainside. A dozen teams of horses leaned into their traces, leather straps creaking, straining to pull fallen logs out of the way. Black armored soldiers clustered at their sides, goading them on with kicks and prods.

There were soldiers everywhere—hundreds of them—driving the horses, standing sentry along the line, and wielding whips against the hunched backs of bedraggled souls slaving to fell trees and level the ground.

The slaves drew Birdie's gaze. She could not look away. Men, women, and children from every corner of Leira, faces stained with dirt and blood and tears.

The dull *thock* of biting axes and the *ping* of hammers filled her ears. Chains rattled. Whips cracked. Human voices cried out in pain. Birdie clutched her head as the song assailed her mind. The five notes, beauty masked by suffering, were sung by a multitude of voices pleading for help. All hopeless, despairing, lost. Beneath it all, the black melody gurgled, a pit of quicksand awaiting the demise of its next victim.

"Poor devils."

Amos's exclamation broke through the dark cloud surrounding her. She startled back to the midmorning sunlight. Clutching a hand to her chest, she fought to control her wild breathing and the silent sobs racking her throat.

What was this? What was happening to her?

"I know that man." Amos's voice was a husky whisper. He pointed at a stout man wielding a pick. "I traded with him for years. An' that woman—down there—she's a Waveryder, sure an' certain, from the far south by the look o' it. Curse the Takhran an' his wretched soldiers!"

Birdie shuddered. This might have been her fate. Though, remembering the unrelenting hatred in Carhartan's eyes, she couldn't help thinking that it was to have been something far worse.

"Come, lass, 'tis time we left."

"Is there nothing we can do?" Even as she spoke, she knew it was hopeless. It wasn't as if the soldiers would simply stand by and allow her and Amos to set the slaves free. But she couldn't help hoping that maybe Amos, her Protector, would be able to think of something.

He shook his head, lips set in a firm line. "Afraid not, lassie. There's naught we can do against a company of Khelari with only a single blade between us. Best we leave afore we're spotted. Follow me an' keep quiet."

The peddler edged out of the crack and limped into the woods, moving westward away from the workers. Wincing at the twigs cracking beneath Amos's heavy boots, Birdie crept after him, stepping on the balls of her feet to make as little noise as possible.

The forest seemed more open here, now that they had crossed through the gorge onto the northern side of the mountain. Clear patches showed through the trees. It made the going easier, though it also meant they were more likely to be spotted by the Khelari.

A grackleberry bush rustled to Birdie's left, silver seed pods clacking together like clapping hands.

"Amos?"

"Shh." He bent to investigate, fingers stroking the hilt of his dirk.

Raaakhkk.

Birdie jumped at the screech.

A raven shot from the bush at Amos's face, pecking at his eyes. The peddler fell, swearing, blindly trying to bat the bird aside. Birdie snagged the raven's left wing and yanked the bird away. Talons dug into her wrist. The bird transformed into a living tornado of flapping wings and clawing legs, then it wrenched free and soared toward the treetops.

Steel hummed through the air. A wet crunch, and the raven's head flopped to the side, then the body crashed to the ground. Just beyond where the bird had been, the hawk's head of Amos's dirk stared back at Birdie, the point buried in a hallorm tree.

The peddler was already up and running. "Birdie, go!" He raced to the tree, yanked his dirk free, and tore through the forest. "Run!"

Shouts broke out behind. Birdie sprinted after Amos, twigs stabbing her feet. A tall plant thwacked her across the face, and a sharp minty smell filled her nostrils.

"Hold up, lass." Amos grabbed the plant and snapped off four strands, tossing two to Birdie. "Tie 'em on." He dropped to his knees and twisted the strands around both legs.

Shouldn't they be running? Birdie looped the rubbery stems around her ankles and tied them in place with a strip of root that Amos cut from a sapling. "What's this for?"

"Havva plant. Smell disguises our scent."

"From what?" As far as Birdie could tell, Khelari didn't follow a trail with their noses to the ground.

A howl filled the air, drifting on the wind until it seemed to surround them.

"Hounds," Amos cried. "Run!"

Birdie and Amos took off through the forest. In the terror of the chase, the peddler seemed to have forgotten his limp. At least there was no sign of it now as he sprinted along, chin tucked, arms pumping, zigzagging down the mountain.

The forest faded into a blur of trees. Birdie could hear herself gasping for breath, but the sound seemed far away, as if it came from another. Her pulse throbbed to the rhythm of her feet.

But the rhythm grew louder, deeper, until it filled her ears and vibrated the earth.

It was the drumming of hooves.

Birdie risked a glance over her shoulder. Black figures flashed between the trees—mounted soldiers and a pack of hounds bearing down upon them. It was no use. She and Amos could run until their legs failed, and still they could not hope to outdistance their pursuers.

They would be caught, and then . . . what? She still didn't understand why all this was happening. But she had spent her whole life yielding to the will of others, and now that she had tasted freedom—however short—she didn't intend to be captured or controlled again.

And if that meant running until the soldiers wearied of the chase, or fighting until she could fight no more, then that was what she would do.

Amos jerked to a stop. Birdie staggered past him a few steps before she was able to halt as well. Her heart plummeted.

About twenty yards away stood the strangest contraption she had ever seen. It was a sort of wagon, with the stern built up to form a deck equipped with all manner of strange devices. Her gaze skimmed over the wagon to the two black-clad figures that stood atop the raised stern.

Black armor. Khelari.

Trapped again.

Birdie clenched her fists. This time she would not go down without a fight. A fallen hallorm branch lay at her feet. Her hands shook as she snatched it up. It would have to do for a weapon—like the broom she had wielded against Kurt and Miles.

But Kurt and Miles were just two spoiled children, not fierce Khelari with armor and weapons.

"Get down!" Amos yanked her to the side and threw her to the ground.

She struck the earth hard, then Amos's weight slammed onto her back, driving the air from her lungs and replacing it with panic. What was he doing? They couldn't hide here. They would be crushed by the horses. Overrun. She *was* being crushed!

Her fingers tore into the loam. She tried to pull herself out from under his bulk, but she couldn't move.

"Lie still," Amos hissed.

A strange chorus of snapping and cracking broke out, then an odd humming, like a swarm of bees passing overhead. Screams filled the air, along with the sickening crunch of tearing flesh and breaking bones—the sounds of death.

She peered over a layer of dead leaves. The two Khelari in the wagon scrambled from one strange contraption to another, cranking, turning, and shooting a stream of arrows into the air.

Shooting at the other Khelari.

An arrow whistled past Birdie's ear and thwacked into the earth beside her shoulder. She choked back a cry. But in that faint echo of music, the song came to her. The five notes were sung by two bass voices, slow and steady as the drip of time, immovable as the mountains. There was no sense of danger in the melody, no terrifying blackness that ate at her soul. The song was pure and fresh.

The last screams trailed away. The stream of arrows abated.

Then silence.

Amos ripped the arrow out of the ground and lurched to his feet, freeing Birdie of his weight. Glorious air flooded her lungs, and she rolled onto her back, gasping in huge breaths.

"Ye fiddle-faced, mealy-mouthed, slime-lickin' slumgullions!" Amos snapped the arrow in half and chucked the pieces toward the wagon. "Ye nearly killed us."

"Gracious me, it can't be!" a deep voice replied. "Is that who I think it is?"

"Aye." Amos snorted. "Who else? Get yer rotten hides over here."

Footsteps crunched toward them. Birdie pushed up to her feet, still clutching the hallorm branch in one hand, as one of the Khelari approached. She tensed, ready for instant flight. The two strangers may have attacked the other soldiers, rescuing her and Amos, but she still wasn't sure if that made them friends.

The Khelari reached Amos, and her surprise at his size drove all other thoughts from her mind. He was a . . . dwarf. His helmeted head barely reached Amos's chest, but there were two swords strapped to his back, and he moved with a quickness and firmness that whispered *dangerous*.

"It *is* you," the dwarf said, and his face wrinkled into a smile beneath his curly black beard. He spun toward the wagon where the other Khelari still waited. "Nisus, do you see who it is?"

"Indeed," Nisus said. He leapt down from the wagon and dipped his head in salute, thudding a fist against his helm. "It has been too long."

"Ah, ye've missed me, have ye? So the first thing ye do when we meet again, is try t' kill me an' the wee lass? Fine way t' greet an old friend," Amos said.

"Kill you?" The first dwarf snorted. "Well, how do you like that? And here we thought we'd saved your lives."

"Do not bother asking for an apology, Jirkar," Nisus said. "*Or* a thank you. That never was his way."

Birdie watched the scene in growing bewilderment and fear. Surely Amos could not be *friends* with these Khelari!

"An apology?" Amos cocked his head back. "No. A thank ye? Aye, reckon I could manage that. Friends, I'd like ye t' meet Birdie. Birdie, these are brothers Jirkar an' Nisus, o' the Whyndburg Mountains—"

"Come, come," Nisus interrupted. "You know better than that. Introductions, of all things, must be done properly." He marched toward Birdie.

She shrank from him, but he merely thumped a fist to his helm—just as he had done to Amos—and bowed his head.

"I am Nisus Plexipus Molineus Creegnan, Xanthen Chancellor to the Caran. And this is my brother—"

"Jirkar Mundibus Icelos Creegnan, Commander of the Fifth Cohort of the Adulnae," Jirkar finished, with a helmet thump and a bow.

At a loss for words, Birdie simply nodded and studied the two dwarves. They looked almost identical with their weather-beaten faces, short-cropped, curly, black beards, and coiling strands of hair peeping out beneath their helms. But Nisus had dark red tints in his beard, while the criss-crossing smile lines woven around Jirkar's eyes aided Birdie in telling them apart.

She turned to Amos. "But . . . their armor?"

"A disguise. Nothin' more. They're not servants o' the Takhran, lass. Ye needn't fear that."

"Speaking of the Takhran's servants," Jirkar said, "it's high time we left this place. More Khelari are sure to come."

"And who was it said this would be an uneventful trip home?" Nisus chuckled and shoved a hand toward Jirkar. "Pay up. Two dicus as wagered."

Jirkar sighed, tugged a coin pouch from his belt, and dropped two bronze coins into Nisus's hand. "It would have been uneventful if our old friend here hadn't barged in. I think he should pay up instead of me."

"I wish you the best of luck with that. Since when have you known him to have money?" Nisus pocketed the coins, then turned to Amos. "Where are you headed?"

"West. T' my mother's house."

"That works out well, then. We can start you on your way," Jirkar said. "Long as you promise the rest of the trip *will* be uneventful. Those were my last dicus."

The two dwarves hurried toward the wagon with Amos at their heels, but Birdie followed at a slower pace, still hesitant to trust the strangers in their hateful garb. Disguise or not, it was the armor of the Khelari, the armor of Carhartan, and she wanted to stay as far away from it as possible.

She cast a glance over her shoulder, and her gaze fell on the bloody aftermath of the battle. Bodies littered the ground—men, horses, hounds—all bristling with arrows and lying in the pale, cold sleep of death.

So still. So silent.

A shudder seized Birdie's limbs. She closed her eyes and shoved the horror inside. Deep inside, where she could ignore the numbing terror that slithered through her veins.

"Time t' go, lass."

She forced her limbs to obey Amos's call and stumbled over to the wagon. With a grunt, Amos hoisted her up. Nisus smacked the reins against the backs of the four horses hitched to the front, and the wagon jolted off into the forest.

Westward. Toward Amos's mother.

And home.

14

Birdie may have thought the dwarves odd, but they were nowhere near as unusual as their wagon. She had never seen anything like it. She sat with Jirkar and Amos on the raised deck at the back of the wagon, while Nisus perched on the driver's seat at the front. Unruly stacks of crates and barrels fastened with rope netting cluttered the space between, while the raised deck bristled with all sorts of odd levers, pulleys, and strange contraptions.

Amos whistled between his teeth. "What d' ye call this thing?"

"It was a stonebarge until recently," Jirkar said. "We made a few minor alterations so it would be more suitable for our needs."

"Minor alterations? It's practically a battle ship. Mounted crossbows, ballistae, catapults—small scale to be sure, but still . . . ye could fight off an army!"

The twinkle faded from Jirkar's eyes. "Hardly. But if the Takhran's forces reach my homeland, we may have to."

The wagon lurched to the left and broke out of the trees onto a rough-hewn road lined with fresh stumps still leaking sap and fallen limbs clad in green leaves. Birdie's mind jumped back to the slaves toiling beneath the lash to clear the road further up the mountain.

"Ironic, isn't it?" Amos chuckled. "The Takhran builds a road so his armies can destroy our people, but we use it t' escape his soldiers. Fate has a curious sense o' humor."

"Fate?" Jirkar snorted. "Call it the mercy of Emhran. We'd be dead without it."

Birdie turned away. Her head whirled from the events of the past few days, and every word out of Amos and Jirkar's mouths only raised more questions. She needed time to think. She slipped over the side of the deck into the bed of the wagon where she would have more privacy.

Wedged between two barrels, she rested her arms on the side of the wagon. Below, beyond the marches of the forest, dunes rose in a succession of golden brown waves fading into dusky blue on the horizon. To the right, the mountain sloped and then rose again to join a chain of smaller mountains winding off to the east.

She released a trailing breath and slid back until she sat against the stern deck.

The world was so much bigger than she had imagined. So much more frightening too. Back at the Sylvan Swan, she had never dreamed of a world where Khelari roamed, griffins flew, and the swift flight of an arrow could snuff out a life before her eyes.

"Birdie?" Amos dropped beside her.

She pulled her legs in to give him room to stretch his out, and sat with her knees tucked up beneath her chin.

"Just think, lass, in a few short days, ye'll be safe an' sound at my mother's house. An' the only thing ye'll have t' worry about there will be decidin' what sort o' oatcake ye want for breakfast." He grinned at her. "Though I reckon I should warn ye. It's a more difficult decision 'n it sounds."

Birdie tried to smile back. Amos was so excited about taking her to stay with his mother, she knew she should be excited as well. For as long as she could remember, *this* was what she had longed for. A home. The hope of belonging. Of finding someone who truly cared.

It was almost too good to be true.

"Best oatcakes you've ever tasted," Jirkar added from his seat on the raised deck. His feet dangled over Birdie's head. "Dripping with honey, or bursting with blueberries, or topped with cinnamon, all steaming hot from the oven. You know what? Change of plans. How about Nisus and I stop off with you both for a few days before we head home, eh?"

"My mother's got better things t' do 'n fill yer empty stomachs. Last time ye came, ye stayed fer two weeks an' nigh ate her out o' the house."

Amos and Jirkar continued bantering back and forth, but Birdie blocked her ears to the noise. Who was to say that Amos's mother would care for her when no one else ever had? She had nothing to offer. There was nothing special about her save the Song, and that seemed to frighten people and turn them against her more than anything else. Only the griffin had been unafraid. He'd even called her curse a gift, claimed he was supposed to protect her, hinted that he knew more of her past.

A clever tactic, if he was trying to manipulate her, as Amos insisted. It made her want to trust him, if only to find out more about the cursed melody and how she might be free of it. But the griffin had gone to fight the Khelari, and the dwarves' wagon carried her farther away every second. Closer to the promise of a home, farther from promised answers.

Unless . . .

Birdie sat up straight.

Amos.

He had his share of secrets and a mysterious past that continued to befuddle her. He recognized the Song, knew that it was dangerous, was familiar with the Khelari. He knew more than he had admitted. She was sure of it.

She turned to the peddler, but he and Jirkar were in the middle of an argument.

"Nay, 'twas ye an' Nisus that lit the campsite afire with yer burnt hotcakes."

"Did not!"

"Aye, ye did. 'twas right after the raid on Mettertwig."

This could go on for hours. And if Jirkar was half as stubborn as Amos, it would. Birdie interrupted the peddler before he could continue. "Amos, we need to talk."

"What's that, lass? Talk about what?"

"About everything that's happened. About the soldiers and Carhartan and the So—"

"Quiet, lass!" he hissed in her ear, and his whiskers tickled her cheek. "We can't talk about that here."

"I thought you said they were friends. We could trust them." She snuck a glance up at Jirkar, but he didn't seem to be paying attention to their hushed conversation.

"Aye, I did. They're friends in so much as they're enemies o' the Takhran an' the Khelari, an' I knew 'em a long time ago. But folk are superstitious, lass. Ye can't mention the cursed melody t' anyone, or they'll turn against ye faster 'n ye can say *boggswoggle*. They'll try t' manipulate an' control ye, use ye for their own purpose."

Couldn't he at least tell her why? "But Amos—"

"Promise me ye won't say anything."

Birdie stared at Amos in silence, frustration seething below the surface. The peddler had that hard, jaw-set look on his face. A look that declared his determination to be done with the current subject matter as clearly as if he'd spoken the words.

Just be quiet like a good wee lass, don't ask questions, an' everythin' will be all right.

The Birdie back at the Sylvan Swan had nodded and promised readily enough, but the Birdie who had been kidnapped, escaped, captured again, and was doubtless even now being pursued by soldiers for something she didn't understand, wasn't quite so ready to admit defeat.

She shook her head. "I have to know more."

The peddler grunted and started to rise, but Birdie grabbed his arm.

"If you won't talk about that, then at least explain the rest. About you and the dwarves and the griffin."

Amos lifted her hand off his arm. "Some things are best left alone." Gripping the side of the wagon for balance, he picked his way through the crates to the bench seat in the front where Nisus sat as he drove. A moment later, Jirkar hopped down from the stern deck and joined Amos and Nisus, leaving Birdie alone with her thoughts.

"Well, that went marvelously, didn't it?"

Birdie jumped at the unexpected voice, knocking over an unfastened stack of crates, and scrambled away. A yowl set her skin tingling, then a fluffy yellow face poked around the side of a barrel and glared at her.

"Can't you watch what you're doing? Nearly broke my tail. Imagine! Me, George Eregius Waltham the third, wandering around with a crooked tail! Horrors. Unthinkable horrors."

"George?" Birdie realized that her mouth was hanging open and snapped it shut. "What on earth on you doing here?" She gestured vaguely at the forest so far removed from the Sylvan Swan where she had seen him last.

"Shh!" George hissed. He cast an anxious glance past her toward the front of the wagon. "If you must know, I'm a stowaway and don't wish my presence announced to the entire world."

"But I thought you were in Hardale . . ."

"*Were* being the key word in that sentence." The cat shuddered. "Ghastly town. Not a charitable soul in sight after your departure. It wasn't long before I set off for more hospitable parts, believe me."

"As a stowaway?"

"Only way to travel."

The wagon swerved, and Birdie clutched at a barrel to keep from falling. She glanced over her shoulder at Amos and the two dwarves on the driver's seat. "You couldn't just ask for a ride? They seem decent enough."

"Decent enough to you, I daresay. You're a two-legs, like them. In any case, it's not as if the blighters could even hear a word I said."

Birdie blinked. "I hear you." For some reason, it didn't really surprise her to discover that she was the only one. It wasn't as if she had ever seen anyone else wandering around carrying on random conversations with four-legged critters.

"I know." The cat twitched his whiskers. "You're special."

Cursed, rather. And a pointless curse at that—a melody no one else heard, a talking cat no one else could understand. Birdie sat down with her legs crossed beneath her. "How do you know that I'm *special*?"

"You're talking to me, aren't you?'

She twisted a strand of hair around her finger, trying to force the loose waves into some semblance of a curl, as she pondered George's response. So this *ability* to understand the cat must somehow be wrapped up in the fact that she heard the melody.

Could she understand other animals as well, or was the cat somehow special too? And what of the griffin? Amos had heard Gundhrold speak. It stood to reason that if she alone was able to understand animals because of her curse, than Amos shouldn't have been able to understand the griffin, unless the griffin was different in some way.

George stretched until his fur stood on end, then sat back, considering her with wide, unblinking eyes. "You hear things that ordinary two-legs cannot, but you're not the only one of your kind. There are others. People like you."

"What?" The question fell half formed from her lips, more a breath than a word.

The cat's face hovered before her, his nose only inches away from her own. "The peddler doesn't want you to know about them. He wants to keep you from becoming . . ."

George's head flicked up, his eyes narrowed, then in a flash of orange, he darted behind the barrel and was gone.

"Becoming what?"

"Everythin' all right, lass?"

Still seated, Birdie spun around, nearly knocking into a second stack of crates. Amos stood behind her, brow furrowed, one hand resting not so casually on the hilt of his dirk.

"Ye all right?" he repeated.

"Yes . . . yes of course." She dropped her gaze to her hands so he couldn't read the lie in her eyes. If Amos could have his secrets, than she could have hers.

The wagon jostled, and Amos caught himself with his free hand. "Good . . . good. Right then." He turned and made his way back to the front of the wagon.

Birdie scooted back until she felt the firmness of the raised stern deck behind her once more. She hugged her knees to her chest and rested her chin on her forearms. How had things become so complicated? She felt like the dunce in the dice game travelers often played in the Sylvan Swan's common room, where everyone understood the current rules of play save the one who drew the fool's cap for the round.

Everyone else seemed know what was going on. And if Amos wouldn't tell her the truth, she would have to find someone who would.

15

Birdie tiptoed away from the fire where Amos and the dwarves sat digesting their soup over pipes and mugs of brew. She hadn't seen the orange cat since their cryptic conversation earlier. There were plenty of places to hide amidst all the boxes and crates aboard the wagon, and she suspected that if the mysterious feline didn't want her to find him, she wouldn't. In any case, she couldn't exactly go poking about in search of him without arousing suspicion.

But he had given her an idea.

Even before she reached the tethered horses, she could hear the whisper of swishing tails and leaves crackling underhoof. A horse nickered a soft musical rumble and softer still, in four harmonizing voices, the freeborn melody rose and fell, like a Karnoth winging through the moonlit glow.

She saw them and her skin tingled with excitement. Four pairs of crystalline blue eyes gazed at her beneath the shadow of dark manes. Muscles rippled through a cloak of dappled gray hair, like a stream shimmering in the starlight.

She reached out to stroke the nearest horse, but her fingers scarce grazed the silky coat before the horse jumped back. It snorted, nostrils flared, head erect, ears pricked forward.

"It's all right," she said. "I'm a friend."

There was no welcome in those piercing blue eyes, nor any hint of understanding. She hesitated, tempted to flee back to the safety of the fire and the wagon and blissful ignorance. But bliss proved false when ignorance was a cage.

"I won't hurt you."

As if she were anything more powerful than a worthless orphan with a cursed song. And yet both the griffin and the cat seemed to think her song was something special. Perhaps creatures viewed it differently than "two-legs," as George called them.

It was worth a try at least.

"They say I am the Songkeeper."

Still, she received no response. Nothing but gazes as blank and expressionless as one of Madame's pewter mugs. She moved in among the horses, hands clasped in supplication, suppressing her embarrassment and doubt. "Please, I need help."

"That much is obvious, miss. Care to be a bit more specific?"

Birdie jumped at the bass voice. It was such a decidedly "two-legged" voice that she didn't bother looking at the horses. She spun around and spied Jirkar sitting with his back to a tree a few feet away, arms crossed over his mail-clad chest.

"I'm not entirely sure that it's their help you need." Jirkar scratched his chin. "Exactly how long have you been trying to talk to animals?"

"I . . ."

Don't speak of the melody, Amos had said. *They'll turn on ye.* But perhaps there was a way to find out what she needed to without asking the dwarf directly.

She flung her head back, trying to exude more confidence than she felt, and tossed Jirkar a question of her own. "Are you spying on me? That *is* what you and Nisus do, isn't it? Spy on the Khelari."

"Where did you hear that, miss?"

In the darkness, she could not read the accuracy of her guess in his expression, but his voice sounded more amused than anything else.

"I figured it out," she said. "Why else would you wear such a disguise?"

The dwarf shrugged. "Well, if you already have it figured out, then there's no need for me to say any mo—"

"What can you tell me about Amos?"

This time the sudden question seemed to catch the dwarf unawares. He was silent a moment before answering. "Now, that there is a strange question, miss. Hear tell he's a peddler now, though you'd know better than I. Back when I knew him, he was a bit of a wild rover, so I suppose it's no surprise to learn that the dust still hasn't settled beneath his feet. If you want to know any more, you'll have to ask him. It's not my story to tell."

As if Amos would actually *tell* her anything. She suppressed a sigh. The peddler seemed to hoard secrets like treasure. "It's just that I can't help wondering what with everything that's happened, with you and the Khelari and Gundhrold—"

"You've seen the old cat-bird?" Jirkar whistled. "By Turning, will wonders never cease? To think that he's still alive after all this time . . ."

Birdie's legs trembled. She thrust a hand against Jirkar's tree to hold herself steady. "You *know* the griffin?" No wonder Amos had warned her not to speak of the Song. If the dwarves were in league with the beast . . .

"Know *of* him," the dwarf corrected. "We've never met. Not sure I'd care to either. Griffins are rumored to be unpredictable creatures—though, they are also said to be fierce enemies of the Takhran, so I suppose that would make us allies."

The Takhran.

Birdie shivered at the name. Thanks to him, her life felt like a piece of Madame's washing, scrubbed, beaten, wrung out, and hung up on the line to dry. And beyond the fact that he was Carhartan's master and someone everyone seemed to dread, she didn't even know who he was. Or why he was interested in a worthless orphan from Hardale.

She sat beside Jirkar and tipped her head back against the tree, gazing at the canopy of interlaced leaves overhead. "Can you tell me more about the Takhran?"

Jirkar fiddled with a dry twig for several seconds before snapping it between his fingers. "What do you want to know? He's a murderer. A tyrant. Look as far back in history as the records go, and you'll find his black name marring the pages. He seems to have just always *been* in his fortress in Serrin Vroi.

"The Leiran tribes have always been independent, each ruled by their own chief, none answering to another. But now most of the northlands are under the Takhran's rule, save for my homeland, and he's reaching out in all directions, subduing the peoples of Leira, tribe by tribe."

"Why doesn't someone try to stop him?"

Jirkar chuckled—a soft, sad chuckle. "Some do. But few have the heart after what happened at Drengreth. Unless the tribes can be united, one by one they will be forced to submit or fall."

The weight of the dwarf's words settled on Birdie, crushing her spirit as surely as she would have been crushed by the hooves of the Khelari horses. "But . . . what does he want with me?"

"Do you mean you don't know?"

She shook her head.

The dwarf released a long breath. "Give Amos time, miss. There is much he could tell you . . . and will, if you bear with him."

Just be quiet and wait. Birdie clenched her fists so hard that her nails dug into her palms. "Why can't you just tell me and be done with it?"

"It's not my place and I've no desire to face *his* wrath! Now, come along, miss." Jirkar stood and held out a hand to pull her up. "If you're going to have those pesky Khelari tailing you, it's best you learn how to defend yourself. Really defend yourself, I mean. What *were* you planning to do with that hallorm branch earlier? Knock my brains out? Might have been more difficult than you thought— dwarf skulls are notoriously hard."

Before she could think to answer, or even fully grasp what he'd said, the dwarf hurried off to the wagon and began rummaging through the stacked crates.

She climbed up and sat on the side rail, biting her lip as the dwarf methodically searched the wagon. What if he discovered George? Unlike the cat, she doubted that he would be in any danger from the dwarves, but if he were found, she might be forced to admit that she knew him—had talked to him even—and that confession could scarcely end well.

Out of the corner of her eye, she caught a glimpse of a fluffy, orange tail retreating between two crates. She gave a relieved sigh. The cat was there, but would remain in hiding for the moment.

Jirkar swung open the lid of a chest. "You have good instincts, miss. Plenty of spirit. But without training that won't save you in a battle."

Birdie caught her breath. At first he'd simply been talking about self-defense, but now she was supposedly going to be fighting a battle? "Who said I would ever be in a battle?"

"Mm-hmm." The dwarf dug through the chest. "Now, let's see. Not much light here. Should've grabbed a torch. Given your size, I'd suggest a long-range weapon . . . ah, this should do the trick." He held up a strange contraption that looked like a bow fixed sideways to a piece of wood. "Bit dark for that right now . . . best to wait for daylight. Reckon a little short sword practice shan't go amiss tonight, though I suggest when it comes down to it we keep you out of the fray as much as possible. Here."

He held out a sword and slapped the hilt into her palm. The twisted iron grip felt cold and unfamiliar. She suppressed a shiver.

"You needn't worry," Jirkar said. "The blade is dulled for training." He slammed the lid of the chest shut and waved her along. "Over to the fire, where we can see better."

Birdie held the sword so that the descending moonbeams rippled across the blade. Dulled it might be, but it was a weapon, and the thought was both terrifying and a little thrilling at the same time. With the sword in her hands, she no longer felt the outcast drudge of the Sylvan Swan. She was free. Strong.

But this wasn't how she had wanted it. She asked for answers, and he handed her a sword? She lowered the blade. "Don't you understand, Jirkar? I don't want to fight them. I want to be free of them."

Jirkar's hand settled over hers, tightening her fingers about the hilt. "Don't *you* understand, miss? You were born to fight them."

The bronze hawk stared up at Amos as he flipped his dirk in the air, catching it by the tip of the blade each time. Fierce green eyes, uncannily like his own, blazed in the light of the fire and burned deep within his soul. A flick of the wrist, and the blade snapped up, rotated twice, and he caught it again without having to move his hand.

The action—so simple—brought back dozens of memories. The rush of adrenaline before a raid—muscles tight, lungs burning from shallow breaths—and then the slow, calm train of thought made possible by performing this mindless task to release the nervous energy.

Distant shadows flitted across his vision, carrying him farther back in recollection. He held the dirk for the first time, the carved wooden handle odd to his touch, the strange hawk's head, unnerving. A gift. A kindly face bent over him, lips parted as if to speak, but Amos pulled away.

The hawk's gaze met his own, unblinking. *Liar.* Amos stiffened at the whispered accusation. *Coward. Deserter.* Balderdash. *Betrayer.* "Boggswoggle!"

He plunged the dirk into the log he was sitting on, catapulting himself back to the present. Back to the forest, beside the fire, with Nisus seated across from him and plates, cups, and remnants of their meal scattered about.

Nisus pulled his pipe from his mouth and thumped it against the log, knocking the ashes out. "You have not been exactly truthful with us."

"What d' ye mean? I'm in no mind for foolishness."

"I assumed you were running from the Khelari because of the past . . . but that isn't it, is it? It's because of the girl. Because of *what* she is."

Nisus knew.

Somehow—Amos didn't know how—Nisus knew about Birdie. Heat crawled down Amos's neck and into his arms. His nostrils flared. He bolted upright, caught Nisus by the collar, and threw him up against a tree. "I don't care who ye think she is, but I'll have no more o' such talk. She's my lass, an' I won't let the likes o' ye fill her head with lies."

"Amos? Is everything all right?"

At Birdie's voice, Amos released Nisus, allowing the dwarf to fall into a heap at the base of the tree, and staggered back, stumbling for something to say.

Birdie stood with Jirkar at her back, a drawn sword in her hand. The sight of his wee lass with a weapon in her fist set Amos's skin bristling and drove all other thoughts from his mind. It was all well and good that she learn to defend herself—though he planned on doing any necessary protecting—but if Nisus and Jirkar intended anything more than that, he would put a stop to it.

He started forward. "What's the meaning—"

"Everything's fine." Nisus scrambled upright and laid a restraining hand on his arm. "Do not mind us, miss. We were just reminiscing about old times." The dwarf bent to retrieve his pipe from where it had fallen at Amos's feet and spoke to him in a low voice. "Surely there's no harm in the little miss learning to protect herself? Let them be."

Amos glowered at Nisus, but sat down again, watching as Jirkar led Birdie to the far edge of the fire's glow and began to instruct her in the art of the blade. The lass's movements were stiff. She held the sword gingerly, as one might hold a snake, and her sweeping strokes hinted of a life spent wielding a broom.

But she would learn soon enough.

And that worried him.

Amos tugged his dirk from the log, sheathed it, and pried his fingers from the hilt. "So, Nisus, are we—the last survivors of the *old days*—to quarrel with one another? Fine gift for the Takhran that would be."

Nisus knelt beside the fire and set a kettle over the flames. "Tea?" From seemingly nowhere, he produced a pewter tea bowl, saucer, and a bag of tea leaves. He plucked a pinch of leaves, rolled them between his fingers, then dropped them into a mesh pouch that he set in his tea bowl. "Imported all the way from Langoria. Care to have some?"

Amos shook his head. He'd forgotten Nisus's strange fondness for the watery, grass-flavored commodity. "I prefer a som'at stronger drink."

Steam puffed from the kettle's spout. Nisus lifted it and poured a stream of boiling water over the leaves in his tea bowl. He removed the leaves after a few moments and sat down across from Amos, cupping the bowl in his hands. "I am surprised you dare mention the old days. From what I have heard, you seem to have forsaken them."

"I have."

"You were once a follower of Artair—"

"I was a fool. Deceived. Blind." He rolled the words across his tongue, savoring the bitter taste. "I know better now."

Nisus sipped his tea. "Sounds like the *fool* is talking now. Since when is willful blindness better? Jirkar may be a mite bludgeon-headed, but he is not deaf. He overheard you two talking. Will you deny that the girl has the same skills that Artair had?"

"Artair failed us. Everything he led us to believe was a lie."

The fire popped and crackled in the silence following Amos's words. He could feel Nisus's gaze resting on him and could picture the accusatory squint of his eyes. Not that it mattered. Let Nisus think what he would. "What d' ye want from me?"

"War with the Takhran is coming. Regardless of your feelings about Artair, you know what the Takhran is. You know what he can do. We need your help."

The words were familiar. Amos had used almost the exact same argument in an attempt to persuade Dalton only days before. So much had changed since then. "What *we*? Yer kin from the mountains?"

"Not just my kin. Warriors from all over Leira are ready to take up arms. We may not be united yet, but we will be."

Amos pursed his lips and released the stale air from his lungs with an audible hiss. He stared into the flames. "An' . . . what . . . does it have t' do with me?"

"Our Caran was murdered last year. His son, the new Caran, is young, inexperienced, a mere beardling. We have allies, but they will not come to our aid without a strong captain to unite us. They will not accept the Caran's leadership, nor will the Xanthen bow to one of their generals. Armies, weapons, and equipment we have in abundance. All we lack is a leader."

Amos's head shot up.

A fire smoldered in Nisus's gaze. The dwarf leaned forward, hands clasped in front of him, tea bowl forgotten. "After Artair's death, Hawkness led us into battle, earned the undying hatred of the Takhran, and swore never to rest until his reign had ended. Yet today the Takhran remains, but Hawkness has disappeared."

"Aye." Amos's throat tightened. "Hawkness disappeared, an' he's long gone by now. Just like Artair. Just like the rest o' them."

Nisus nodded slowly. "*That* is why we need you. Consider it, Amos. The tribes would hail you with open arms. The Xanthen would accept your authority as one of Artair's oldest followers. *You* could unite us and lead us to victory."

Amos studied the web of scars covering his hands. He should have known there was no escaping the past. One could only hope to evade it for a time before it came snapping at the heels like one of the Takhran's cursed hounds. Still, at the thought of once more standing against the Takhran, his chest tightened and he felt the coolness of the dirk's hilt beneath his fingers without intentionally moving his hand.

"The Takhran's armies march on my homeland as we speak," Nisus said. "He will come south when the north is defeated, if not before. You're running out of places to hide. And you cannot conceal the girl forever."

A chill swept over Amos. Had he so soon forgotten his responsibility to Birdie that he would even consider resuming his old life?

Steel rang on steel. Across the fire, Birdie blocked Jirkar's stroke and danced away from his next attack. Her forehead pinched in concentration. She might not be skilled, but she moved with a grace and rhythm that could well prove deadly with experience. It reminded Amos of a flowing stream. Of music.

"In the mountains, among my people, she will be safe."

A bitter taste flooded Amos's mouth. "With an army upon yer doorstep? Aye, that sounds like a safe place t' me."

"We will protect the Songkeeper."

Amos clenched his fist around the hawk's head until the sharp beak drove into his hand. "Oh an' is that why ye're teachin' her t' fight? Ye'd lead her t' her death."

"You cannot keep her from what she is, from what she must become! You cannot deny her gift."

"But I can protect her from those who'll use her for their own gain."

Nisus thudded his fists against the log and pushed to his feet. "You see monsters in everything and everyone. Cannot trust anyone, can you Amos?" He stalked away, then stopped. "We will lose, you know. Unaided, our army might as well be weaponless for all the good we can do against the Khelari. We're defeated before we start."

The denial stuck in his throat, but he forced it out. "Whatever I once was, I'm not that now."

Words he had spoken only a few days earlier tore through his mind: *Amos McElhenny won't change. The Takhran can bet his life on it.*

Had he, the *great* Amos McElhenny, changed?

"We need a leader." Nisus was pleading now, and hope shone in his eyes.

Amos couldn't look, couldn't bear to see the hope snuffed out like a candle into darkness. He studied the sun-bleached toes of his boots.

"I'm not yer leader. I never was."

16

By all rights, he should be dead. Nothing more than a rotting corpse lying in the gorge while carrion fowl feasted on his remains and that cursed griffin sheared the flesh from his bones. The thought was enough to instigate a treacherous quiver in Carhartan's reining hand, a quiver that persisted despite his attempts to resume mastery of himself.

Amos had been there, too.

It wasn't every day one survived both a griffin attack and a visit from a ghost in the flesh.

Misty though his vision had been as he'd emerged for a moment from unconsciousness before slipping back, he had *seen* the man's wild green eyes and flaming hair and that cursed dirk in his hand. Amos had called him by name—Oran Hamner.

A name he had believed buried in the depths of the past.

The burn scar on his neck started throbbing again, and a hiss of pain escaped his lips. He dropped his reins to his steed's neck, plucked the pipe from his side pouch, and balancing it against his chest with his left arm, managed to light it. He took a long pull. The familiar action brought a sense of steadiness to his shattered world.

Amos once vowed to kill him.

So by what mystical alignment of the stars was he still alive?

The steady tapping of the horse's shoes on the cobbled street jerked Carhartan from his thoughts. Above, a thin strip of star-studded sky showed through the narrow gap between overhanging buildings. Firepots dangling from iron poles highlighted the dirt and grime covering the city of Serrin Vroi. A few ragged peasants shuffled past, eyes downcast and faces averted.

Carhartan emptied his pipe and gripped the reins again, fighting to quell the tide of anxiety threatening to dash him to the ground in the face of ruin. This was the second time he had tried unsuccessfully to capture the Songkeeper. Finding her after all these years had been the wildest stroke of luck in his career. Her capture would have restored to him the favor he had enjoyed for a brief period following that first success, so long ago.

The discovery that both Amos and the griffin still lived, coupled with the Songkeeper's escape, struck a double blow against his ambitions. It must not happen again. The Takhran would not look kindly upon a man who failed a third time.

He forced his sagging posture erect and spurred the horse to a faster pace. The steed snorted, and the tempo of the iron-shod hooves increased. Even if death awaited him, there was no sense in lingering.

He preferred to meet danger head on.

Gray dusk shattered before the approach of night, and the last faint gleam of Tauros's rays faded. Just ahead, the city changed. The overhanging houses fell back and the narrow street opened into a paved road across a square lined with zoar trees. Beyond, the serrated peak of Mount Eiphyr stabbed the night sky, and along its base— ablaze with red light—ran the wall of the Takhran's fortress.

The road passed through a circle of fountains in the center of the square, long silent, now broken and filled with dust and leaves. Carhartan craned his neck back to look up at the ebony trunks towering overhead, straight as columns until they spread into a canopy of silver green at the very top. Fallen leaves clumped at the bases of the zoars and skittered across the square, pursued by a chill breeze.

Ahead, the outer wall of the fortress wound down the side of the mountain in serpentine fashion. Protective battlements, a four-towered gatehouse, and a massive double portcullis guarded the gate, but the gate itself stood open.

Once Carhartan had dared remonstrate the Takhran over the strategic fallacy of leaving the portcullis raised and the entrance unbarred at all times. His master had simply laughed and ignored his suggestion. A *closed* gate, he said, was a sign of weakness.

Carhartan, riding now across the drawbridge toward the open gate, was impressed by the wisdom of his master's plan. The gaping hole, rather than appearing to be a chink in the impregnable defenses of the wall, seemed a warning that here was strength too great to fear attack. Arrogance, perhaps, but the Takhran's armies stood unopposed.

Hounds bayed as Carhartan approached, sending the rumor of his coming deep within the fortress. As he rode beneath the gleaming spikes of the first portcullis, two bristling hounds sprang toward him. Chains clinked, yanking the ravenous beasts back. Saliva dripped from their fangs, and their white eyes gleamed in the light of the torches.

His horse trembled, nickering and pawing the ground, but Carhartan waited in silence for the Watchman to appear.

The black-cloaked figure materialized out of the shadows, torchlight glinting blood red off the curved blade of the double-headed battle axe he bore on his shoulder.

A dozen soldiers clattered after him and fell into line just within the entrance.

"Who goes there?" The Watchman's deep voice rebounded off the gatehouse walls.

"Lord Carhartan, Second Marshal of the Khelari, bearing a message for the Takhran."

The cloaked figure shoved a torch in his face, and the light blinded him for a moment. Then the Watchman stood back and lowered his axe, the metal-studded shaft thudding against the stone floor. "Let him pass."

A cranking winch sounded from the darkness within the gatehouse towers, and the chains receded, dragging the slavering hounds backward, inch by inch. The soldiers parted, and Carhartan rode through the tunnel-like entrance. Garbled voices muttered overhead, and through narrow arrow slits and murder holes in the ceiling above, he made out the flickering light of a fire and shadowy forms pacing back and forth.

He emerged from the gatehouse into the castle bailey where rows of wattle and daub buildings served as barracks for the Takhran's ever-growing army, stables for his steeds, storehouses, and smithies. The massive keep, built into the side of Mount Eiphyr, stood before him. He dismounted, handed his steed to a waiting soldier—along with his broken sword and instructions to have it repaired—and climbed the stairs to the entrance.

He followed the familiar path to the oak door at the end of the main passage and clanked into the great hall in the midst of the supper hour. White-aproned serving lads bustled to and fro along the lines of tables, bearing enormous platters covered with the proceeds of the hunt on their heads. Scarce a vacant spot remained at the tables in the lower portion of the hall, but the great table on the dais stood empty, a refuge of quiet in the chaos. The savory aroma of the meal mingled with the far less pleasant scent of unwashed clothes, sweaty humans, and drooling hounds.

Carhartan felt a light touch on his arm. A soldier stood at his elbow, helmet in hand and head bowed. "If you please, Lord Carhartan, the Takhran sent me to fetch you. He said you were to come to the Pit the moment you arrived. The cage is waiting at the top."

Carhartan swallowed the bile rising in his throat, and as the man started to lead, thrust him aside. "No need. I know the way."

Stammering his obedience, the soldier drifted back into the crowd. Carhartan crossed the great hall, turning a blind eye to the disturbance his appearance caused among the line of feasters, and left through an arched door beside the dais.

The fact that the Takhran had known of his imminent arrival did little to settle the quiver of apprehension in his throat, though it scarcely surprised him. Winged spies kept the Takhran well informed.

Feet thudding on the stone steps, Carhartan descended the narrow winding staircase past three levels until he came out onto a ledge. The cage hung before him, creaking and swaying on its chains in the shaft. It shuddered and dropped a few inches when he stepped in. His left hand settled on the winch, metal grated on metal, the chains groaned, and the cage slowly sank.

Minutes marched past, each rotation of the winch bringing him deeper into the bowels of the earth below Mount Eiphyr. The square of light marking the entrance grew smaller and smaller above. He cursed his own forgetfulness for neglecting to bring a torch

The cage came to rest against the cavern floor with a shock that threw him off his feet. He slammed into the wall of the cage, catching the bars just in time to keep from falling. Forehead burning, he stood tall, straightened his cloak and sword belt, and strode out into the cavern.

In the center of the subterranean room, a single torch guttered and rustled in a twisted bracket at the top of an iron pole. It cast a ten-foot circle of dim light, swallowed by pitch black on the far side. Carhartan stumbled forward, spurs jingling, boots catching on unseen rocks. He hesitated, toes just touching the golden ring, and then forced himself to walk beneath the torch to the far side of the circle overlooking the Pit.

A shudder seized him. He hated this place above all others.

The vast crater spread before his feet, walls sloping down into blackness. A thick cloying scent filled his nostrils and clogged his throat. He resisted the urge to gag. Crimson drops flashed in the torchlight, spiraling down to rest in the empty streambed hidden below by distance and darkness. The steady drip fell upon his ears, like the beating of a heart.

It whispered his name. *Oran. Traitor.* Condemning him. Reminding him of all he had once been, and all that he had become. Breath hissed through his gritted teeth. He reached for his sword before remembering that the blade was being repaired.

"So many years after the rebels were crushed, and the blood still flows."

Carhartan's spine tingled at the cold voice. It seemed to emanate from the Pit. "My lord, I have returned."

"What of your mission?"

"A success. King Earnhult pledges his allegiance and the Midlands to your service."

"And the Songkeeper? Your spy sent word that she was in your charge."

Was it just his imagination, or was there a hint of laughter in the Takhran's tone? "I regret that—"

"I have already been apprised of your failure." The Takhran's voice hissed beside his ear, and it was all Carhartan could do to avoid starting. The torch sputtered, and the flames fizzled out until only a tiny spark remained. Wings fluttered overhead. The croaking cry of a raven tumbled down.

"The Songkeeper lives and roams free," the Takhran said.

"Not free, my lord. Not yet. But there is more." Carhartan cleared his throat. "Amos McElhenny guards the Songkeeper in the guise of a peddler. You know what he used to be. He may be an old fool, but he is no less dangerous than he once was. He should not be underestimated."

Not as Carhartan had when he'd assumed Amos had become so lost in his new identity that he would not dare give chase when the little Songkeeper disappeared.

"The griffin lives as well—he attacked me in Dwimdor Pass and helped the Songkeeper escape, then waylaid the patrol I summoned and slew half of them before he retreated. We believe him to be injured but still alive, possibly in the company of the Songkeeper. I alerted the army under Marshal Varon's command and posted a line of sentries along the northern border of the forest. If they try to leave that way, they'll be spotted."

The Takhran was silent a moment before he spoke. "So the mindless beast evades you again. Did he take your other hand this time?"

"No, he did not." Carhartan bit off the word at the end. The Takhran was baiting him, but a man who had failed could not afford to rise to the challenge. His life hung in the balance as it was.

"Pity. Perhaps I shall be forced to do it for him."

An iron grip seized his left hand. He heard the ringing of a blade drawn from a metal scabbard, then the cold edge stung his wrist.

"Shall I take it as recompense for your failure?"

The Takhran's grasp tightened. The blade slid forward across his wrist, slicing so fast that he scarce felt it. Blood welled from the cut, trickling down his hand and dripping from his fingers to the ground. Carhartan waited in frozen silence and made no attempt to staunch the bleeding.

The Takhran's will was law.

"No, I suppose not." The Takhran sighed, and it was the sigh of a world-weary old man. "I will leave you your hand, Lord Carhartan. There is still work for you to do."

A chance to redeem himself and regain the Takhran's favor? It was a rare offer.

"You have been my right hand for many years . . . despite the fact that you have none." An unpleasant chuckle twisted the Takhran's voice. "I will give you one last chance. Are you ready for your task?"

"Yes." Emboldened by the Takhran's words, Carhartan continued, "It will give me great pleasure to find my lord's enemies and slay them."

"Undoubtedly, but your private revenge will have to wait. I want you in Kerby, at the River."

"The River?" He groped to understand. His failure deserved punishment, but this was far worse than death. A failing task assigned to an already failing man. How could he hope to redeem himself? "But my lord, that search has been going on for years."

"And you will end it soon."

"But . . ." Carhartan choked back his anger. "Do you mean to let the Songkeeper go free?"

"The search in Kerby is of the utmost importance. Let the Songkeeper revel in her supposed freedom for a few days before we strike. The net draws tight about her. There is no hole, no shelter, no crack into which she can crawl that can help her escape us for long. Already Marshal Varon prepares to march upon the Midlands as soon as the road is complete, and if the griffin may yet be found in the forest, he will be dealt with, along with the Songkeeper *and* dear Amos."

"But if they leave—"

"There is nowhere they can go that will be beyond my reach. It is only a matter of time, and time is ever in my favor."

Carhartan forced himself into a stiff bow, but his words still came out as a growl. "As you wish, my lord."

Beating wings approached. A raven swooped down, brushing Carhartan's face as it passed. The bird croaked something, and the Takhran responded, but both spoke so quietly that Carhartan could not distinguish the words.

Then the Takhran addressed him again. "Krakov will go to Kerby with you, to serve as your messenger. When you find it, send him to me with the tidings. Only then will you be free to hunt down those who have wronged you and bring them to me."

Carhartan bowed in acknowledgement. The extra incentive was hardly necessary. As much as he burned for revenge, he knew what would happen if he failed at the River. That was reason enough to succeed. The crimson drops drew his gaze, and Carhartan suppressed a shudder. The Takhran's decision to hear his report in the Pit was not an idle threat. "I will leave at once, my lord."

Soft footsteps retreated toward the Pit. The torch flickered and came back to life, casting a yellow glow over Carhartan. He stood alone beside the pole with the raven perched on the crossbeam above him. Pain sliced through his wrist; he pressed it to his chest. The cut was deep. It needed bandaging, and unless he planned on using his teeth, he would require assistance.

He cast one last glance around the cavern and at the Pit, the place of his glory and his shame, and then stumbled back to the cage. The raven screeched, soaring above him, as he painfully cranked the winch.

Fate had a twisted sense of humor. If things had worked out as planned at Drengreth, the Takhran would already have his treasure, and Carhartan would not have been sent on this doomed mission. Yet another failure to add to the already haunting list.

Another reason to hate Amos.

The cage reached the top, and he ascended the narrow staircase. The Takhran's parting words drove him through the Keep and out to the main barracks. He pushed through the door. Chairs fell over, bunks creaked, and armor rattled as the soldiers scrambled to attention.

"Captain," he said to a silver-cloaked officer. "Order a company of soldiers saddled and mounted at the gate. We leave within the hour."

17

"To load your crossbow," Jirkar said, "set your foot in the stirrup—that's the square piece at the tip of the bow—and turn the crank to pull the string back."

Birdie blinked to clear the sleep from her eyes. Misty dawn hung over the campsite where Nisus and Amos slept beside the dying fire. She would still be asleep too, if Jirkar hadn't awakened her at first light for a shooting lesson

She studied the strange contraption in her hands—a crossbow, Jirkar called it—and ran a finger along the smooth grain of the wooden stock. Weapon training may not have been what she'd originally hoped to gain from Jirkar, but after her experience with the sword last night, she was eager to learn more. With a good weapon in her fist and the skill to wield it, she wouldn't have to answer to anyone ever again.

"Still asleep, miss?" Jirkar tapped her on the shoulder. "Come on, now—stirrup and crank."

"Yes, sorry." Fingers fumbling at the unfamiliar tasks, she followed the dwarf's commands.

"Good. Now drop the bolt into the groove."

Bolt—another unknown word. The groove was fairly easy to spot running down the length of the stock, but she had no idea what the bolt was. Perhaps another lever? She flipped the crossbow over.

"No, no, not there." Jirkar plucked the crossbow from her hands. "By Turning, miss, you don't know overmuch about weapons, do you? The bolts are sitting at your feet."

"At my feet?" She glanced down. A quiver full of arrows lay on the ground, but she saw no sign of the mysterious bolts. "Where?"

Jirkar sighed and nudged the quiver with his toe. "There."

"But I thought those were arrows?"

"No, miss, a crossbow shoots bolts—they're a bit shorter and heavier than arrows. So take a bolt, drop it in the groove"—he demonstrated each action as he described it—"lift the bow and set the stock firmly against your shoulder. Put your other hand beneath the lathe—that's the bow part right here—to stabilize the crossbow. Look down the bolt, take a deep breath, and when you feel good and steady, squeeze the lever to release the bolt."

The string snapped forward, a blur of motion, and the bolt *thunked* into the trunk of a zoar tree fifty feet away.

"Like so. The crossbow's fairly easy to learn. You just point and shoot. Now," he dropped the weapon into her hands, "your turn."

Birdie took a deep breath, and running through the steps in her mind, reloaded the crossbow. She raised it to her shoulder—it was heavier than she expected—and bent her head over it. Her cheek tingled at the coldness of the wooden stock.

She aimed at the zoar tree, but her arm trembled beneath the strain, and the tip of the bow bobbed up and down. That was no good. How could she hope to hit her target if she couldn't even hold still?

She tensed, muscles tightening in her back and shoulders, and pulled the lever. It resisted, so she tugged harder. The crossbow jerked, and the bolt shot wide of her target and plunged into a thicket of dragon's tongue.

"Hmm." Jirkar scratched his chin. "Missed. Try breathing this time, and don't tense so. Squeeze the lever, don't yank it."

She reloaded—quicker this time—forced air into her lungs, and raised the crossbow to her shoulder once more. The tip quivered for a moment and then became still. She exhaled and slowly squeezed the lever. A rewarding *thwack* sounded out.

"Good shot."

The bolt quivered in the side of a rowan tree behind the zoar. "It's the wrong tree. I missed again!"

"Ah, but you hit *something*. That's marked improvement. It's the small victories that count in the long run, miss. Let's try again, shall we?"

"Birdie, Jirkar, time t' head out."

The peddler's brogue carried over the creaking of the crossbow. Birdie gave the crank a final turn, locking the string back, and dropped a bolt into the groove. She was still nowhere near as fast or accurate as Jirkar, but after an hour of practice the actions had begun to feel more natural.

"Last shot, miss. Make it count, eh?"

She pulled the lever, the bolt shot away, and a moment later, appeared as if by magic in the midst of a cluster of bolts protruding from the zoar tree.

"Fine shot," Jirkar said. "Fine shot, indeed." He stumped over to the tree and began plucking the bolts out. "What do you think of our young warrior maid, Amos?"

Birdie twirled around to face Amos, rocking back and forth on her heels in expectation.

But the peddler didn't answer. He stalked toward Jirkar, face as hard and expressionless as stone. "Birdie, won't ye go an' see if Nisus needs any help?"

"Amos—"

"*Now*, lass."

There was no point arguing when Amos spoke like that, but nor was it necessary to race to meet his demands. Birdie collected the bolts and quiver from Jirkar and strolled toward the wagon where Nisus was busy harnessing the horses.

"Look here, dwarf, I don't mind ye trainin' the lass t' defend herself, but I don't want ye fillin' her head with this warrior maid nonsense or any—" Amos's voice faded behind her.

Birdie stashed both crossbow and quiver in the weapon chest, and slumped down amidst the crates with her back to the raised deck. Amos had always been somewhat prone to dramatic outbursts, but his moods were becoming more and more difficult to understand. His reluctance to answer any of her questions, the antagonism he displayed at any mention of the Song and now toward Jirkar . . . did she truly know him anymore?

"Psst."

Even in a whisper, there was no mistaking that voice. It was about time the cat showed himself—perhaps now she would get her answers. "George, where have you been?"

"Pardon me if I don't credit such a ridiculous question with an answer." The cat's head poked out between two crates at her feet. "Where do you suppose I've been? Hiding, of course. As if there were anything else to do on this hideous conglomeration of disaster that they have the effrontery to call a wagon."

"You can come out now, if you like. There's no one here but me."

The cat's upper lip curled into a tight smile. "There's about to be. Yon dwarf is nigh finished harnessing, and the other two approach as we speak."

He had scarce fallen silent when Amos and Jirkar climbed into the wagon and took their seats at opposite ends—Amos behind the driver's seat, Jirkar passing Birdie to resume his usual position on the deck. A moment later, Nisus hopped up as well, snagged the reins, and the wagon jolted off into the forest.

"What did you mean the other day—" Birdie turned back to the cat, but he was gone. Again. "George?"

"Gracious me, there's no need to shout," he hissed into her ear. "Hiding, remember?"

She jerked away. The cat sprawled across the lid of a barrel beside her, chin resting on his paws. "But how did you . . ."

George winked. "That's why I'm the master and you're the pupil.

Hmm, *master* of the Songkeeper. I rather like the sound of that."

"And what makes you the master?"

"Simply because, my dear girl, I know more than you do." The cat curled a paw over his mouth to conceal a yawn. "And in this splendid world of ours, information is currency. You should know that by—"

The wagon jerked to a stop, slinging Birdie off balance. She crashed into the side of the wagon, and George landed on top in a yowling bundle of fur and claws. Boots thumped beside her, and George dashed away. She started to rise, but a hand—Jirkar's hand—settled on her shoulder.

"Stay low, miss. Khelari ahead."

He crept toward the front of the wagon, and Birdie crawled after him, halting beside Amos. Nisus crouched over the driver's seat in front of them.

"Would ye look at that," Amos muttered. "It's a blaggardly army."

Birdie peered past Nisus. The trees ahead petered out into a graveyard of fallen logs and stumps hacked by axes and scorched by fire. Beyond, rows upon rows of tents stretched in rigid lines across the plain. Black-armored soldiers milled about the tents like Madame's chickens scurrying through the inn yard.

"So this is it, then," Amos whispered. "This is war."

"Nearly ten thousand men," Nisus said. "Mostly infantry, some cavalry from the look of it . . ." He continued speaking, but the words seemed to dissolve into meaningless mutterings before they reached Birdie's ears.

A painful beat pulsed in her head. She closed her eyes and rubbed her temples, struggling to think. Why the army? Why here . . . why now? Had they come to capture her? That seemed a bit ridiculous. Why send an entire army to capture one girl?

The beat grew louder . . . deeper . . . and she recognized the discordant notes of the other melody—the song she had heard when Carhartan was near.

Her eyes sprang open. There. At the edge of the tree line, a dark figure lurked in the shadows.

Carhartan?

She gripped the back of the driver's seat with both hands and fought to remain calm. Whoever he was, he didn't seem to have noticed the wagon yet. At least, the dark figure hadn't moved since she spied him.

Focusing on the gloomy melody, she heard what sounded like a duplicate or an echo—faint and farther away, but still recognizable and undoubtedly sung by a second voice.

Two Khelari. In the woods.

She touched Amos's shoulder. Holding a finger to her lips, she whispered, "Soldiers. In the forest."

"Where?"

She pointed. "One to our left. Another farther away to our right—at least one. I don't think they've seen us."

"Bilgewater! Nisus, get us out o' here. Back the way we came. Hurry."

Without a word, Nisus steered the horses into a tight turn. It was no easy matter with such a massive wagon, but the dwarf managed it somehow, and a moment later they rolled back up the road away from the edge of the forest.

Birdie scrambled to the back of the wagon and scanned the woods behind. Seconds slipped by, and still no movement came from the patch of trees where the dark figure had been. The melody gradually faded.

Then silence.

The Khelari was not following—he must not have seen them.

Birdie crawled to the front and slumped with her back to Nisus's seat. Amos glanced at her, but didn't speak. There was no need. She could read his disappointment in his gaze. He knew—or guessed—how she had known of the soldier's presence.

And he wasn't happy about it.

Her cheeks burned, and she hugged her knees to her chest. Amos could stew in his wrath, because there wasn't anything she could do!

She hadn't asked for this curse, hadn't asked to be the Songkeeper—or whatever she *was* or *wasn't* supposed to be—and she couldn't *not* hear the melody, so she might as well make the best of it.

"Turn right here," Amos said. "Head west."

Birdie glanced up as Nisus steered the wagon off the road into the woods. The horses were forced to move at a slower pace now, winding their way through thickets and stands of trees set so close that the wagon scraped bark on both sides.

After a few minutes, the dwarf cleared his throat. "Care to explain what we're doing?"

"Gettin' away with our necks intact. Those soldiers back in the woods—what did ye make o' them?"

"Sentries guarding the road. Common sense. Of course the Takhran would want to protect his route. We should have foreseen it—or at least my cohort commander brother should have. Predicting troop placements is his job."

Jirkar snorted. "Oh, if we're going to point fingers, why not point at the Xanthen strategist steering the—"

"I fear they had word o' our comin'," Amos interrupted. "If they placed sentries elsewhere 'long the border o' the forest, we may yet have trouble. In any case, our best hope lies in headin' west inside the forest 'til we're past their watch posts, then we can break out onto the Westway Road."

A thread of harsh music drifted toward Birdie and she tensed. It was distant, so faint that she could scarce hear it, but terrible nonetheless.

Amos bent over her and whispered in her ear, "What is it?"

The answer faltered on her tongue. It would only anger him further, and she had enough trouble to deal with.

"Speak, lass. Our lives are at stake."

So now he wanted her to use her ability? Her tongue stuck to the roof of her mouth, but she managed to get the words out. "Another one—"

"Where?"

"To our right. A good ways off, I think . . . maybe on the edge of the forest . . . I don't know."

Amos straightened. "Keep heading west, Nisus. Don't go any closer t' the edge o' the forest 'til I tell ye."

Over the course of the day, Birdie heard the dark melody five more times, none closer than the first, and most farther away. Each time she mentioned it to Amos, his scowl deepened, but he simply nodded. At last, as the shadows lengthened through the forest, Amos tapped Nisus on the shoulder, and the dwarf altered course to the right.

Half an hour later, they broke out of the woods. The army was nowhere in sight. Rolling yellow dunes sprawled before them, miles upon miles of grass unbroken by tree or stump or city. The Westway Road carved a dark line through the dunes. Far off, the dunes faded into a jagged blue mist—more mountains, Birdie realized.

She looked back over her shoulder in the direction of the Khelari encampment. Surrounded as she was by the vastness of Leira, it seemed ridiculous to think that an entire army had been sent to capture one orphan. "Amos . . . the army? What is it doing here?'

"Invading the Midlands. What else?" Amos shrugged, but the bitterness in his voice belied the casual gesture.

No one spoke.

In the sudden silence, the rattle of the wagon wheels seemed abnormally loud—a death rattle, it sounded to Birdie, like the noise Master Dalton had made when Carhartan stabbed him in the chest.

Horrible images passed before her eyes. Smoke hanging over Hardale. The Sylan Swan burning with bodies scattered about the yard—Madame, Kurt, Miles, Master Dalton. Screams rang in her ears as soldiers streamed over the hills. Behind them all was aflame, and everything in their path withered. At the front of the black horde, Carhartan marched with his red sword aloft.

Birdie staggered to her feet to escape the choking melody that seized her head and tightened around her throat. "No, we have to do something! We have to stop them."

Amos's firm hands settled around her shaking shoulders—strong, steady, comforting. But his gaze was as hard and cold as stone. "We're doin' the only thing we can, lassie. We're runnin'."

18

Amos was avoiding her. There was no other explanation.

Birdie huddled beside the unlit campfire, arms hugged to her body in a vain effort to ward off the cold. Winter Turning was approaching—the season change would come in the next day or two. But even the chill northern wind seemed warm compared to Amos's behavior.

Three days had passed since the discovery of the Khelari army, when her curse/ability—she still didn't know what to call it—had enabled them to slip past the sentries undiscovered. Now with the forest and Khelari behind them, they followed the Westway Road toward freedom.

There was so much she wanted to ask Amos, but he had become silent and distant. Even now he stood *across* the fire from her as he snapped twigs and tossed them onto the stacked wood. For a moment their eyes met, then he stumped off into the gray evening in search of more wood.

"Ah, there's nothing like a spot of hot tea to complete the day." Nisus pottered past with his arms full of tea things. "Would you care for some, miss?"

"No, thank you."

The peddler doesn't want you to know, George had whispered.

Didn't want her to know what? And how did the cat know what Amos did or didn't want, in any case? In the end he had offered her even less than Amos, since he disappeared after their last conversation. Yet again.

Amos trudged over and tossed another handful of twigs onto the pile. "Should about do it. Tinderbox, Nisus?"

"My dear fellow, since when have *I* ever needed a tinderbox?" The dwarf reached into a pouch at his belt, pulled out a flint and steel, and sprinkled a pinch of red flakes onto the wood. He struck the flint and steel. A spark flew into the flakes, there was a puff of blue smoke, then the kindling ignited in a spurt of flame.

Birdie jumped, barely suppressing a cry, and scrubbed at her eyes. Orange circles danced across a field of black, obscuring her vision.

Behind her, Jirkar chuckled. "Startling isn't it? Nisus never could light a fire without putting on a show."

She blinked and found to her relief that her vision was returning. "What is it?"

"Ryree powder—made from the roots of the fire flower. Very flammable, very dangerous, and very handy. Now, stir your stumps." He dropped a sword into her lap and grinned at her, wrinkles splaying from his eyes like clefts scarring the surface of a rock. "Time for practice."

She stifled a groan and pushed to her feet. Ever since sighting the army, Jirkar insisted on spending every spare moment in practice. Her back and arms hadn't ached this much since Madame's last beating. But still more painful was the knowledge that Amos would simply watch in silent disapproval.

Even an argument was preferable to that.

She refused to look at the peddler as she picked up her sword and followed Jirkar away from the fire. Thrusting her problems to the back of her mind, she fell into position and awaited the attack.

Jirkar bowed, thumping a hand to his helm, and then struck. Not too fast, giving her time to respond. A slash at the head, then a downward stroke toward her side.

She blocked both. After only three days practice, she could hardly be considered a swordswoman, but at least her weapon no longer threatened to fly from her grasp, and the basic guard positions felt less awkward.

There was music in the clash of the blades, a rhythm hidden beneath the pattern of slash and parry, offense and defense, advance and retreat. The melody was faint, seeming just beyond reach. But Birdie sought it, and as she listened, her movements felt more fluid. Natural. Thought and action occurring in synchronized harmony.

She attempted a slash of her own.

Jirkar turned aside her blade, throwing her off balance. She stumbled and lost the rhythm. The dwarf winked at her, eyes twinkling in the shadow of his black helm. Then he pressed forward, forcing her to retreat, strokes coming faster and faster, until she could no longer see his face, only the black of his armor.

The armor of the Khelari, of Carhartan, of murder and death.

Hatred surged within her, and her hands shook with anger. She thrust blindly, sword stabbing the air.

A jolt ran up her arms. She staggered back, her hands empty, the sword lying on the ground a few yards away, and glanced up at Jirkar's smirking face.

"Not bad." He swaggered over to retrieve her weapon. "I've seen far worse—and that from a dwarf who'd been studying swordsmanship for three years trying to join the Adulnae. Poor Tymon. Terrible fighter, excellent chef."

Birdie's hands were still shaking. The dark melody throbbed in her ears, and the world seemed to tilt, dipping first one way then the other. She sat down—hard—and clasped her hands in her lap to hide the trembling.

Jirkar bounded to her side. "Did I frighten you, miss? I went a bit hard on you at the end, I know, but you handled it well—"

"No, no, I'm fine." Her tongue felt thick and clumsy, but she forced it to form the words. "I'm tired, that's all."

A poor excuse, but how could she explain? She *was* frightened, but not of Jirkar. The depth of the hatred brewing within her was like a monstrous pit looming before her feet, waiting to swallow her. And in that moment, she knew she could kill . . . would kill . . . *wanted* to kill if it meant being rid of the Khelari.

The thought sickened her. She hid her face in her hands lest the terrible desire be written on her face for all to read. Jirkar jabbered on, and though she couldn't make out what he said, the relentless droning of his voice comforted her.

At last, she spoke. "I didn't think I'd care so much. I grew up in the Midlands, but it wasn't home. Nobody cared for me, and I didn't much care for them. But seeing that army . . ."

Jirkar let out a long breath and sat down beside her in a clatter of rattling armor. "I understand, miss. Believe me, I do. The same sort of army marches on my homeland. Seeing it just tears your insides and sets your blood to boiling in your veins."

He fell silent a moment, then cleared his throat. "We split off tomorrow, Nisus and I, to head north and prepare our people for battle. You don't . . . don't have to *run*, miss. You could come with us. Do something. Fight."

Birdie jerked her head up. "What do you mean?"

"With you on our side, the peoples would rally to our cause." He pressed his sword into her hand and wrapped her fingers around the hilt. "The tribes could be united. We could defeat the Takhran."

"I told you, I don't want to fight them." Not before, and certainly not now. In Bryllhyn, Amos promised her a home. Safety. Freedom. "I want to be free of them." She tried to release the sword, but he held her hand between both of his.

"Up north, you can get your answers. The Xanthen are the wisest scholars in Leira—except Nisus, of course, but he's considered a bit of a bad egg really, more strategist than sage. The Xanthen could tell you all you need to know."

Her throat tightened. If experience was any guide, no one would simply *tell* her anything. Even now it was all secrets, mysteries, and promises, but no answers. According to George, information was currency.

No doubt the Xanthen would have a price as well. "In exchange for what? Becoming who you want me to be?"

"No, miss, becoming who you're *meant* to be."

Birdie closed her eyes. Amos had been right all along. No one else cared for *her*, only what she could *become*. Jirkar had seemed different, treating her as a friend, not the orphan drudge, or mad girl with insane fantasies, or even the cursed Songkeeper. Yet the whole time, he'd been manipulating her to become what his people needed. "And who is that?"

"The Songkeeper."

A frustrated sigh brushed her lips. "I don't even know what that is, and none of you will tell me."

"It's . . . complicated. I don't fully comprehend it all myself. Not well enough to explain to you. That's why you must come with us and speak to the Xanthen. I'll tell you plain, miss, Amos will be difficult to convince. We've asked him to come along, but he'll have none of it. He may be more reasonable now, seeing that you're willing. Else you may have to come on your own."

And leave Amos behind?

Never.

Birdie pulled free and shot to her feet. The peddler might not have been himself lately, but he had followed her and rescued her from Carhartan. She couldn't abandon him now, not even to get the answers she desired. Not when he alone cared for her. Not when he alone had followed her.

The dwarf called to her, but she ignored him and stumbled away from the fire glow toward the wagon and the cover of darkness.

The wagon came to a creaking stop, and Birdie peered over the side. Golden dunes surrounded them on all sides, rising ever higher to the north until they faded into the blue of the mountains. Ahead, the road marched west toward Tauros's descending rays.

"I'm afraid here's where we part ways," Nisus said. "Time Jirkar and I headed north."

Amos hopped off first and offered his hand to assist Birdie down. "Come, lass. Only a few more days o' travel, then we'll have hot oatcakes, warm fires, an' motherin' aplenty."

He twirled her through the air, then set her down with a wink and a grin. For the first time in days, the peddler seemed his old jovial self, and Birdie couldn't help staring as he trotted to the front of the wagon to bid Nisus farewell. She didn't know what had caused the change, but it was nice to have the old Amos back.

One of the horses nickered, drawing Birdie's attention. It tossed its head, dark mane flapping against its muscled neck, and whinnied. It was a pity she had never been able to discover if the horses could—

"Little Songkeeper," a husky whisper interrupted the thought.

Birdie gasped. Intelligence flooded the horses' faces. Their eyes were bright and clear, so different from the dull, empty gazes she had seen before.

The closest one nodded at her. "May Emhran be with you."

She started toward the horse, still too stunned to speak, but Jirkar's voice stopped her.

"Miss . . . wait!" He slipped over the side of the wagon and set two bulging packs at her feet. "I meant no offense last night. I didn't mean . . . well, that is . . . I packed supplies for you and Amos— food, warm cloaks, and the like. A spare pair of boots for you. Might be a bit large, but you'll want something with Winter Turning just around the corner."

Her hurt and frustration melted before the kindness of the deed. "Thank you, Jirkar, for everything."

"Please, miss." He shuffled his feet, pulled something from behind his back and pressed it into her hands. "I thought this might come in handy in case you run into any more of them wretched varmints. Don't misunderstand me—don't mean to change your mind—just reckon it might be useful."

He stepped back, relinquishing the object to her grasp, and she saw that she held a short sword. A brown leather sheath, complete with a belt, concealed the blade. Her hand settled on the carved wooden hilt, and she slid the sword halfway from the sheath. A scale-like pattern scrawled the length of the blade, while the hilt and crossguard were engraved with intricate figures. It was oddly beautiful in a harsh, deadly sort of way.

"Oh, Jirkar, I can't—"

"Of course you can, and you will, else I'll be very much offended.

And miss," he lowered his voice, "it's not a curse. Remember that."

Jirkar pulled away and scurried back to the wagon, pausing beside Amos to thump his fist to his helm and say farewell before he climbed aboard and sat beside Nisus.

It's not a curse.

Even at a whisper, Jirkar spoke the words with such conviction that Birdie wanted to believe him. But if the Song wasn't a curse, then what was it?

"Farewell, friends." Nisus snapped the reins and shouted to the horses, "Hy-hup!" The wagon lurched off the road into the dunes. "Amos, tell your mother the Creegnan brothers send their greetings."

"I will." Amos laughed. "And be sure ye stop by next time ye travel through the Westmark, or she'll ne'er forgive me!"

A flash of yellow slipped over the side of the wagon and vanished into the golden grass, then the wagon jolted over the top of one of the dunes and disappeared from sight. Apparently George had his fill of a stowaway's life. She wouldn't mind the cat's company, so long as he kept his presence a secret. Amos would hardly be pleased at this new demonstration of her curse.

"Ye ready, lass?" Amos hefted the larger of the two packs and slung it over one shoulder. He took a deep breath, puffing out his chest. "We've supplies aplenty, the wind at our backs, an' the open road before our feet. What more could a man wish for?"

Nothing. Nothing at all. Birdie smiled as she buckled the sword belt around her waist. With Amos she was free to be just *Birdie*. He didn't care about the cursed Song or forcing her to become one thing or another. She was just his wee lass.

Of course she still had questions, and she didn't doubt that Amos had answers, but that could come later. For the moment, she was content.

She tugged her pack up on her back and tried to settle it into a comfortable position, a task made more difficult by the unfamiliar bulk of the sword strapped to her side. "Where to, Amos?"

A grin tweaked the corners of Amos's mouth, and he took off

down the road at a half jog, calling back over his shoulder. "How d'
ye feel about inns? Stayin' in one, I mean—not slavin'. If we hurry,
we can shelter from the Winter Turnin' in Kerby tonight. I know the
perfect place—the Seaman's Chase—has the finest brew this side o'
the forest."

Birdie ran to catch up with the peddler.

"Then tomorrow or the day after, we'll reach Bryllhyn and my
mother's house by the Great Sea. Just think of it, lass. We'll be
home."

PART FOUR

19

Ky shivered and tucked his elbows closer to his sides, trying to trap in as much warmth as he could. The chill, northerly wind sighing across the hillside and the mud seeping into his clothes drained the heat from his body, while the pale afternoon sun offered little relief.

Four days on watch now, for Cade's little army. Four days of spying on the soldiers rowing up and down the River Adayn, casting nets from the banks and bridge, and eating and sleeping—all the while racking his brain trying to figure out what they were up to—aside from rowing and fishing and eating and sleeping, of course.

And still nothing had happened.

Ky clenched his teeth to keep them from chattering and tugged the muddy cloak tighter around his shoulders. The dripping cloth did little to keep him warm, but at least it offered some protection from prying eyes.

Maybe Cade was wrong. Maybe the dark soldiers weren't any closer to finding what they were searching for. Maybe they weren't even searching for anything, just doing some sort of intense river training.

"Hoi!"

Ky tensed at the cry and peeked over the shivering stalks of grass. A black-clad figure stood on the shore, shouting and pointing down at something he had hauled out of the water. Ky couldn't make out what he said, but his words produced a flurry of excitement among the other soldiers. They scurried over like so many ants and huddled around him.

Naw, can't be.

A quiver of excitement stirred Ky's stomach, and he couldn't help inching down the slope in the hopes of hearing better. The grass crackled when he moved, and mud squelched beneath his hands and feet. Sure not the stealthiest approach he'd ever made, but it would have to do.

The voices grew louder as he neared, until he could distinguish individual words. He slithered behind a weeping thrassle bush and peered through the tangle of delicate strands hanging about his face. Sounded like the soldiers were debating whether they had actually found what they were looking for.

A silver-cloaked officer pushed into the ring, and the discussion faded into a rumble of consternation, succeeded by a deadly quiet. Amidst a scramble of head bobs and fisted salutes, the soldiers backed away, yielding the officer freedom to conduct his inspection.

Ky held his breath as the officer knelt down and lifted something in his gloved hands.

"By Delian's fist!" A flash of shimmering gold—some type of metal—and then the officer stood, his cape concealing the object from Ky's view.

A few barked commands sent four soldiers scurrying off, returning a moment later with a long, flat, wooden box and a bundle of cloth. The officer stooped, wound strips of cloth around the object—still, Ky couldn't see what it was—and placed it in the box.

His toes itched to run, and he fought the urge to break out of his hiding place and race back to the Underground with the news.

The officer straightened and dusted off his hands. "Who was on duty here?"

"I was, sir." A soldier stepped forward and removed his helmet.

Ky bit his lip to keep from gasping. It was the light-haired soldier who'd nearly ruined Meli's first apple-bobbing run.

The officer nodded. "Well done, Hendryk. The Takhran will be informed of your admirable service. The Second Marshal is due to arrive this evening. Transport this to the Keep and guard it until he does."

"Yes sir." The soldier—Hendryk—bobbed his head as the officer walked away, then picked up the box, holding it gingerly as if the least upset would ruin it. "Fetch the wagons."

That was all Ky needed to hear.

He wriggled up the hill on his belly, taking great care to remain sheltered by the overhanging weeds. *Wagons to the Keep.* Given that the dark soldiers would want to travel quickly through the afternoon crowds, there was only one route the heavy wagons could take.

And that was where the Underground would be waiting.

He reached the top of the slope and scrambled halfway down the other side on hands and knees before lurching to his feet and breaking into a full run. He should have about fifteen minutes before the wagons were loaded and ready to travel. Time enough to alert Cade and get into place.

This would prove a fine feather in his cap! Cade's treasure discovered on his watch. His previous misgivings about Cade's plan faded beneath the drumming of his feet against the ground. Cade would smile proudly when he heard the news, clap him on the back, and make him one of his captains.

And that, of course, would be pleasant, but not nearly as pleasant as watching Dizzier's smirk fizzle into disappointment as he, Ky, won Cade's approval . . .

. . . and destroyed the Underground.

The thought crashed into his mind, and Ky staggered to a halt, breathing hard, in the middle of a field with the slope behind him and the city walls ahead. That's what this would do—destroy the Underground. Cade would start his so-called *war* against the dark soldiers, like the famous outlaws of old, and it wouldn't end until some of them—maybe all of them—were killed.

It was beyond his control . . . wasn't it? A chill sliced through him. Or maybe, just this once, matters were in his hands. He could prevent the robbery from happening. All he had to do was turn around, walk back to the river, and allow the wagons to pass unheeded, spoiling Cade's big plan.

He could pretend ignorance, claim to have fallen asleep on watch. So simple. So easy. Yet *so* hard. How Dizzier would crow when the "mistake" was discovered. The dozens of slights and snubs Ky had received over the past three years from his assigned "older brother" materialized and assumed physical shape before his eyes, grinning down at him, that cold one-sided smirk that Dizzier delivered so well.

Ky started running. He couldn't just hand Dizzier more fodder for insults, and if he meant to alert the Underground in time, he would have to hurry. Head thrown back, arms and legs pumping, he ran until the cold gnawed his cheeks and the wind blurred his vision and a dull cramp settled in his side.

The walls of the city loomed before him. He sprinted the last few yards and flung himself against the walls to catch his breath and plan his next move. The measured tread of a sentry on the wall-top thudded through the stone to his listening ear. A steady flow of villagers, merchants, and peasants streamed through the open city gate about a hundred yards to his left. He could slip in with the crowd easily enough, but it would take time.

Time he didn't have.

Rattling wheels caught his ear, and horses' heads bobbed over the top of the hill. He spun to face the wall, sliding his belt around beneath his cloak so the short sword Cade had given him hung in the back. He pressed his fingers to the stone, sand crumbling beneath his touch, and instinctively found handholds. A last look over his shoulder to make sure no one was watching, then he scrambled up and clung spider-like to the wall just below the top.

The sentry's footsteps grew fainter. Judging by the sound, he should be approaching the far corner of his section of the wall.

Ky gripped the top of the wall, swung himself up and over the edge, scrambled across the platform, and dropped fifteen feet to the ground. The jolt of the landing ran up his legs and jarred his teeth. He rolled backward and sheltered beneath the overhanging platform, studying those who passed to see if he had attracted any attention.

No one so much as glanced his way.

He crept through the shadows at the base of the wall. According to Cade's instructions, the messenger should be waiting here.

Something rustled overhead.

Ky froze, one foot off the ground. A dark figure dropped in front of him, and before he had time to react, seized him by the collar. He choked back a cry and tore himself free, but he tripped over his own feet in the process and slammed back into the wall.

The figure flipped a hood from its head, revealing Paddy's freckled face and bright red hair. His slight frame shook with uncontrollable mirth. "You should see your face, laddy-boyo!"

Ky expelled the pent up breath from his lungs. At least it wasn't Dizzier. "What were you doin' up there?"

"Up in the support beams? Waitin' to scare you. Grand place for a nap, too . . ."

Then again, Paddy was fond of jabbering away. Least Dizzier might have listened.

". . . I like this whole "war" business. Far easier than bobbin' apples, if you ask me."

"Don't speak too soon," Ky burst in before Paddy could continue. "It's about to get rough." He rattled off his report, trying to put all the force and urgency he could into his words. "We have to hurry."

"Right," Paddy said. The levity faded from his face, and he knuckled his forehead in salute. "I'll gather the others. We'll meet you there." He started to dash off and then stopped and spun around. "Good luck, Ky."

Ky forced a smile to his face. "Yeah, you too." Hollow words paired with the danger they were about to face. He took cover beneath a broken barrel and settled down to wait for the wagons to roll through the gate.

Cade's plan *was* good, he had to admit that. The Underground leader had carefully plotted out the probable routes, identified potential escape paths, and assigned each runner his role in the raid. He seemed to have thought of everything . . . everything but the possible consequences, of course.

"Make way!"

The crowd parted, allowing a pair of wagons—each drawn by two horses—to creak past. Ky scurried after the wagons, mechanically using any cover that the crowd and setting afforded as he scanned his targets. There were four . . . five . . . six men in each wagon. A dozen all told, armed with swords and spears, but no long-range weapons.

The Underground might have a chance after all.

He waited until he was sure the wagons were headed in the right direction, then darted down a spider-web of alleys and by-ways. At last he stumbled to a stop in the middle of a deserted street lined with ramshackle stone buildings. A narrow alley bisected the street about five feet away and another a little farther down.

He trotted to the first alley and peered down it. All was in place, the barrels and crates stacked innocently against the wall on either side. In the second alley, on the right, he found a pile of straw moldering at the base of the corner building beneath the sign of the hawk. He kicked the straw aside, wrinkling his nose at the musty reek that clogged his throat, and pulled out the sections of rope that Cade had stashed there four days ago.

He knotted one end of the rope around an iron railing set into the corner building, played the rope out across the street—taking care to smudge it with mud so that it blended with the cobblestones—and wrapped it twice around an iron railing in the opposite alley. He did the same with the second rope, tying that one higher up and then leaving slack in the line so that it would lay flat against the cobblestones.

The click-clacking of ironbound wheels pricked his ears. Still distant, but drawing nearer.

Where was Cade? The raiding party should have arrived by now through the trap door at the end of the opposite alley. He studied the spot—though even he had a difficult time picking it out from the surrounding cobblestones—willing it to open and the harvesters to emerge.

"Lookin' for us, Shorty?"

20

Prickles ran down his back, and he stiffened at the harsh voice. "Dizzier."

"Yeah. We're all here and ready for action, so you can stop sweatin' and leave it to the masters."

Ky ignored the sting of Dizzier's taunt and turned around. The raiding party filed out of one of the buildings, packing the alley. He stifled a snort. Looked like even after three years in the Underground, there were *still* tunnels Cade and Dizzier hadn't thought fit to show him.

He took a closer look at the runners Cade had chosen—sixteen of them, all clad in dark cloaks, faces streaked with black mud, armed with the crude spears, bows, and slings that the Underground had managed to make. It was difficult to discern their features through the mud, but he didn't need to identify the runners to realize that these were the oldest and biggest boys and girls.

"Forget your disguise, Shorty?" Dizzier knelt and then straightened suddenly, arm flicking toward him. "Here you go."

Splotch. A clod of mud engulfed his face, blurring his vision. Droplets trickled down his cheeks onto his neck. He spluttered and tried to wipe the mud away from his nose and mouth and eyes.

"Nope, not quite enough to hide your ugly mug. Looks like you'll need a bit more."

Through watering eyes, he caught a glimpse of Dizzier bending over. He scrubbed his face with his sleeve and regained his sight just as Dizzier scooped up a second glob of mud and chucked it at him. He dropped to his knees and the mud whizzed past his head.

"What're you doing?" Paddy demanded. "We're about to start a raid!"

Dizzier's smirk filled Ky's vision. Anger throbbed in his forehead. His fists tightened, and he lunged toward his older brother.

A firm hand fell on his shoulder. He struggled against the restraint until Cade's voice cut through his fury. "That's enough."

The two simple words recalled him to his senses, the renewed knowledge of where he was and what they were about to do hitting his mind like a hammer blow.

One of the other runners restrained Dizzier with an arm across his neck. Ky took in the runner's curly brown hair, blue eyes, and white teeth flashing a dangerous smile in the midst of his blackened face, and recognized Rab.

"You too, Dizzier," Rab said. "Focus on the objective."

Dizzier elbowed Rab in the ribs and broke from his grasp. He tugged his cloak back into place. "Wasn't doin' nothin'. Shorty here hadn't put his disguise on yet."

Cade said nothing, but his glare must have been a true scorcher. It reduced Dizzier's blustering excuses to muttering and tinged his face red beneath the layer of dirt. Then Cade spoke in clipped tones, "Wagons are on their way. Everyone to their places. Ky, Dizzier, Paddy, you know what to do?"

Ky nodded. Beside him he could feel Dizzier and Paddy doing the same while the other runners skittered across the street and into the alleys.

Dizzier slapped Ky on the back, "Let's go, Shorty," and shuffled across the street to the opposite alley where eight runners were already in position by the ropes, waiting for Cade's signal.

It was a simple enough plan. After they forced the wagons to stop, half the runners would remain on the ropes while the other half would swarm around the soldiers to distract them as Cade and Dizzier's teams crept up, disposed of the drivers, and stole the wagons.

Ky could hear the staccato clip-clopping of the horses' hooves now. He peered around the corner of the alley just in time to see the first wagon turn onto the street. He jerked back, the roar of his hammering heart filling his ears. "They're coming."

The other runners pounced on the lines, four to each rope, all grins and jabbing elbows and muffled laughs.

Ky blinked. Was this just a game to them?

He closed his eyes, forcing his breath through pursed lips, trying to think about nothing at all but finding his thoughts inexplicably seized by images of Meli and Aliyah and all the other little ones in the Underground who would be helpless before an attack.

Cade's shrill whistle tore through his thoughts. His eyes snapped open as the lead wagon came abreast of the alley. The runners hauled back on the lines, bracing their feet to keep from sliding on the slick cobblestones.

"Shorty!" Dizzier barked.

Ky jumped into place on the lower rope. Now was not the time to have second thoughts about the raid. Now was the time for action.

The first team of horses struck the ropes, catching at the chest and knees. They reared back, but the weight of the wagon drove them forward into the line, the impact jerking Ky and the other runners around like puppets on a string.

Then the left horse was down, throwing the horse beside it into a plunging fit. Hopefully Dirk and Paddy would be able to get them sorted out when it was time to leave. But for now, at least the wagon was stopped.

Ky strained his ears to hear the next signal above the racket of clattering hooves, screaming horses, and shouting men. A tremendous crashing and bumping rang out—the Underground members hidden in the first alley had done their work, tumbling crates and barrels behind the wagons to block the escape.

"Now!" Dizzier shouted.

Ky let go of the rope, jumping aside as half the runners snatched their weapons and swarmed into the streets. The four runners still holding the rope skidded forward a few steps under the strain but managed to hold on.

Cade's instructions cycling through his head, Ky tugged his sling from his waist and raced toward the second wagon. He tried to ignore the skirmish around him, tried to focus on the objective—wait until the wagons were mostly empty, then take out the two soldiers in the driver's seat—but the horror of the fight set his stomach churning.

Stones and arrows hissed through the air, clattering off armor, biting into wood and flesh. A sword swiped past Ky's head. He flung himself to the ground, rolled to his knees, and crouched behind the forewheel of the second wagon.

Most of the soldiers were on foot now, fighting the Underground hand to hand. Tilting his head back, Ky peered up at the two remaining soldiers striving to control the wild-eyed horses from the driver's seat.

Dizzier dropped beside him, a sneer etched into his features even in the midst of the battle. He clutched a broken spear like a club. "Ready, Shorty?"

Ky stretched the leather straps of his sling taut and released them with a snap. "Ready."

"On my signal . . . Go!"

He dove away from the wagon, rolled, and came up on one knee, sling spinning around his head. He released the strap, sending the stone crashing into the driver's helmet. His second stone pummeled the driver's nose, releasing a fountain of blood. The driver crumpled to his knees, presenting a perfect target for Dizzier's club.

Ky shot underneath the wagon and belly-crawled between the front wheels, breath catching in his throat as the horses' flashing hooves narrowly missed his hands. Then he leapt up onto the wagon tongue.

The second soldier was leaning over the side of the wagon to yell at the others. "Back to the wagons! We'll fight the curs later."

Ky fingered his short sword but didn't draw it. The sling was his true weapon. "Oi, you!"

The soldier spun around, and Ky's loaded sling clubbed him in the forehead, ripping his helmet away to reveal a pale face framed by shaggy light hair. It was his soldier—Hendryk.

Hendryk staggered back, catching the side of the wagon to keep from toppling over. An arm reached up and knifed around his throat, slamming him to the ground. A dull *thwock* sounded out, then Dizzier clambered up into the back of the wagon. "What're you waiting for?" He motioned to the reins. "G'on!"

Ky scrambled into the driver's seat and grabbed the reins. Only then did he have a chance to check on Cade and Paddy's wagon in front of them. Both horses were now standing, and the two boys hopped up onto the driver's seat as he watched.

Cade's whistle pierced the air.

The fight ceased. The Underground runners halted mid-stroke and ran, releasing the trip lines to free the horses, then scattering down the side alleys into the maze of streets beyond. Some of the soldiers raced after the thieves, others stood bewildered, and still others started back toward the wagons.

The front wagon rattled away, rapidly picking up speed with Cade and Paddy in the front, whooping and hollering and making more noise than an army of drunken soldiers.

Ky cracked the reins against the horses' hindquarters. "Hyah!" The wagon jolted forward, and he urged the horses on with another thwack of the reins, weaving left then right to avoid trampling two downed soldiers. Both seemed stunned rather than dead, and for that he felt a strange sense of relief.

He leaned into the right rein, and the wagon drifted around the turn onto the next street. At least there didn't seem to be any Underground casualties. Amazing really, considering the numbers . . .

Ky's breath jammed in his throat at the sight of a cloaked form sprawled at the base of a stone stoop on his right. Brown hair hung in blood-matted clumps over a blackened face. Sweat marks streaked white through the mud, exposing the runner's identity—Rab.

Ky hauled back on the reins and tugged the brake lever until the wagon slowed, iron-bound wheels screeching.

"What're you doing?" Dizzier shouted in his ear.

Rough hands tore at his, trying to loosen his grip on the brake lever. Ky's gaze locked on Rab's open eyes. Lifeless, staring up at him like ice-crusted pools of water. Dead. The realization struck like a blow to the stomach, and he doubled over, gasping for air, fingers slipping from the reins and the brake lever.

Dizzier leaned over him and shoved the reins back into his hands. "Go, go, go! Drive. Drive!"

A gray fog surrounded him, deadening sight and sound, slowing movement until time itself seemed to dangle like a water droplet on the tip of the breaking point. Ky's limbs moved as if by their own volition. He had no recollection of the thought before the action, or of performing the deed himself, but the next thing he knew he was leaning forward in his seat, the reins flying loose in his hands, shouting and goading the horses on, while the buildings blurred on either side and the wagon creaked and groaned beneath him.

Rab's empty gaze haunted him. The sight of those blue eyes frosted in death sent a shiver through his body. He blinked to clear the fog from his vision, ears tingling at muffled shouts and the clatter of iron-shod feet behind. Something nagged at him—something was wrong. But he couldn't figure out what it was.

"Hah!" Dizzier thumped a long, flat, wooden box down on the seat.

Ky glanced at it, then turned back to steering the horses. *Of course* the box was on their cart. Hendryk had been there, and he was sure to keep his find within reach.

The sounds of pursuit swelled behind.

"The soldiers know where it is." The words slipped from his mouth of their own accord, but somehow vocalizing the thought made its reality all the more apparent.

"Huh?" Dizzier clambered over the back of the seat, shifted the box out of the way, and slouched down beside Ky.

"The soldiers, Dizzier. They knew which wagon the box was in. Don't you see? Our distraction was pointless. They won't bother chasing any of the others—they're all home free." Except Rab, of course. "The soldiers knew the box was in our wagon, so they're going to focus on finding *us*. All of them after you and me."

The smirk withered on Dizzier's face. His fingers tapped a restless tattoo on the wooden box. "Turn left here. Do it now!"

Ky jerked the horses down the narrow alley Dizzier had selected. The buildings on either side were set so close that he could easily reach out a hand in both directions and touch the moss-clad stone. "What're we doing?"

The shouts behind grew closer. Looked like their sudden change of direction hadn't confused the soldiers.

"Take the next right," Dizzier said.

"Why?"

"Just do it."

A latch clicked open and hinges creaked. Out of the corner of his eye, Ky saw Dizzier pull the cloth-wrapped bundle out of the box and conceal it beneath his cloak. It was long and bulky, but Ky couldn't make out what it was.

He turned down the next right. Dizzier stood, balancing with one hand on the back of the seat. "So long, Shorty," he said, and leapt from the moving wagon, landing in a roll that carried him back up to his feet.

"What're you doing?" Ky dragged on the reins to stop the horses.

Dizzier patted the bundle beneath his cloak. "Gettin' this safely to the Underground. You decoy 'em, lead 'em on 'til I can reach one of the tunnels." Then, as Ky still hesitated, Dizzier waved him on. "Go on! Before they get here!"

With a rustle of his cloak, Dizzier spun around and disappeared through the open window of one of the dilapidated buildings lining the street.

Ky cracked the reins, harrying the horses down the street. Maybe if he went fast enough he'd be out of sight before the soldiers rounded the corner, and then he wouldn't have to bother with being bait.

"Hoi! There he is!"

He risked a glance over his shoulder. A dozen dark soldiers clattered around the corner, and behind them, a mass of slobbering jaws and flashing teeth: the hounds of the Takhran straining against their chains.

The beasts howled, and Ky's skin tingled as if one hundred ants skittered down his arms. There was no need to urge the horses now. Blowing panicked breaths from their nostrils, the horses settled into a run, ears pinned to their skulls, hooves pounding.

The wagon skidded around the next corner, bumping and thumping as the wheels slipped and then caught again. The impetus of the turn nearly flung Ky out of the wagon, but he shoved his feet against the dashboard, dropped the reins, and clutched the seat with both hands.

The discarded reins wriggled around his feet like living creatures. He pried one hand loose and snagged the quivering strands, throwing himself back into the seat as the wagon tottered around another curve. He tugged with all his strength to slow the horses, but he might as well have been trying to pull down a stone wall for all the good it did.

He forced his eyes away from the road and glanced over his shoulder. The soldiers were nowhere in sight. But he had no time to feel relieved. He was nearing the marketplace . . . and what would he do with a runaway team in the middle of the crowd?

The wagon jolted, throwing Ky off the seat and tangling his cloak around his arms and legs. He tore free of the constricting cloth and pitched the cloak over his shoulder into the bed of the wagon. Nursing a bloody lip, he picked himself up.

The left hind wheel rattled with an off-beat thump. The horses were approaching a sharp corner far too quickly to clear it safely.

An idea ignited in Ky's mind, and he acted.

No hesitation—no time for that. He hopped up onto the front edge of the wagon, arms jerking to keep himself balanced, and then he jumped.

A vivid image of the cobblestones and the horses' pounding hooves flashed through his mind. Then he landed, swaying, on the wagon tongue between the two horses, fingers clutching the leather harness on either side.

He forced himself to stand upright on the bucking wooden spar, grasped the left horse's collar and clawed his way up onto the horse's back. The corner was less than a hundred feet away now. Ky fumbled with the straps of the harness.

Only fifty feet.

He needed something sharp! One of his slingstones maybe? His hand flew to his pouch and struck something cold and hard in passing—the short sword Cade had given him.

He yanked the sword from its sheath and sliced through the harness for both horses. The straps snapped just before the left hind wheel collapsed and the cart tipped sideways.

It skidded fifteen feet before wrapping around a lamppost and smashing into pieces.

The air whooshed from Ky's lungs, and he collapsed against the horse's neck, stroking its sticky coat. Gradually the horse slowed to a shuddering trot, then a heaving walk.

Ky sat up. He was in a curving alley that spilled into the market place about a hundred yards farther down. The market-day hum droned in the background. A few bystanders cast curious glances at him, but none asked any questions.

He slid off the horse's back and nearly crumpled when his feet hit the ground. Leaving the horse, he staggered down the alley toward the market on quivering legs, only too glad to be nearing the Underground and safety.

"Make way! Make way for the Takhran's soldiers!"

The cry propelled Ky back up the alley, scrambling to a makeshift hiding place behind a set of stone steps. Cobblestones dug into his knees and elbows. He crouched, neck tilted back to peek over the top of the steps.

A soldier stalked past on the main street, sword drawn, shoving a cloaked form before him. The figure tripped and fell, hood flipping back to reveal the wide-eyed, still-sneering visage of Dizzier.

21

"Dizzier." The mumbled words left Ky's lips before he realized he had spoken aloud. He ducked his head, resting his forehead against the cold step. Shallow breaths puffed from his mouth, heating the stone in front of him and bouncing back to warm his cheeks.

Moments passed without a cry of alarm. Slowly, he raised his head. The street was clear. The soldier and Dizzier were both gone.

He sprang to his feet and darted down the street, pausing at the corner to pinpoint the tall soldier and Dizzier in the crowd. Then he slipped into the masses and half-ran, half-walked after them, tugging his sling from his waist.

"Go on!" The soldier shoved Dizzer, and again the boy stumbled and fell.

What was wrong with him? Was he hurt? Ky pressed forward, selecting a stone by feel and slipping it into the pouch of his sling.

"Get up!" The soldier's boot connected with Dizzier's stomach.

Dizzier groaned and struggled up to his knees, bent forward with his head brushing the ground. Cords bound his hands at the wrists, and a longer rope hobbled his feet, leaving him just enough slack to take short steps.

Now less than five yards away, Ky slipped inside a fishmonger's three-sided stall, nearly tripping over the old man's feet. The fisherman just blinked, and drawing a long puff from his pipe, propped his feet on a stool.

Ky took his silence as an invitation to stay. He pulled a pebble from his pouch and flicked it so it bounced off the top of Dizzier's *thick-skulled* head.

Dizzier's gaze shot up from the ground.

"Need some help?" Ky mouthed, dangling his sling over the side of the stall.

Dizzier's face darkened. "Get out o' here." He jerked his head toward the far side of the market where the empty seller's stall concealed the Underground tunnel. "G'on! You have to get—"

The soldier tugged Dizzier to his feet. "Move along, cur."

There was something familiar about the soldier's voice. If he would just turn his head, Ky would be able to see his face through the open visor of his helmet.

"Hoi, whatcha got there?" Two more soldiers clustered around Dizzier.

Dizzier's captor spat on the ground. "Caught this little vermin thievin' in the square. He's one of the ones who attacked us earlier."

Ky blinked at this revelation. He'd made himself a decoy so Dizzier could palm a few coins when he was supposed to be delivering their take to the Underground?

"Does he have it?"

"No, but I'll wager he can tell us where it is."

Ky shook his head, trying to focus. He had to forget about the prize and focus on Dizzier. There were three soldiers now. Not tremendous odds, but he couldn't just let them take Dizzier.

The rules of the street ran through his mind, finishing with: *Keep up or get left behind.*

Dizzier glanced back as the soldiers shoved him through the crowd. The condescending sneer was gone, replaced by fear.

Suddenly, Ky knew that he could not . . . no, he *would* not allow Dizzier to be taken away without a fight. Swinging the sling around his head, he vaulted over the side of the stall and landed in a crouch.

"Hoi! There's another one." A soldier jogged toward him from the right.

The two soldiers standing beside Dizzier's captor spun around, and one started toward him. He released a stone with a snap of his wrist, and it thudded against the closest soldier's helmet with an audible clang. Reloading and slinging again took only a few seconds, and both soldiers stumbled back, half stunned.

Ky dropped another stone into his sling and turned toward Dizzier's captor. He could see the soldier's face now. It was Hendryk. That cursed soldier was becoming a nuisance.

Another three soldiers thundered toward him from the side. There was no way he could fight all of them and hope to rescue Dizzier, but he couldn't just leave . . .

Could he?

Look out for yourself.

He ran, dodging back toward the alley through the crowd, wishing he could forget the look on Dizzier's face. A crack sounded behind him, and a crossbow bolt shattered on the wall, inches from his head. He skipped sideways, trying to see who was shooting at him.

Dizzier grappled with Hendryk, struggling to yank the crossbow away from the man's hands. Before Ky had time to think about helping him, Hendryk tore the crossbow free and bashed Dizzier in the head with the stock. Dizzier pitched forward onto the bolt that the soldier held.

A cry caught in Ky's throat. Even from a distance, he could see Dizzier convulse as the shaft pierced his side and hear his agonized scream. Hendryk jumped back and Dizzier crumpled, the wind expelling from his lungs in a breathy groan that Ky heard over the market din.

"Dizzier!"

Soldiers hurtled toward him. He knew he should run, hide, do *something*, but his limbs seemed encased in granite. He forced himself to move, and somehow the spell was broken. Heat returned to his body, filling his legs with desperate energy, allowing him to escape into the maze of alleys. He ran until his lungs failed, and he collapsed on a pile of rags in the corner of a doorway set deep in the wall of a crumbling house.

His chest ached. But he forced himself to breathe slowly . . . evenly . . . and listen for pursuit. There was no sign that the soldiers were still on his trail. Doubtless they'd given up long ago and continued searching for the stolen prize—whatever it was.

Curse Cade's foolishness for meddling in the dark soldiers' plans. And curse the fate that brought the dark soldiers to Kerby in the first place.

The image of Dizzier, bound hand and foot, fighting to keep the soldier from shooting him in the back, haunted him. Why would Dizzier do such a thing? For once Ky had followed the rules of the street. He had survived and escaped the soldiers. He had looked out for himself.

But Dizzier hadn't. The thought struck him as if he had been punched in the gut. Dizzier had looked out for him, Ky, the annoying "younger brother" that he had always delighted in tormenting. He had fought for him. Died for him.

Tears welled beneath Ky's eyelids, and he blinked to hold them back, then surrendered the fight. He pressed his head against his arms and rested them on his knees.

Thunder rumbled and a flash of lightning lit up the darkened alley. It was going to be a long, cold night. Ky thought of the warm, dry caverns below the city where the Underground runners would be settling down, boasting of the day's adventures, little realizing the terrible price that had been paid.

How could he break the news? Rab, Dizzier, both lost. And for what? Cade's precious treasure was lost too. No, he couldn't go back. Couldn't face the questions or the sympathy or the blind support for Cade's reckless war.

Not now. Maybe not ever.

22

The peddler halted in front of Birdie, standing as stiff as a zoar tree, head tipped back, forehead wrinkled in concentration. Sunset painted the dunes with a ginger brush, and his figure cast a long shadow across the earth.

"What is it, Amos? Soldiers?" She listened for the discordant strains that heralded the approach of one of the Khelari. But all she heard was the jouncing five-noted melody in Amos's hearty baritone, with a reedy tenor—George's voice—singing in the background. Odd how the longer she was around someone, the easier she found it to ignore their "singing," until she only heard it if she listened for it.

"No, not soldiers," Amos said in a low voice. "Somethin' else." His hand inched toward his dirk. "I do believe we have a spy on our tail."

Birdie fumbled to grab her sword. "What do we do?"

"Don't move."

The peddler's arm flashed, and the dirk sliced through the grass a few feet away from her. Amos dove after it. There was a short scuffle that rattled the dead stalks, something yowled, then Amos emerged with a triumphant grin, his dirk in one hand and a quivering orange cat in the other. "Ha! Got it."

"George!" The word slipped from Birdie's mouth before she could stop it. So much for keeping the cat's presence a secret. But there was no point in pretending now. "Don't hurt him, Amos. He's not a spy, he's a friend."

Amos scowled. "Ye mean ye know the filthy creature?" Disgust streaked his voice. "Sneakin', crawlin' little pests. I can't abide them."

"Filthy?" The cat reared his head back, fur bristling on his neck. "Now that's a bit too much coming from a nasty, lumbering, malodorous, old two-legs like you!"

Birdie bit her lip, half expecting a thunderous response from Amos—the peddler never took an insult without rising to the challenge—but his expression remained unchanged. George was right. The peddler must not be able to understand the cat's speech.

"Just when were ye plannin' on tellin' me about our little tag-along?" Amos gave the cat a shake.

George launched into a string of complaints, but Birdie ignored him. She couldn't carry on two conversations at once. "I didn't think you'd want to know—"

"Want t' know what? That ye invited a spy into our midst? Lass, don't ye understand how dangerous this all is?"

"Yes, I know . . ." Birdie broke off. Why would Amos think George was a spy unless he knew George could talk?

It only made sense. In order for the cat to be a spy, there had to be some way for him to report the information he was supposedly gathering. Which meant that Amos knew she could talk to animals . . . knew there were others who could do the same. And he hadn't told her.

She snatched the cat away from Amos and hugged him close. The rapid beat of his heart fluttered against her fingertips. "His *name* is George Eregius Waltham the third. A friend. I met him at the Sylvan Swan, and then he stowed away on the wagon. We've had several very pleasant conversations—did you know I could talk to animals?"

"Of course not," he blustered, but she saw the truth in his downcast eyes. "It's sheer boggswoggle. Foolish twiddle twaddle an' drivelin' poppycock. Ye're imaginin' things."

"No, I'm not." She set the cat down on the ground, and he rubbed up against her legs, purring. "You may not want to talk about it,

Amos, but I have to know what I am. Why do I hear these things? You call it a curse, but what does that mean?"

"I told ye, lass, it's dangerous. It's powerful an' deadly, an' it'll turn everyone against ye. I'm just tryin' t' keep ye safe. Away from those who'll try t' use ye. Can't ye trust me?"

She narrowed her eyes, studying the peddler's face. This was Amos. Her dearest friend. The only one who had ever come after her. "Yes, I can. But I want you to trust me too. Please just tell me the truth."

Amos sighed, running both hands through his hair until it stood up about his head like a bristling fire flower. "Aye, lass, I'll tell ye the truth. But not here. Not now."

"Amos—"

"When we're safe in Bryllhyn, I swear I'll tell ye all ye want t' know about the Song an' the Songkeepers."

Birdie crossed her arms. "And the Khelari?"

"Aye, the Khelari too. Is it a deal?"

Only a few more days until they reached Bryllhyn . . . surely she could wait that long. "Yes, it's a deal." She shook Amos's hand, her tiny hand swallowed by his great gnarled one, and smiled up at him.

In the distance, thunder crackled and the air prickled with energy. Tauros slipped beyond the edge of the horizon to sail the forgotten seas of night. The Turning was coming.

"Fantastic." George yawned. "Now that this dreadfully boring conversation has finally come to a close, do you suppose we might be moving on before the Turning hits and we're all turned into frostbitten icicles?"

Birdie glanced up at Amos. Caught up in their "dreadfully boring conversation," they hadn't actually settled on what to do with the cat. "Can he come with us, Amos?"

"What? Screechin' like that the whole way?" The peddler shuddered. "We'd have the soldiers on us in no time." He shoved his dirk into its sheath. "Fine, have it yer way. If he is a spy, it's best t' keep him close where I can slit his throat if he turns on us."

George chuckled and dipped his head. "I assure you, my good peddler, treachery is the farthest thing from my mind."

Light flashed across the sky, and a brilliant sphere floated aloft—Fallandine, the winter star—bathing the dunes with a white glow. A tingling melody radiated from the north: soft, but growing in volume and breadth.

Winter Turning had come.

Birdie pulled the cloak and boots Jirkar had given her out of her pack and threw the cloak over her shoulders, burying her hands in the warm woolen folds to guard against the sudden cold. She tugged on the boots—they were a little large, as Jirkar had feared, but not enough to cause discomfort.

They started off again as snow began to fall. Gently at first, a whisper in the wind, then whipping and twisting on the breath of a gale, until it coated the ground and frosted the grass. Tiny pellets of frozen rain stung Birdie's cheeks. She lost track of time. It seemed the night was endless, a pitch-black maelstrom of sleet and cold.

At last Amos stopped on the crest of a hill and stepped to the side, revealing a shimmering array of lights nestled in the basin below. "Here we are. Kerby."

"Come along, lass! Told ye we'd find it eventually." Amos jogged up to the door of the Seaman's Chase and waved to her to follow.

Birdie cast an anxious glance over her shoulder and hurried after Amos with George at her heels. They had not seen a soul since sneaking into Kerby over a gap in the wall, but she felt vulnerable and exposed in the empty streets.

The inn stood at the meeting of two narrow alleys and had a wide stoop mounting to an arched door deep-set in the rounded corner. An oval sign, dimly lit by a dying lantern, hung above the entrance. Rain and snow obscured Birdie's vision, but at last she was able to make out the faded portrait of a black-hulled ship running before a storm with the words *Seaman's Chase, proprietor Jon Tildman*, inscribed below.

Amos grasped the brass handle and shoved the door. It didn't budge. "Och, what now?"

"Perhaps they're closed for the night?" Birdie said. "Or shut up against the storm?"

At her feet George shivered, and his teeth chattered like soldiers marching down the street. "*Perhaps* we could save this fascinating conversation for a more opportune time?"

"Closed or not, they'll simply have t' open again." Amos hammered on the door with his fist, then stood back, waiting. He tugged a soggy kerchief from his pocket and swiped it across his face.

Footsteps clumped inside, locks rattled, then the door scraped partway open, a narrow space just wide enough for the man who appeared in the crack. Jon Tildman, Birdie supposed. He was clad in a white apron that seemed rather too large for him. A mop of black hair crowned his head, hanging down so far in front that it almost covered his eyes.

"Blisterin' barnacles, took ye long enough, didn't it?" Amos started forward, but the innkeeper forestalled him with a raised hand.

"What do you want?" Tildman stood with the door braced against his foot, thin arms crossed over his narrow chest.

"Lodgings, o' course."

"Can't let you in. I'm sorry." Tildman started to close the door, but Amos thrust a hand forward and held it open. The innkeeper struggled a moment and then gave up, though he still barred the door against their entrance.

Birdie peered past the innkeeper into the yellow glow. Muted voices came from within—merry voices lifted in raucous song. She took a deep breath, and her stomach ached at the tang of roasting meat.

Amos dangled a little pouch before Tildman's eyes and shook it so that it jingled. "I've coin. We're honest travelers, don't want any trouble."

Tildman tried to slam the door again, but this time Amos got his foot in the way.

Please," the innkeeper said. "You're breaking curfew simply being out this late. I shall have to report you. I only answered the door because it might have been one of the soldiers."

Amos seized the innkeeper by the collar and dragged him out of the doorway. The innkeeper's arms hung stiff at his sides like twigs, jerking awkwardly as the peddler shook him. "What's this about soldiers?"

"I can't let you in!" Tildman shouted, struggling to extricate himself. "It's against regulations!"

"Whose regulations?"

"The Takhran's." The harsh word, spoken in a quiet voice, sliced through the ruckus.

Birdie spun around, mind reeling under a sudden assault of the dissonant melody. A lone Khelari stood in the middle of the street, helmetless, sword drawn. Ice drops pattered against his armor, and snowflakes left white splotches on his fur-lined cloak.

"Out after curfew, are we? Molesting upstanding citizens, possessing unlawful weapons within the city limits . . ."

Birdie's gaze drifted to the tip of her scabbard poking out below the edge of her cloak.

"All serious offenses."

Amos dropped the innkeeper and turned to face the soldier. "So, this is what it looks like, eh? When the Takhran takes control o' a city." He spread his arms wide to encompass the city and then, inexplicably, sauntered toward the soldier. "I didn't know his armies had moved this far west."

Birdie reached inside her cloak and wrapped her hand around the carved wooden grip of her sword, half drawing it from its sheath.

"Where's he headed next?" Amos demanded. "Caacharen? Holbright? Dumendorf?"

The soldier thrust his sword toward Amos. "Stay back, you hear? Don't come any closer."

Amos raised his hands. "We don't want trouble. Just let us be on our way."

There was something odd about Amos's left hand. Birdie squinted at it in the dim light. Something dangled from his fingers . . . something metal.

"Who are you?" A hard edge crept into the soldier's voice. "You and the girl? Where are—"

Amos's left hand shot forward. Something whirled through the air and smashed into the soldier's forehead. The man crashed to the ground and Amos sprang to his side.

"Did you . . . kill him?" Birdie shoved her sword back in its sheath.

"No, more's the pity." The frost in Amos's voice sent a chill of fear racing through her. "Hilt was slicker 'n I thought—just struck him with the pommel. He'll recover." He sheathed his dirk and stood.

Behind them, wet footsteps slapped against stone. The inn door slammed.

"Tildman!" Amos spun toward the sound and took off running, clearing the steps in a single bound. He rammed into the door, but it held shut. "Tildman! A thousand vengeful poudrins upon ye an' yer hideous mog."

Pressure built at the back of Birdie's skull. The dark music began, a deep pulsing chant, sung by dozens of voices. "Amos . . ."

A hound bayed, and the chilling sound echoed from the tall buildings lining the street. In the silence that followed, Birdie heard the thudding of feet running toward them. "Amos, Khelari!"

The peddler pounded down the steps and grabbed her hand, tugging her after him. Down the alleys they raced, twisting and turning and doubling back, until Amos skidded to a stop in front of a ramshackle, three-story house. He pried open a shutter with his dirk and motioned for Birdie to climb through.

She slid in and crawled to the side to give Amos room to land. He dropped beside her, the shutter snapped closed, and his footsteps shuffled away. A moment later she heard another creak and a groan, then his hand settled on hers, guiding her forward.

"Careful, lass. Watch yer step. There's a hidden cellar below us. I'll help ye through the trap door. We can spend the night down there an' wait for this trouble t' pass."

It wasn't until they were both safe in the hidden cellar that Birdie realized that something was missing.

George.

23

Ky bolted awake to the sound of howling. He staggered to his feet in the doorway, blinking in the dull gray of dawn. The howls seemed to come from all directions at once, and they were drawing nearer. He froze, listening.

A dark soldier appeared at the end of the alley with a hound at his heels. "Hoi! You. Stay where you are."

The hound tore toward him. Ky leapt for the stone wall of the building. Clinging to every available projection the crumbling stone offered, he scrambled up onto the roof. The hound's teeth grazed his heels, and it fell back, howling its disappointment.

The soldier fumbled with the crossbow strapped to his back. "In the name of the Takhran, halt!"

Not likely!

Ky dropped to his hands and knees, and the first bolt hissed past his ear. Then he took off, racing along the edge of the tiled roof. A dull twang, and a second bolt whistled past, followed by a third that splintered against the stone by his foot.

Ky gulped back a twinge of fear.

A few yards ahead his path vanished in a sheer drop where the line of buildings ended as an alley intersected the street. Looked like he was going to have to jump. Filling his lungs with air, Ky sprinted forward, nerving himself for the leap.

The crossbow twanged again. It sounded different this time . . . closer. Ky threw himself flat, bounced and rolled upon impact, and then watched the bolt screech past a few inches from his face.

Funny how the soldier's aim was improving. At this rate, the next would probably kill him. He staggered up and charged for the drop off. Ten feet . . . five . . . three, two, one! He sprang, throwing himself across the gap with every ounce of strength he had left.

He yelled as he twisted through the air, then he landed, rolling on the peaked roof with the wind knocked out of him. He skidded to a stop on the slick tile, and his feet shot over the edge. Gasping desperately for air, he crawled up away from the drop, bright specks spinning before his eyes.

He gulped in a breath of frosty air that stung his throat as it went down and, spurred on by the soldier's shouts, scaled the steep roof, hopped across the ridgepole, and slid down the other side where the soldier's crossbow could not reach him.

Whizzthunnnkkk.

Ky stumbled back, nearly slipping on the icy roof, and stared at the crossbow bolt quivering in front of him. Where had that come from? Cries from the street to his left echoed the soldier's shouts from the right.

"Hoi! On the roof!"

Looked like the dark soldiers were out in force. Ky ducked behind a stone chimney that resembled an overgrown pottery jar. A volley of bolts zipped through the air and rattled against the tile roof like hail stones. Hoping that it would take the soldiers a few moments to reload, he charged the end of the line of houses and steeled himself for another jump.

He landed rolling, kept his breath this time, and again nipped behind a chimney—a square one, the top level with his head.

A bolt grazed his right side and he yelped. He peered over the edge of the roof and caught sight of the first soldier and hound below. Three more bolts clattered off the left side of the chimney. Ky instinctively ducked.

His hands trembled, and his breath caught in his throat. He might as well admit defeat. Capture would follow, maybe even death, but at least it would be over and done with, rather than sitting here waiting to see who would shoot him first.

Dizzier's face flashed through his mind, and the tremble left his hands. Dizzier had gone down fighting, and he could do no less. He slipped the sling from his belt and stretched it, noting the satisfying snap of the leather, and then fumbled in his pouch for a stone.

He heard the bolt before it struck.

A scream tore from his throat, and he stumbled back, gazing uncomprehending at the black feathered shaft sticking into his hand ... through his hand and into his side, binding his hand in place. Pain roared up his left arm into his shoulder. Below, the soldiers sent up a shout. The sound swelled in his ears, and the roof seemed to rush up at him and then fall away again.

He lurched to keep his balance, and the bolt tore out of his side. An agonized groan scraped his throat. Warm blood seeped into his shirt and trickled down his side.

A clap of thunder exploded overhead, and the noise jolted him to his senses. Down to his right, the soldier waited while the hound clawed at the wall. To Ky's left, a party of three soldiers trotted up with a ladder on their shoulders. The soldiers would climb up now ... they would climb up and capture him ... or shoot him. And there was nothing he could do.

He slumped forward, defeated, resting his head against the chimney. The cold stone soothed his burning forehead.

He jerked back. *Cold. The stone's cold.*

That meant there was no fire beneath. It was a long shot, sure, but it just might work.

Careful not to disturb the bolt protruding from his hand, he tucked the injured limb against his chest and clasped the top of the chimney with his right hand. Groaning with the effort, he managed to hook his left elbow over the top and hung there a moment, feet scrabbling against the stone. Shivers of pain clenched his side and arm. Then with a final tug, he scrambled on top of the chimney.

For a moment, he crouched on the edge, exposed to shots from both sides of the street. The narrow hole yawned at his feet—it would be a tight squeeze. Yelling broke out in the streets, and he knew he had been seen. He took a deep breath, dropped to his knees, and lowered himself into the hole.

Soot engulfed him as he scrambled down the chimney, feet wedged against one wall, back pressed against the other. Ragged rock ripped through his worn coat and tore at his skin. The broken shaft in his hand scraped against the wall, and he gasped at the pain. And all the while, he told himself to hurry, hurry, hurry.

The house was tall, at least two—maybe three—stories. Even now the soldiers could be breaking down the door—they might even already be waiting for him at the bottom.

Something crunched beneath his toes—ashes. Squirming like a fish trapped in a net, he wriggled loose and dropped into the fireplace.

He crawled out into a dark room. Three rusty pots sprawled beside the hearth. A table stood in the center of the room, cluttered with knives, spoons, chipped plates, and various odds and ends, all covered in a thick layer of dust.

Something skittered in the far corner. He twisted to face the noise. A dozen rats scampered across a stack of empty casks and rustled through torn grain sacks.

"Open in the name of the Takhran."

Ky jumped at the muffled voice and the rats scattered. A loud crash echoed over his head, followed by the thud of booted feet dispersing through the house. The noise of the search filtered down to the kitchen—the thump of overturned furniture, doors yanked open, shutters left to swing in the wind, shouts ringing down empty corridors. And nearer, footsteps clomping down a flight of stairs.

Ky raced toward the stacks of barrels in the corner, but the earth suddenly gave way beneath him. Too startled even to scream, he tumbled into darkness.

• • •

Ky wandered in fog. Garbled voices drifted around him, and dim figures flickered across his vision. Calloused hands tended his wounds—there was a flash of pain in his hand, then a dull throbbing that gradually eased.

"Is he going to be all right?" A girl's voice spoke beside him. It sounded musical, like a stringed instrument.

"Aye, he's not sore hurt." The second voice was deeper, rumbling. "Bleatin' bollywags, but I'd like t' get my hands on the slitherin' slumgullions who'd shoot a wee lad like this."

Ky groaned, trying to open his eyes.

"Amos, I think he's waking up." An icy hand rested on his forehead.

He jolted awake and tried to scramble away, but pain lanced through his side and arm, and he fell back, dizzy.

"Not so fast, lad. Ye've had a nasty fall." Firm hands held him down, and a weathered face surrounded by unkempt red hair beneath a feathered cap loomed over him. Green eyes blazed beneath the shadow of heavy brows. "Aye, that's it. Take it easy. We're friends. Ye've naught t' fear from us."

Ky doubted that was true. Scars on the man's hands labeled him a warrior. He was obviously dangerous and—

Blue eyes peered at him over the man's shoulder. Cold blue, like frost floating on the River Adayn. Ky shivered and tore his gaze away from the eyes to a pale, round face framed by dark hair.

The girl stared at him in silence a moment and he stared back. Then she scooted past the man, revealing ragged, mud-spattered clothes draped over a small frame. She didn't look much like one to fear, but something about her eyes made him uneasy.

And the Underground was proof that even the smallest could be deadly.

Right now though, the best he could do was lay quiet until the dizziness passed and then be on his way. He studied his surroundings in search of an escape route. Looked to be a small underground room lit by a candle set against the far wall. A few empty casks were scattered haphazardly across the floor. The only way out appeared to be a trap door in the ceiling, and it was wedged shut.

"I'm Birdie," the girl said at last. "The grumpy one is Amos." She paused and looked to be waiting for a response, but she wasn't going to get one. Didn't she know better than to throw names around with strangers?

He checked for his sling. It was still looped around his waist, and he had his sword too. Odd if he was a prisoner. Maybe he had fallen in with honest folk—that would explain the odd behavior. At least it couldn't hurt to ask a few questions.

"How'd I get here?"

Birdie's eyes flickered up to the trap door. "You fell through there a few minutes ago, bloody and covered in soot. Amos treated your wounds. Do you remember what happened before that? Who did this to you?"

Ky forced his left hand to rise, wincing at the pain, and eyed the blood-stained bandage. Recollection flooded his memory as the boards overhead creaked with the weight of footsteps. Pots and pans clattered, barrels tipped, something heavy was dragged over the wooden floor and then overturned with a massive thud.

The dark soldiers were still looking for him.

Birdie's face turned the color of ice. "Khelari."

The man—Amos—inched to his feet and drew a bronze dirk from his belt. He crept over to the far wall beside the candle and ran his free hand along the stone, muttering to himself.

Ky pushed up to a sitting position, blinking as the blood rushed from his head. Was there another way out, a tunnel of some sort? He didn't trust the trapdoor to withstand the dark soldiers' search, and he didn't want to be in this cellar when they found it.

From the looks on Birdie and Amos's faces, neither did they.

Amos grunted and pressed against the wall in two different places. Something clicked, and a three-foot section slid back, grumbling on rusted tracks.

Gritting his teeth against the pain, Ky limped over and ducked his head inside. The tunnel didn't look familiar, but if it *was* one of the Underground tunnels, then how did this stranger know about it? The Underground survived by staying invisible.

"Those Khelari brutes will have heard that," Amos said. "Quick, lass, grab the packs. Birdie?" He hastened to her side and hovered over her kneeling form. "What's wrong?"

The girl clutched her head in her hands, eyes closed, lips pressed together as if she were in pain. Then her eyes flew open—round, haunted eyes—enormous in her white face. "Carhartan's here," she whispered.

"Bloodwuthering blodknockers, how could ye possibly know that?"

"Please trust me, Amos. I *know*."

Overhead, steel-shod footsteps clanked down a flight of stairs. Scrambling feet thundered across the floorboards, and then a soldier stammered. "Lord Carhartan, Marshal, sir. You're . . . we . . . expected you at the Keep . . ."

Ky didn't waste any more time. Dark soldiers close enough to overhear were too close. Clutching his injured hand to his wounded side, he snatched up the candle and crawled into the tunnel. A moment later, the girl slipped through, followed by Amos with both of the packs. The man pushed the section of wall back into place and squeezed past Ky to the front.

Amos took the candle and led the way at a brisk walk with the flickering circle of light bouncing down the tunnel before him. The noise of their breathing and the slap of their feet echoed in the enclosed space.

Each step sent renewed pain flaring through Ky's injuries, but he had to stay alert. Focused. Now was his only chance to find out what the stranger knew about the Underground. He cleared his throat. "Where's this tunnel lead?"

"It's an old smuggling tunnel," Amos said without turning. "It'll set us out on the street a few blocks away."

Birdie's clear voice piped up behind Ky. "What will we do after that, Amos?"

"Find *somewhere* t' hide 'til we can get clear o' this blaggardly city. Look, lad." Amos halted, puffing for breath, and gripped Ky's shoulder.

He fought the impulse to break free and waited to hear what the stranger would say.

"That was a Khelari bolt in yer hand, so it's no use pretendin' those soldiers had naught t' do with it. The lass an' I are none too fond o' them ourselves. It just so happens that there's an entire network o' tunnels beneath this city, leadin' t' a central cavern, an' there's an entrance not too far from where this tunnel lets out. I reckon we can wait in the cavern for things t' settle down, an' ye're welcome t' join us if ye've a mind."

Ky's heart sank. So they *did* know about the cavern. He couldn't just allow them to barge into the Underground on their own, but if he accompanied them, Cade would hold him responsible for revealing their secrets to strangers. "Wouldn't it be better to just wait here and avoid risking the streets? Could be patrols everywhere by this time."

"No." The hardness of Birdie's tone surprised him. "We're too close to the Khelari. They'll be searching this area. They could find the tunnel and then we'd be caught."

"Aye, best t' put as much distance between us an' this place as we can." Amos started off again at a swinging trot.

"Wait!" Ky called after him, struggling to keep up against the pain and weakness that made his legs tremble and his breath catch in his throat. "How did you know about the tunnels, anyway?"

There was a long pause, then Amos grunted an answer. "Friend o' mine owned a smithy not far from here. He knew about them."

Ky stopped so fast that Birdie ran into him, bringing a pained groan to his lips. She stammered an apology and slipped past, hurrying to catch up with Amos. The weight of the stranger's claim sank in. Cade's father, Lucas Peregrine, had been a swordsmith, and the ruins of his smithy concealed the nearest Underground entrance.

"Lucas Peregrine," Ky burst out. "He was your friend, wasn't he?"

Amos came to a halt and swung around, arms folded across his broad chest. "How did ye know that?"

Chuckling, Ky slumped against the tunnel wall, grateful for a chance to relieve the weight on his legs. He let his head tilt back until it thumped against stone and closed his eyes, trying to think straight through the fog clouding his brain. If this *truly* was an old friend of Lucas Peregrine returned to Kerby, Cade would be thrilled to meet him.

Ky could only imagine what it would be like to have the chance to talk to an old friend of *his* parents. It put things in a new light. Of course Amos and Birdie must go to the Underground.

He took a deep breath. "Follow me. I'll show you the way."

24

"This is it." Ky halted in front of the ramshackle building that had once been Cade's home. With a shaky hand, he wiped away the sweat beading on his forehead, then hugged a displaced column for support. Stones blackened by fire and scarred by weather, the old smithy sprawled beside the street in a jumbled heap of collapsed walls and sagging roof. The place looked about as weary and pain-ridden as Ky felt.

"Blithering barnacles, what happened here?" Amos demanded. His forehead furrowed and the muscles stood out along his jaw. "I'd scarce recognize the place. *This* was Lucas Peregrine's smithy?"

"Until the dark soldiers burned it down. Now it hides one of our secret entrances." Ky tilted his head toward a large boulder on the edge of the ruin, inviting Amos to take a closer look. He had explained the workings of the Underground on the way, about the coming of the dark soldiers to Kerby and the fight to survive.

Amos knelt and traced the flaring *V* etched in the stone. "This is your symbol?"

"Yes." Ky started to draw himself up tall, but thought better of it when pain shot through his wounded side. "A hawk for the hero Hawkness. His example taught us that we aren't made to bow to the dark soldiers. That we could fight back, be free!"

He released the column and picked his way painfully through the ruin until he stumbled to a stop in the middle of the pile of broken stone and twisted metal pipe. An old wooden door lay at his feet, half buried in the mound of rubble. He grasped the curved handle with his good hand, spun it in a circle, and pulled, gasping at the strain in his injured side.

The top half of the door swung open, revealing the Underground entrance.

"George!" Birdie cried out.

Head still reeling from the exertion of opening the tunnel, Ky tottered around and watched the girl run over to a yellow cat strolling atop a porch railing at the edge of the rubble.

"Where have you been?" Birdie scooped the scrawny beast into her arms, oblivious to his attempts to squirm free. "How did you find us? I've been so worried."

The cat purred when she set it down and rubbed up against her legs.

Ky shuffled back and motioned to the entrance. "Here it is."

"Good." Amos called Birdie over, then turned back to Ky. "D' ye have a name, lad?"

"Yeah, it's Ky . . . Ky Huntyr." He knelt and pointed into the entrance shaft. "There's a ladder built into the wall. Whistle when you get to the bottom."

Birdie nodded her understanding and made her way down, her dark head melting into the underground blackness. Amos dropped into the narrow entrance next, wriggling to free himself as his pack jammed against the sides.

Leaving Ky alone in the company of the bedraggled yellow cat. Whiskers twitching, it trotted over to the entrance and sniffed the air. A shadow smudged the ruins for an instant and then was gone. Ky glanced up, and out of the corner of his eyes, saw a large black bird swoop down and perch on the ridgepole of a house farther down the street.

The cat hissed at Ky and sprinted away, fur bristling like an exploding fire flower.

Far as he was concerned, the feeling was mutual.

A whistle drifted up from below, signaling that Amos had

reached the bottom. Setting his teeth to endure, Ky tucked his left arm against his body so that the elbow provided support to his side and his wounded hand rested on his chest. Then he sat beside the hole, swung his legs over, and clambered down as best he could one-handed.

He paused halfway down and peered up at the open square of light above him. *This is going to be tricky.* He tried to grip the iron bar with his injured hand and reach for the trap door with the other, but fire flamed in his palm, and he bit his tongue to keep from crying out.

Stifling a sigh, he continued down.

As soon as his bare feet scraped the bottom of the tunnel, he explained the problem to Amos. The man climbed back up the ladder and yanked the trap door shut. It thudded into place, blocking all light from the tunnel, and Amos dropped back down.

"There, closed up nice an' tight."

Ky started off, but a rough hand seized his good wrist.

"Hold up a moment, lad. We'll link arms."

After a moment's scuffling while Birdie and Amos tried to locate one another, Ky received the go-ahead. They proceeded single file down the twisting tunnel, Ky leading the way with a confident step. As they neared the Underground, the passage widened and became visible before them, lit by the glow of the main cavern ahead.

A sense of wrongness settled in Ky's stomach. He slowed his pace and cast a glance around the tunnel. It was odd they hadn't met any sentries. Cade usually kept a runner posted in all the main tunnels, just to be safe, but Ky didn't see any sign of lookouts in the usual crannies and hidey-holes.

What if there had been a raid?

His steps quickened to a shuffling run, tugging Birdie and Amos after him, grunting with every aching breath.

Light flooded the tunnel.

Ky jerked to a stop, blinking in the sudden orange brilliance of a dozen torches. Familiar faces pressed in on all sides—Cade, Paddy, all the oldest runners in the Underground. He took in the accusatory squint of every eye, the hard press of every mouth, and the weapons drawn in every hand.

Guilt struck like a blow to the stomach, driving all thought of speech from his mind. Dizzier should have been standing here with the rest of them, the same old, hateful sneer twisting his face. Not lying dead in the marketplace.

"Explain yourself, Ky." Cade pushed to the front of the crowd. "Where have you been all night, and where is Dizzier?"

Ky swallowed, trying to moisten his dry mouth. "He's gone, taken by the soldiers. He's *dead*."

A murmur rippled through the circle, and one of the girls whimpered.

"Dead?" Cade's gaze roved across Ky's face as if to read the truth in his eyes, then the older boy shook his head and a lifeless mask slipped over his features. His voice was hard when he spoke again. "How did it happen?"

"He was captured. I tried to rescue him. A soldier shot at me and Dizzier fought him." Ky heaved a breath and let his eyes drop to his dusty toes. He should stop talking now, but somehow the bitter words refused to be held back. "Dizzier's gone . . . the mission failed . . . what do you think of your war now?"

Torchlight flared in Cade's eyes. "It's not *my* war. It's *ours*. And what of the sword, did you lose that too?"

Ky touched the leather grip of the short sword belted at his waist before realizing that Cade was talking about something else.

He tilted his head to look Cade in the eyes. "How'd you know what was in that box?"

Cade shifted positions, and Ky caught a glimpse of uncertainty on his face.

He pressed his advantage. "I never saw what we stole. Dizzier took it away while I kept the soldiers busy, but he didn't have it with him when he was captured in the marketplace. And if it isn't here, then how do *you* know what it was?"

Cade didn't reply, but that was answer enough. In that moment, Ky knew. Somehow Cade had known all along what the treasure was, known what they were getting themselves into, and yet he hadn't told them. His silence had cost Dizzier and Rab their lives and put the Underground at risk.

But something still nagged at Ky.

He scuffed a foot against the tunnel floor. If Cade didn't have the sword, and it hadn't been seized with Dizzier, then where was it? Dizzier's capture replayed in his mind. He shrank from it, but the memory persisted.

And suddenly he knew where the sword was.

The words sprang to his lips and then died unspoken. He just *couldn't* tell Cade where it was. As long as the sword remained in the Underground everyone would be in danger, and he couldn't risk that—not for an independent thieving run, or a captaincy, or all the *approbations* in the world.

Cade folded his arms across his chest. "I don't have to answer to you. You allowed Dizzier to be slain, abandoned us after the raid, and now you've returned, leading strangers into the Underground. You betrayed us, Ky."

With a start, Ky realized he had forgotten about Birdie and Amos. He started to speak and explain the stranger's identity as a friend of Lucas, but a distant crash from the entrance passage interrupted him.

Cade's gaze flickered around the circle and settled on Paddy. He sent the redhead scrambling up the tunnel with a jerk of his head, then turned to face Amos and Birdie. "Now, who are you and what are you doing here?"

"Look here, laddie." Amos took a heavy breath that reeked of longsuffering patience. "I roamed these tunnels before ye were born, so I suggest ye show a bit o' respect."

He squeezed Ky's shoulder. It was oddly comforting and constraining at the same time.

Ky wriggled free.

"You *roamed* these tunnels?" Cade's eyes narrowed. "Now that's mighty strange. My father told me that the only ones who knew about these tunnels were outlaws, thieves, and smugglers. Is that what you are then? An outlaw?"

Amos pursed his lips. "Ye're Lucas's son, aren't ye? Ye sound just like him. I'd know that tone o' voice anywhere."

Cade faltered for just a moment. "You knew my father?" Then he spun around and scowled at Ky. "Is this some sort of ill-conceived jest?"

Before Ky could answer, a soft moan came from his left. Birdie stood with her head in her hands, staring unseeing at the floor. "Amos, the soldiers are coming . . . now."

Silence overtook the circle of runners. All eyes swept first to Birdie then to Amos. Even Cade seemed at a loss for words—something Ky would have found mighty satisfying under any other circumstances.

Bare feet slapped down the tunnel toward them, and Paddy burst into the midst of the circle, red hair aflame in the torchlight, freckles standing out on his nose and cheeks like splotches of mud on his white face. He blurted his report, gasping for breath in between words. "Dark soldiers . . . in the tunnel . . . comin' fast."

Steel sighed against leather and wood, and the sharp tip of a blade pricked Ky's neck. Slowly, he turned his head to meet Cade's furious gaze.

"You led them here."

His stomach roiled at the accusation. Cursed fool that he'd been, walking through the streets in the company of strangers in broad daylight. How had he not realized they had been followed? That *he* had led the soldiers to the Underground and all the little defenseless ones in the cavern just around the next bend.

He fumbled for something to say.

A small, white hand settled on Cade's blade, slowly, gently pushing it away from Ky's throat. "It's our fault the soldiers are here, not his. I'm sorry."

Cade shifted the blade toward Birdie.

"Don't be a fool, lad, there's no time for it!" Amos's voice broke through the tension like the snap of a bowstring. "The soldiers are comin'. D'ye intend t' fight or run?"

"We can't run," Paddy said. "There's nowhere to go."

"Then stop standin' around like a bunch of seaswoggled slumgullions! Ye must fight *now*."

Cade sprang into action and began issuing orders. "Paddy, assemble the runners and issue weapons. Jena, take the little ones down the other tunnels, out of bowshot. Be prepared to scatter throughout the city should we be overrun. Neil, you and three others build a barricade at the entrance to the cavern. We'll hold them off there. Hurry!"

The runners scattered to do his bidding. With his good hand, Ky slipped his sling from his belt and patted down his stone pouch. Still a few left, though not nearly enough to make much of a difference against the soldiers. He would have to make each shot count.

"Look, lad." Amos gripped Cade's arm. "I helped build these tunnels. I fought in 'em. I can help. But I don't have time t' explain everythin'. Ye'll just have t' trust me. There's a section o' this tunnel, right before the main cavern, that's rigged t' collapse. I know where 'tis. Build yer barricade here, not at the entrance t' the cavern, an' hold 'em off 'til I call the retreat. Then everyone needs t' run straight back t' the cavern 'cause the walls are comin' down."

Arms crossed, Cade stared at Amos a moment, then finally nodded. "Do it, but don't expect to get off so easily. We *will* speak later. Ky, help him. Signal when you're ready."

Ky started to object, but Cade was already racing away, shouting for Neil to hurry with the barricade. Runners scurried past, toting barrels, crates, chests, tables—anything they could find—along with their weapons. In just moments, a makeshift barricade had been erected, and the runners crouched behind it, waiting for the soldiers.

That was where Ky should be. Defending the Underground alongside the other runners, not running errands for some stranger!

"Quick, lad." Amos propelled him down the tunnel with a hand to his back. "Ye too, lass. There isn't much time."

Cade barreled past with Paddy at his heels, both carrying bows and bundles of arrows. "To me, Underground!" Cade cried.

Down the tunnel, like the rush of the River Adayn in the spring floods, came the clatter of iron-shod feet and the hoarse war cries of the soldiers.

25

"Fire!" Cade shouted, and the snap of bowstrings, the whine of slings, and the clatter of missiles filled the air. Screams reverberated off the walls of the tunnel, bouncing back and forth until the horrendous din surrounded Birdie as if she stood in the very center of the battle.

"Hurry, lass." Amos tugged her forward. He stopped a short way down the tunnel, about a hundred feet behind the barricade, and ran his hands over a section of the wall that had not been shored up with stone. He spoke to Ky without turning. "Is there a fire within?"

Focused on the fight at the barricade, the boy did not respond. His sling swung back and forth as if impatient to join the fray.

Amos spun and gripped him by the shoulders. "Is there a fire within the cavern?"

"A fire, yes."

"Good. Fetch me three burning brands. And quick."

Ky grunted and—clutching his side—raced toward the cavern end of the tunnel, returning a moment later with three flaming brands. Birdie accepted hers gingerly and turned her attention to Amos.

The peddler gestured as he spoke. "We built the tunnels with an eye for defense. 'Twas always a possibility that an enemy would find their way in, so we left two sections in each o' the main tunnels un-shored with stone or wood: one right before the cavern, the other at the mouth of the tunnel. And we planted packets of ryree powder throughout the wall in the un-shored sections."

221

Birdie remembered the virtues of the red powder only too well. The few flakes Nisus had sprinkled on his tinder had been enough to start a roaring fire. Several packets in the wall could prove deadly.

Amos motioned them over. "See here?" He pointed to a gummy black strand poking out of the wall. "Fuses—a tarred string attached t' the packet. We light the fuse, it burns t' the packet an' ignites it, an' the combined force o' the flame weakens the wall t' the point o' collapse. Ye got it?"

Ky nodded. "Let's get it done with and join the *real* battle."

A shrill scream yanked Birdie's attention to the fight raging around the barricade. One of the Underground girls staggered back, struck by an arrow. She fell to the ground, and a tall Khelari burst through the barricade where she had been standing and charged down the tunnel.

The carved wooden hilt filled Birdie's hand, and the blade whipped from the sheath before she realized she had drawn her sword. Amos's dirk whistled past her head and pierced the soldier's throat. At the same time, one of Ky's slingstones smashed into his face. He crumpled to the ground.

Amos ran to retrieve his dirk, shouting over his shoulder. "G'on, lass!"

Birdie sheathed her sword and rushed over to the wall. Scattered at uneven heights, the tarred strings looked like tree roots poking their knobby fingers through the earth. She blew on her brand to raise the smoking embers to life and touched it to the first strand.

Nothing happened.

She held it there a moment longer, willing it to catch. The strand sizzled and ignited, and she dashed down the length of the wall, lighting the rest of the strings on her side. She had scarce finished when Amos thundered toward the cavern bellowing "Retreat!" at the top of his lungs.

An ear-piercing whistle from Ky skittered down the tunnel.

Instantly, the Underground runners broke away from the barricade and raced toward the cavern at full speed.

Birdie spun to follow Amos and almost tripped over two dead

Khelari lying in the tunnel, their blood turning the earthen floor to mud. She'd been so focused on her task, she hadn't even heard them coming. But from the looks of it, Amos had.

She ran to the end of the tunnel and skidded to a stop beside Amos and Ky, behind a stack of barrels just within the main cavern.

"Here." Amos tossed her a crossbow, and she barely caught it. A quiver of bolts rattled at her feet. "Borrowed it from a Khelari. Load up." He cranked back the string on a second crossbow. "Time ye put that trainin' o' yours t' use. We'll cover 'em as they come in."

Birdie's hands shook, but she forced herself into action. She shrugged her pack off, set her foot in the stirrup of the bow, and started cranking. When the string was drawn, she dropped a bolt into the groove and raised the stock to her shoulder, ready to fire.

Her arms trembled so much that she had to lower the bow. There was no chance yet of shooting without fear of hitting one of their own runners retreating from the barricade.

She had never fired at anything living before, let alone a person! And that was a terrible thought. But worse still was the fear that she *wanted* to fire at the Khelari, wanted to kill the terrible, black-armored soldiers.

She shoved the thought from her mind and raised the bow to her shoulder.

The runners retreated into the cavern, dragging the wounded with them. Cade and three older boys hung back, loosing volleys of arrows to cover the retreat.

"Cade!" Ky's shout caught the older boy's attention, and he looked back for half a second. "On three drop!"

Cade nodded.

"One . . . Two . . . Three!"

Cade and his fighters dove to the ground.

Birdie squeezed the lever, and the bolt shot from the bow. She couldn't see where it struck, but two soldiers fell before the combined volley of the two crossbows and Ky's sling. Mechanically, she followed Amos and Ky's lead, reloading and firing again, then advancing a few paces into the tunnel to cover Cade and his fighters as they raced to the cavern.

Then Amos gripped her and Ky by the arm and dragged them back. "Go, go, go!"

The ryree powder!

A sweet smell, like apples and cinnamon steaming in a pot, saturated the air. Tiny trails of fire flickered across the walls, like night moths luminous in the light of a torch. Birdie dove into the cavern at Amos's heels.

A thunderous roar shook the Underground as the sides of the tunnel caved in and the roof collapsed, filling the passage with earth and completely blocking the entrance.

Ky's lungs burned. With a ragged groan, he pushed up from the ground and clutched his left side. Fresh blood stained his bandaged hand.

Dust blanketed the cavern and stung his eyes. Through the ringing of his ears, he could hear the dull clanging of weapons somewhere to his left. Next to him, Birdie sat up, gasping for breath. A stocky form bent over them, then Amos gripped Ky's good arm by the elbow and hauled him to his feet before assisting Birdie to rise.

Ky scanned the cavern. The cave-in didn't look to have harmed anything beyond the main entrance tunnel. A fire still blazed in the central stone ring, while the storeroom and armory were intact. On all sides the runners stood, or lay, or sat in clusters, stunned expressions on their faces, weapons dropping unnoticed from their hands. Some had tears in their eyes. Others clutched open wounds with blood seeping between their fingers.

He could just about smell the fear choking the cavern.

The clanging stopped, a cry rang out, and a soldier fell dead at Cade's feet. The Underground leader wiped his sword on the body and then sheathed it.

Ky started toward Cade, but Paddy intercepted him and clapped him on the back. "Well done, laddy-boyo! We did it!"

The truth slowly sank into Ky's brain. "Yeah, Paddy, guess we did." He glanced toward Birdie and forced his lips into what he hoped would pass for a reassuring grin.

She did not smile back.

Her gaze fell to the tip of a soldier's boot sticking out from beneath the pile of rubble, and she looked like she was about to be sick.

Across the cavern, Cade barked an order, and the runners started back to work without a word—cleaning weapons, restoring things to their rightful places, and tending to the wounded. Ky wrapped his sling around his waist, tied it in place one-handed, and laid out bedrolls beside the fire for the seriously injured. He took in the pain-seared faces, the ragged moans, and the blood spilling from jagged wounds, and any ounce of relief he'd felt vanished.

The soldiers might have been defeated, but this was no victory.

"Aliyah!" Cade's breathless voice startled Ky. The Underground leader pushed past him and dropped beside one of the bedrolls.

Ky crept to his side. An arrow pierced Aliyah's chest, blood staining the front of her ragged dress. Her eyes were closed, and her breath rasped in her throat like the rattling of the stones in his pouch. Beneath the hem of her dress, one leg was twisted and scarred.

Cade's fingers trembled as he brushed strands of blonde hair out of her face. "She was supposed to leave . . . down the tunnels with the others!"

"Step back lad, let me see what I can do." Amos's deep voice carried a note of calm assurance that eased Ky's fears, but his face—when he looked up from examining Aliyah's wound—dashed all hope. "I . . . I'm sorry, lad."

"No . . . no, don't say that." Cade clutched her hand in both of his own. "You have to help her."

"There's naught I can do." Amos's voice was hard, but pity showed in the lines of his face. He shook his head. "All this time, an' I never even knew Lucas had a daughter."

"That's because you abandoned this city before she was born." Cade's eyes rolled up to meet Amos's, and his voice dropped to a low, dangerous pitch that Ky could barely hear. "I know who you are, so it's no use denying it. Not with that dirk in your belt. My father said you were dead. *Hawkness* was dead."

Ky started and searched Amos's face for the truth, but the man's expression might as well have been carved from stone for all he could read in it.

"But we couldn't give up, not my father and I." Cade grunted as he pushed up to his feet. "*We* could never give up. You left us to stand alone, and look where it's gotten us."

"All right, lad, c'mon. Not here." Amos gripped Cade by the arm and steered him away from Aliyah's side. Ky tried to follow, but a glare from Amos kept him rooted to the spot.

There was no denial in Amos's eyes.

No surprise at Cade's accusation. No hint that he was offended. And that was enough to convince Ky that it might be true. Blinking, he ran the oiled leather strings of his sling slowly between his fingers. To think he'd spent the morning yammering on like a fool in the company of one of the greatest outlaws of all time.

The legendary Hawkness.

Surrounded by the wounded, Birdie bowed her head, choking on the lump lodged in her throat. She couldn't look, couldn't bear to see any more, but no matter where she turned it was the same—suffering, sorrow, death.

And it was all her fault.

Pain followed her wherever she went, shadowing her like the cursed Song. Why should others suffer because of her?

A few feet away, Amos pulled Cade from the side of a wounded girl, and the Underground leader allowed himself to be led, taking stiff, cautious steps as though he expected the earth to crumble beneath him. She could not hear their whispered conversation, but she could not help watching as Amos drew his dirk and pressed it into Cade's hand, speaking in his earnest, dynamic way. Beside her,

Ky's forehead wrinkled, and he scuffed his toes across the dirt floor, studying the patterns in the dust.

Cade's shoulders straightened as Amos spoke, and his stance shifted from that of the broken and defeated to that of a warrior. He clutched the dirk in his hands for a moment, then returned the blade to Amos who clapped him on the back.

There was a hard cast to Cade's features when he knelt again by the girl's side, but even the firmness of his mouth could not hide the wet streaks beneath his eyes.

Tears rolled down Birdie's cheeks, blurring the images of suffering. She closed her eyes and allowed the shadows to engulf her. A soft humming throbbed in her ears. She sought to quench it, but the melody would not be stopped. Quiet at first, a whispering candle flame, then it spread through her, tingling and warm, a ray of sunlight after an endless cold winter.

Her heart ached at the sound of it.

The Song welled within her, a river, an ocean, then it burst forth from her opened mouth. The melody sprang quavering from her lips to blend with the beautiful melody filling her soul, rising keener and broader, louder and stronger, rippling forth in a pattern of dazzling light.

She spread her arms wide. Brightness grew around her, driving the shadows back, until in a blinding flash, the darkness melted away.

Then she gasped, and the Song faded.

She stood, blinking in the red glow of the fire-lit cavern, striving to understand what had just happened. For she had heard a voice speaking to her out of the melody, out of the light. A whisper, not even words, a distinct melody that she somehow understood, forming thoughts out of the notes, grasping the Singer's intent.

The voice had called her *Songkeeper. Child. Beloved.*

"Who *are* you?" Cade looked up at her with awe and terror in his eyes. He swallowed hard, and his gaze shifted to the girl at his side.

Birdie glanced down, and a cry slipped from her lips. The girl was sitting up, staring around her through eyes liquid with tears, but where the arrow had protruded from her chest, nothing remained but a damp blood stain. The arrow . . . the wound . . . were both gone.

Shouts of joy and delight broke out behind her. She spun around. The other injured runners were sitting up, clutching bloodied rips in their clothes where the skin underneath was now new and whole.

The thrill of hope that had spread through her at the first sound of the notes faded, replaced by cold terror.

Who *was* she?

"How'd you do it?" Ky tugged the bandages from his left hand and held it out, palm up, working his fingers back and forth to display the unbroken skin.

Cade stood. "What are you? Some kind of a sorceress?"

"You don't understand." Birdie backed away, shaking her head. "I didn't do this. This wasn't me." She looked to Amos for help, but the peddler refused to meet her gaze.

The Song was dangerous, he claimed. Dangerous because it was powerful. A power she didn't control, hadn't asked for, wasn't even sure she wanted.

No wonder he'd warned her to keep it a secret.

Amos stood. "We're leavin'. Now."

Birdie made no attempt to argue. She collected her pack in silence, but left the crossbow where she had dropped it when the tunnel collapsed. Children scattered before her like Madame's chickens at feeding time. As if they were afraid of her. She didn't blame them. She was a bit afraid of herself.

She only half listened as Amos instructed Cade to light the ryree packets at the other end of the tunnel they had collapsed to destroy it forever, and to lay low for a while until things settled down. Then Amos turned in a slow circle. "Ye've made some changes since my day. How d' we get out o' here?"

"That way." Ky nodded toward a tunnel opposite them. "Follow me." He started to walk off, but Amos grabbed him by the collar.

"We can find our own way out. Ye needn't worry."

Ky shook himself free. "Sure you can, but I'm going with you."

"What?" Two voices spoke at once—Amos and the red-headed boy, Paddy.

"You wish to leave us?" Cade folded his arms across his chest, and the glare he directed at Ky would have put Madame to shame.

"No! No, you can't do that," Paddy said. "We need you 'ere."

"I have to." Desperation tinged Ky's voice. "I'm sorry, Paddy. I can't explain now, but there's something I have to do. It won't take long. A few days. I'll come back soon, I promise." He gripped his friend's wrist, then looked hesitantly at Cade.

Cade glanced at Amos and something indiscernible flickered in his eyes. Then he slowly turned back to Ky and nodded.

"Ky!" A little brown-haired girl dashed out from one of the other tunnels and threw her arms around his waist, sobs muffled in his shirt. "Ky, you cain't leave! You just cain't!"

Ky patted her on the back and turned back toward the others, a look of helplessness on his face. "I'm sorry, Meli. I have to. Just for a little while."

"No, you have t' stay here with me!"

Paddy stepped forward and gently pulled Meli away, kneeling so that his head was on her level. "Come 'ere, love. It'll be just fine. I'll look after you 'til Ky gets back."

"Good—Goodbye." Ky dashed into the tunnel without another word.

Amos paused before following and turned back to Cade, fumbling with the dirk at his belt. His voice, when he spoke, was soft. "Yer father would be proud o' ye, lad."

Something passed between them then, an unspoken message that Birdie wished she could understand. Cade's head lifted, eyes burning with the light of battle, and he seemed to stand straighter than before.

Then Amos ducked into the tunnel, and Birdie could feel the eyes of all the children on her, watching as she trailed behind.

26

A faint breath of air trickled across Ky's cheek, pulling him up short. To his left, a side tunnel branched off toward the empty stall in the marketplace. He must have been moving faster than he thought. They had made incredible time through the passages.

He flung up a warning hand. "Stop here."

Birdie and Amos stumbled to a halt, the former outlaw breathing hard with his hands resting on his knees. Ky felt a smile crack his dry lips. Being short did have *some* advantages, like not having to run stooped through the tighter tunnels.

Amos puffed a long breath. "Ye goin' t' tell us where we're headed, lad?"

"You wanted to get out of the city, right? I'm going to get you out." After that, Ky had his own plans to save the Underground. Plans that required a couple minutes of freedom from any watchful eye—even if that watchful eye belonged to Hawkness. "Wait here. I'll be right back."

He ducked into the tunnel and took off running, with Amos's shouts ringing in his ears.

"Come back! What d'ye think ye're doin'?"

His thoughts sped in time with the steady fall of his feet down the well-worn track in the center of the tunnel as he struggled to wrap his mind around the situation. If Dizzier had been captured while trying to *reach* the stall, then he should have had the sword on him, and it would have been reclaimed by the soldiers when he was taken. But there had been no sign of the sword during the struggle in the marketplace.

It just didn't add up.

His foot struck something, bringing him to a stumbling halt beneath the stall entrance shaft. Hazy light filtered into the tunnel from the cracks surrounding the trap door, but the glow petered out halfway down the wall and didn't quite reach the floor.

He squatted and groped along the ground. Cloth met his searching fingertips—cloth wrapped around something long and hard. He hefted it in his hand, gauging the weight and balance.

It had to be the sword.

Slowly, the pieces began to fall into place. Dizzier hadn't been thieving when Hendryk caught him—why stop to pinch trifles when he already had the treasure? No, he must have been caught sneaking into the stall, and somehow managed to toss the sword inside before he was dragged away.

It was a huge risk to take. If the soldiers had arrived a moment sooner, they might have spied the entrance, and Ky gritted his teeth at the thought of what could have happened if the soldiers had attacked before Amos revealed the cavern's secret defenses.

In any case, it explained Dizzier's strange behavior in the marketplace and his insistence that Ky go to the stall. Not to escape—that wasn't Dizzier's way—but to make sure the sword was found. Why go to all that trouble? Sure, Cade was obsessed with collecting weapons for the Underground, but there were plenty of easier ways to acquire them than attacking a party of Khelari.

Ky began to part the wrappings, but stopped just shy of revealing the hilt. There was no point to unveiling the sword in the dark. In the end, it didn't matter *why* the sword was important. All that mattered was keeping the Underground safe, even if it meant he had to leave the city to do it.

The thought brought a lump to his throat. If this was his best shot at saving the Underground, why did it feel like a betrayal?

With a groan, he pushed to his feet, stuck the sword through his belt, and retraced his steps to the main tunnel. He heard Birdie and Amos long before he reached them. Their hushed whispers rebounded off the floor and walls of the tunnel, magnifying the sound.

". . . don't like this. He's been gone too long. A fine trick, leavin' us stranded here in the dark whilst he goes scamperin' off t' who knows where!"

"He's coming back, Amos."

At least *someone* had faith in him. But there was something in Birdie's voice that suggested more than a hope that he would return. It was almost as if she knew that he was actually returning at that very moment. Just as she had known that the dark soldiers were in the tunnel.

Ky shuddered. There was something strange about that girl— strange and downright frightening. The song she had sung seemed to pierce right through him. Not to mention the uncanny way she'd healed the injured runners and his hand. What kind of power enabled someone to do that?

He emerged from the tunnel and stopped a few yards away from them. "Ready to keep moving?"

Amos grunted. "O' course *we* are, but where were ye?"

Ky's hand drifted to the cloth-wrapped sword tucked in his belt. "We should go."

"Where are we headed?" Birdie asked.

"The market."

To his relief, neither Birdie nor Amos asked any more questions as he led the way down the tunnel and up through the trap door into the bustle of the marketplace. The clamor of hundreds of voices concealed their arrival, allowing them to melt into the crowd.

Unfortunately, Ky's plan hinged on attracting attention. So when he spied black armor ahead, he pulled the cloth-wrapped sword from his belt, darted toward his target, and smashed the flat of the blade across the back of the soldier's head.

The soldier collapsed like a felled tree.

Startled cries rippled through the crowd, and Ky fought the urge to disappear. For once, the more of a commotion he made, the better chance he had of succeeding.

He parted the wrappings to reveal the sword's pommel. Then as the soldier groaned and struggled to rise, he shoved the sword at his throat, forcing the man's head back so he could get a good look at the weapon.

The action revealed the soldier's face.

Ky's hand tightened around the sword hilt. It was Hendryk—Dizzier's killer. His gaze drifted to the soldier's unprotected throat. One quick stroke was all it would take—just one—and Dizzier would be avenged.

But he would have failed the Underground.

Right now, that was all that mattered. He stepped back and slid the sword back into his belt, looping the wrappings to conceal the pommel again. Amos's hands settled on his shoulders, and he allowed himself to be dragged away.

"What d' ye think ye're doin'? Are ye tryin' t' get us all killed?"

A horn call blared through the marketplace, spreading the alarm. Just in time.

Ky broke free of Amos's grip. "Wall-top. Hurry!" Without waiting to see if they would follow, he raced to the steps and up to the battlements, halting before a gap in the layers of stone. "Come on! Over here."

Amos handed Birdie over the edge, and then dropped down beside her. Ky could hear their feet scraping against the stone as they climbed down. A flash of yellow caught his eye, and the cat—George—appeared out of nowhere and dodged over the side of the wall.

Ky turned to survey the city. Horns blasted from all directions. The baying of hounds mingled with rallying shouts. Below, soldiers shoved through the crowd, while Hendryk raced up the wall-top steps.

Grinning, Ky dusted his hands on the knees of his trousers. Even Cade's most masterful schemes hadn't worked this smoothly! He hopped up onto the battlements, paused to salute Hendryk, then slipped over the side and scrambled down the wall.

"I'll be back," he whispered.

As soon as his feet hit the earth, he took off running after the others, across the field toward the River Adayn and the Westmark Bridge.

Birdie gasped in a ragged breath. Her feet pounded the earth, cold mud splattering her legs, frozen grasses leaving icy trails on her skin. She struggled up the slope at Amos's heels, with Ky beside her and George dashing at her feet.

The cat seemed to pick the worst time to show up. Apparently he thought so too. A panicked wail spilled from his lips. "We're doomed . . . doomed . . . doomed . . ."

The rhythm of her feet matched the repetition of the word, and she caught herself thinking it along with George.

Amos crested the slope and turned around to face the city, a scowl creasing his brow. "Hurry!" he barked. "Thanks t' yer fool stunt, lad, there's mounted soldiers on our trail."

"I knew it!" George cried. "Knew we were doomed!"

Birdie pushed herself past him and up to the top of the slope, and then stopped in utter amazement at the sight on the other side.

A torrent of white-capped water rushed through a cleft between two hills. The grassy foot of the slope she stood on dropped just below into the curling arms of the roiling flood. This must be the Adayn, the great river of Leira, at flood stage after the Turning.

Ky grabbed her arm and tugged her forward. Together they skidded down the steep hillside to the brink of the river, where Amos stood with one foot on a swaying wooden bridge that arched the lashing water. The bridge creaked and groaned as the Adayn coiled around the wooden pilings, less than a foot beneath the platform.

Amos started across the bridge, shouting something back over his shoulder, but the roar of the river swept his words away.

Birdie strained to hear.

"Once we cross . . . we'll be . . . Westmark!"

The words filled her with an incredible longing. This was the end of her journey, the fulfillment of all her hopes. Here, at last, in the Westmark, she would be safe.

Here she would be free.

Still clutching Ky's hand, Birdie raced out onto the shaking bridge. Beneath her feet, the River Adayn leapt like a bucking horse. Icy water spurted through the slats, coiling around her ankles as if seeking to drag her away.

She glanced back and saw a line of horsemen crest the hill and sweep down toward the river. Ahead, the green shore of the Westmark glimmered through a cloud of mist, only thirty paces away. Everything within her strained to run faster. With each aching breath, she could taste freedom mingled with the spray on the wind. So close, *so close!*

Close enough she could almost ignore the voice whispering doubt in her ear. Almost, but not quite. The soldiers could cross the bridge as easily as she, and once on the other side, how could she hope to evade a mounted enemy?

"We're all going to die!" George wailed.

"C'mon! Keep up!" Ky jerked her arm, and she realized her steps had slowed.

She pushed herself to run faster.

Twenty paces now to the other side of the Adayn. Then ten. Amos stumbled onto solid ground and shouted encouragement. Then George was across, a flying blur of yellow streaking up the bank.

The bridge quivered, and Birdie stumbled, Ky's hand the only thing that kept her from falling. A clatter like the sound of crumbling rocks filled the air. She looked over her shoulder. A dozen soldiers were riding across the bridge, and at the front of the line—her breath caught in her throat—Carhartan, mounted on his massive gray steed.

She reached the end of the bridge and leapt off onto the bank. Ky continued up the side of the next hill, but Birdie slammed to a stop and wrenched her hand free of his grasp.

"What're you doing?" Ky demanded.

Even if they managed to escape here, she would never truly be free. She would always be cursed, always hunted. Carhartan would *never* give up.

Better to face the Khelari with a sword in her hands than be ridden down and stabbed in the back. She turned to Amos and saw the same determination in his eyes. He drew his dirk and stood before the bridge, but his posture was that of a bent and weary man, not the fierce Protector Birdie had come to know.

Birdie planted her feet, drew her sword, and held it upright before her. The soldiers were more than halfway across the bridge now. She could see their faces beneath the shadow of their open helms.

Something thrummed behind her, and hard round objects sliced through the air to pelt the soldiers. Ky was slinging.

She found comfort in that fact. At least she would not die alone. Abandoned.

Then beyond the racket of the approaching hooves, beneath the roar of the river, she heard something else: a low throbbing, deep and haunting. It was the first notes of the Song. And in the Song, a voice called to her. Rich. Strong. Powerful.

It called her by name. *Birdie. Songkeeper. Beloved. You are mine.*

But she didn't belong to anyone.

The dark melody boiled to the surface, but something about it had changed. It was enticing, now. Sweet and bitter at the same time, like honey laced with salt, Madame's frozen smile concealing her acidic tongue.

Be free, it whispered. *Free of pursuit. Free of this madness.* It fueled her wrath, and strength coursed through her sword arm.

You are mine.

Never before had she felt such a rush of light and opposition. The Song tugged her forward, brightness compelling and drawing her into itself, but at the same time, the dark melody pursued, clutching at her ankles like a quagmire seeking to suck her into the depths.

You are mine.

The words caressed her tongue as she repeated them softly to herself. Who was the speaker who claimed her, an orphan, as their own?

Emhran.

That single word—or was it a note?—brought a breath of peace into the chaos, a shimmer of light in the shadows.

You are the Songkeeper.

Sing.

She closed her eyes, allowed the melody to flow through her, and sang.

The melody tore through Ky, a purging fire, rending bone from marrow, unmaking and then remaking anew. His hand stilled, and the sling hung limp from his fingers.

A change came over the river before his eyes. The water swelled around the base of the bridge until the wooden planks groaned beneath the force. A wave dashed across the bridge, knocking one of the mounted soldiers into the river. The rest of the horses skidded on the wet planks, forcing the soldiers to slow their pace.

Birdie sang without faltering.

With every note the stolen sword seemed to grow heavier, weighing down Ky's belt. His hand brushed the pommel, and cold seized his fingers through the cloth wrappings. He took a deep breath, gripped the hilt, and drew the sword from his belt.

The strips of cloth shriveled, as if consumed by fire, and fell back, revealing the sword. Long bluish-white blade, glowing and wet, like flames seen through rippling layers of water. A gold crossguard and pommel. Leather-wrapped hilt. A high-pitched metallic voice emanated from the blade and blended with Birdie's melody.

The sword was singing!

It wasn't a conscious decision, but in that moment—with the soldiers bearing down upon them, the river rising, and Birdie's song flowing through his soul, Ky knew he had to protect her. He pushed past her and Amos and lifted the sword in both hands, point angling down at the bridge.

With a yell, he drove it into the wooden planks.

A blinding flash. A deafening roar. A resounding crack.

Then a firm grip hauled him backward, and he crashed into something solid.

Gasping for breath, he sat up on the river bank, sopping wet, with Amos standing over him and Birdie sitting at his side. The River Adayn rippled past his feet, scarce a current disturbing the smooth surface of the water, but the Westmark Bridge was gone.

He stared in amazement from the unfettered river to the naked blade in his hand, to the soaked girl beside him. His hand still tingled with the power coursing through the sword. He forced himself to release the hilt and stared at his palm, expecting his flesh to be seared from the intense cold radiating from the blade, but his skin was unscarred.

Across the river, waterlogged soldiers and their dripping steeds clambered out onto the bank. Only about half of the soldiers appeared. Of the other half, Ky could see no sign. A few broken planks floating in the water were all that remained of the bridge. Everything else seemed to have been washed away. Even the boats that had been left on the bank after the search for the sword were gone, borne away upon the flood.

Ky hefted the sword in his hand—such perfect balance, so different from the clumsy, lifeless blades he was used to—and slid it into his belt. Then he stood, groaning at the effort, and turned to Amos, expecting the man to take charge and issue commands as he had in the Underground.

But Amos stood as if carven from stone, bronze dirk still held upright in his hand. His skin looked like stone too. All the color had fled his cheeks, leaving them the dull gray of the city's walls. Deep lines marked his face like the intersecting streets of Kerby, all twisting and turning and secrets concealed.

"We have to go," Ky said. The soldiers weren't fools. Even if their means for crossing the river had been destroyed, they would soon recover their wits and their weapons, and he wanted to be far away before that happened.

"Yes, we must," Birdie said. Her voice surprised him—it was so faint.

He held out a hand and helped her up, but her knees buckled at the first step and she sank in his arms. Her short sword lay on the ground at his feet.

Amos roused from his lethargy and stumbled to Ky's side, scooping Birdie up in his arms. Her head rolled back against his chest, dark hair shadowing her white face.

A bolt whistled through the air and plunged into the earth at Ky's feet. He lurched back and scanned the opposite bank for the shooter. There he was, a dark figure kneeling on the bank to reload his crossbow.

"Let's go!" Ky caught up Birdie's short sword and scrambled for cover, squelching up the soggy slope with Amos behind him.

"George," Birdie mumbled, "where's George?"

Ky shrugged but couldn't bring himself to answer. Come to think of it, he hadn't seen the cat since crossing the river, but he failed to see how a cat mattered when soldiers were using them for target practice! Far as he could see, the only thing that mattered at the moment was putting as much distance between themselves and the soldiers as they could.

He paused on the crest of the hill to wave a derogatory farewell to the soldiers, then bounded down the slope with Amos at his heels.

27

Amos stamped his foot against the frozen ground. It felt solid enough, but on the Westmark—a moorland pitted with peat bogs and hidden pools—one could never be too careful. "We'll stop here an' rest for the night."

He chaffed at the delay. They'd made good time traveling, once Birdie recovered from the bridge disaster, and Bryllhyn was only another two or three hours' brisk walk away. But both Birdie and Ky had been lagging behind since evening fell and looked like they would fall over if he didn't stop soon.

Ky threw himself down and seemed to fall asleep almost instantly, sprawled on his back with his arms and legs stretched out. Birdie curled up in a ball, and Amos tucked her cloak around her to keep the winter chill at bay. The poor lass was worn out. Such a wee thing. Too small and frail for the burden she was forced to carry.

If he had his way, she wouldn't be forced to carry it at all.

Pity Emhran never asked him for advice.

He paced beside the sleepers, heavy heart thumping to the rhythm of his dragging steps. His hand sought the solace of his dirk, and he pulled it from the scabbard, flipping it in the air and catching it by the blade again. And again. And again. As the hours slipped by, he kept watch. But the action brought no comfort as it once had. With each rotation of the blade, he saw the brilliant white-blue of the sword—Artair's sword—and heard once more the notes of the Song, and saw yet again that kindly face before him.

Cursed fate. To think that he had forsaken one Songkeeper only to stumble upon another. That he had rid himself of the sword and all the painful memories bound up in the blade only to find it again. What could it be but the stars conspiring against him?

Or Emhran.

Boggswo—Amos bit off the end of the unspoken word. Best not to scoff at things he didn't understand. He shoved the dirk into its scabbard and knelt beside Ky.

The gold pommel of the sword in the sleeping lad's belt gleamed in Mindolyn's pale light. Slowly, Amos extended his hand until his fingertips brushed the burnished metal. A chill seeped into his bones, and an ache settled in his chest.

Befoggling, wasn't it? That the sword should have spent nigh thirty years in the muck at the bottom of the Adayn, yet not a mark of rust nor stain showed upon it.

The lad startled awake and scrambled back, clutching the sword to his side. "What do you want?"

What *did* he want? To revert to life as it had been less than a week earlier, with the past good and buried, and he content to hate the Takhran from afar. A sigh escaped his lips. There was no hope of that now. "How did ye find the sword?"

Ky's gaze assumed a new intensity, and a hard edge crept into his voice. "What do you know about it?"

"I know 'twas found in the river."

"Yeah, and how do you know that?"

Amos took a deep breath. "Because I put it there."

Ky was silent a moment, and when at last he spoke his voice was hoarse. "The dark soldiers found it. Cade wanted to strike back at them, hit them hard, so we stole it. What's so important about this sword anyway? Is it magic?"

"Some might call it that." Though Artair would not have been pleased. He claimed the Song's power and the sword's peculiarities came from Emhran, not meddling with darkness.

For years Amos had rejected the Song and the Master Singer, denied their power, even their existence. Willful blindness, Nisus called it. Yet what he had seen today summoned dozens of memories he had buried beneath a mound of deceit, until the truth at last lay bare before him and there was no hope in denying it.

He cleared his throat. "The man who owned that sword was a friend, Artair. He was captured an' slain by the Takhran long ago. I saw t' it that his sword was kept out o' evil hands."

"So you threw it in the river?"

"Aye." And he had meant for it to stay there too. Forgotten forever.

"But what is it makes this sword so special?"

Bearded pikes and mottlegurds! The lad asked more questions than Birdie. Amos massaged his scalp with both hands. "Because it belonged t' a special man. Now, go back t' sleep, lad. It's late."

"Was this special man a Songkeeper?"

Birdie spoke behind him, and Amos heaved a sigh. He'd supposed the lass to be sleeping. "Why d' ye ask that?"

"Because I want to know the truth." She seized his forearm. "Amos, please, I don't think it's a curse."

He tried to break free, but she wouldn't relinquish her grip, and he had no desire to hurt her. "Lass, I—"

"Please! I want to know what I am."

"Even if the knowing'll do ye harm?"

She released him then and stumbled back. "How can *knowing* do me any more harm?" Her voice trembled on the verge of tears. "I have no home. I've been kidnapped. I'm hunted wherever I go. Something is different about me, and I don't understand it. I've seen people *die*, Amos. And for what? That's all I want to know." Her voice dropped to a whisper. "Why?"

Why? How many times had Amos uttered that word in the dark nights following Drengreth? *Why?* He had whispered it in the pathless tunnels below Mount Eiphyr, and screamed it to the starless sky, and yet he had received no answer. Emhran was silent. As he had ever been.

And yet, the Song continued.

That truth could not be denied. It stood before him in the slim figure of a girl, bewildered and forlorn, awaiting his response.

"Aye, it's true." The words were out before he could halt them, and now that he had begun to speak, he found he could not stop, as if the admission had demolished the wall he'd erected to conceal his secrets. "Artair was a Songkeeper, an' I was one o' his followers. Even then, the Takhran hated Songkeepers an' hunted 'em down like animals. So we lived on the run, always *just* one step ahead o' the Khelari, ever dreamin' o' a day when we would be free o' 'em. We thought Artair would lead us t' defeat the Takhran, thought he would save us. Fools—that's what we were. Deceived by our own vain hopes."

"What happened?"

"One o' our own turned traitor an' led the Takhran's forces right into our midst. We called him brother, an' he brought our enemies t' slay us in our sleep. His name was Oran Hamner." The name tasted like poison on his tongue. "You know him as Carhartan."

Birdie's head snapped up. "You *knew* Carhartan and you didn't tell me?"

"Didn't realize 'til after he'd captured ye."

He should have slain Carhartan when he had the chance. Better that than worrying that the traitor was still out there, somewhere, on the trail of Artair's sword and the supposed Songkeeper. At least the collapse of the bridge would provide them with a few days of safety, since the only other fordable crossings were miles up and down the river. Though hoping Carhartan had drowned would doubtless be asking too much.

"What about your friend, Artair?" Ky spoke up. "What happened to him?"

"Taken alive. The Khelari slew the rest. A few escaped, though I didn't know it at the time. Thought I was the only one left. So I took Artair's sword from his tent, before the Khelari could find it, an' set off t' rescue him."

"Alone?" Birdie's hand crept back to his arm.

"Aye. I followed 'em deep into the Takhran's fortress, but by the time I arrived, 'twas too late." Amos nearly choked on the word. He couldn't bring himself to speak of that terrible journey wandering through the dark tunnels of the Takhran's fortress, or the horrors he had discovered in the caverns below Mount Eiphyr. Artair was dead, and that was all that mattered, because it meant Artair had failed and his promises had proved vain.

"I knew I had t' keep his sword out o' the Takhran's hands, but I couldn't bear the sight o' it. So I traveled t' the Adayn an' there on the Westmark Bridge, I cast it into the deep."

"And then you became Hawkness," Ky breathed.

"Aye, lad, I became Hawkness." It was strange that words so long concealed should come so easily to his lips.

Birdie's grip tightened on his arm. "And who *is* Hawkness?"

"Not is. *Was.* He was an outlaw. Those o' us who survived Drengreth vowed t' fight the Takhran 'til our dyin' breath."

"Jirkar and Nisus?" Birdie asked.

"Aye, they were part o' the original band. Others trickled in after—the Takhran wasn't short o' enemies in those days—an' beneath the streets o' Kerby, we plotted our revenge."

"But none of the others were as fierce and brave as Hawkness." Ky's eyes gleamed in the moonlight. "You're a legend. A hero."

The lad's words pierced his conscience like a poisoned shaft. "Never a hero, lad. For twelve years we warred, fought, lied, stole, cheated, 'til our cause was lost in the horror o' who we'd become an' our own people grew t' hate us. Most o' the Drengreth survivors left after the first few years. The rest dwindled away one by one. Some taken by death or imprisonment. Still more by the lure o' a new life.

"And that's when I forsook the name o' Hawkness an' became who I am, Amos McElhenny, travelin' peddler. But I've never truly forgotten who I've been, or what the Takhran has done."

There. He had said it. The truth was revealed at last, and he felt naked before it. In the silence following his words, he heard the wind creeping over the moor accompanied by the shrill weeping of the night moths.

Then Birdie spoke. "The Song isn't a curse, Amos."

"Lass, I'm tryin' t' protect—"

"No!" She jerked away from him. "No. You have to understand. It's a part of who I am, and I can't deny that anymore. I *am* the Songkeeper."

The way she said it, so calmly, set Amos's teeth on edge. "D' ye even know what that means? D' ye know what a Songkeeper is? Or the Song, for that matter, or any o' it?"

"How can I when no one will explain it to me?"

"It's dangerous meddlin' in things ye don't understand—"

"But don't *you* understand, Amos? *This* is who I am. I didn't see that before, and I don't know what it means yet, but I can't deny it. I have to know more. Please. Help me." Head thrown back, hair tossing in the wind, she seemed as fragile as a fire flower, yet as strong as a zoar tree. Even her plea for aid sounded strangely like an ultimatum.

Images stirred on the edge of Amos's vision. Memories he had thought defeated assailed him once more. The horrors of the Pit. The choking stench of death, so thick it seemed to assume physical form and claw at his throat. Bodies, rows upon rows of them, broken and discarded. And Artair . . .

No! He wrenched himself back to the present and the lass standing before him. "I'm sorry, lass. I can't help ye become a Songkeeper."

28

Birdie sat alone in the dark, huddled beneath her cloak, while the stars sang above her. Ky and Amos had long since fallen asleep, but Amos's words still echoed in her ears. She had been so blind. All this time, she had been so worried about others forcing her to become the Songkeeper that she hadn't realized that Amos was trying to do the opposite.

He'd warned that people would try to manipulate her, all the while telling her that she was cursed. A shuddering breath escaped her lips. She'd thought he cared about her for who she really was, but she should have known better.

No one would ever care about her for her own sake. Only what they could get from her.

Stealthy footsteps crunched behind her. She reached for her sword and slowly turned.

A familiar figure shuffled around the campsite, obviously taking pains to be silent—Amos. Half of her wanted to rush over and reason with him, beg him to understand. Surely she could make him see that her ability was a part of who she was, not a curse—and certainly not something she could ignore. But the other half of her recalled the lies and the hurt and the secrets, and refused to move.

So she sat and watched as Amos knelt beside Ky for a moment and then stood, wrapped his cloak about him, and marched away into the night.

Ten minutes passed, and he did not return.

Then an hour.

Birdie hugged her knees to her chest. He would return. He had to. And in the light of day he would be more reasonable.

He *would* come back.

She said the words over and over to herself, as if the repetition could somehow make it come true. How long she sat there, just her and her thoughts and the airy melody overhead, she did not know. But at last, pale strands of light streaked across the fringes of the sky, heralding the approach of dawn.

And Amos had not returned.

A flash drew her gaze to the eastern horizon where Tauros sailed up over the crest of the earth. A long, clear note, like the call of a horn, hung in the air. The Morning Star, Artair, shot across the sky to herald the rising sun and vanished in a burst of gold.

And Amos did not come back.

Ky stirred in his sleep. Morning light bathed his face with rosy hues. The rise of the river had washed all the mud and soot off him, and shaggy strands of straw-colored hair stuck up in all directions about his head. Birdie could make out his features for the first time. He looked to be around the same age as her, or maybe just a bit older.

How long until he abandoned her as well?

She banished the thought. Amos had not abandoned her. There was still time for him to return. It didn't make sense for him to have come so far, endured so much, only to leave her alone now.

She forced herself to rise and find food for breakfast—anything to distract from the relentless clamor of her thoughts. Amos's pack was still there, lying undisturbed where he had set it the night before. That was a good sign, wasn't it? If Amos had left for good, he would have taken his pack with him.

Not until she had pulled out a handful of bread and dried meat from the bottom of her pack did she realize that Ky was awake and scowling at her. She flinched before the ferocity in his gaze. "Would you . . . like something to eat?"

The boy shook his head. "I want my sword. Where is it?"

"I don't know. I haven't seen it." Her gaze traveled over the campsite, searching for a glimpse of bluish-white or gold.

"This isn't a game." Ky jumped to his feet and began pacing back and forth. He reminded Birdie of a caged animal on the verge of breaking loose. "I need that sword back. What've you done with it?"

"Nothing. I told you, I haven't seen it." But she *had* seen Amos sneaking around Ky in the dark, hadn't she? Could Amos have taken the sword? The idea seemed ridiculous enough to be completely impossible, but the fact that he still had not returned was suspicious.

Ky stopped pacing abruptly. "Hawkness—where's Hawkness?"

"He's not a thief!" She blurted out, but even as she spoke she knew the words weren't entirely true. By his own admission, Amos *was* a thief . . . and worse. But that had been long ago. He had changed, hadn't he?

"Look, I'm not accusing him. I just want to know where he is."

The lump that had been growing in her throat all night long threatened to choke her. A tear spilled down her face. "He's . . . not . . . here."

She couldn't deny it any more. Amos was gone. He had gotten a glimpse of who she truly was the night before, and he had fled. He wasn't coming back. He had abandoned her. Just like everyone else.

"I need that sword." Ky groaned and dropped to the ground, resting his elbows on his knees and his forehead on his fists. "It was my only hope to keep the Underground safe. I figured I could lead the soldiers away from Kerby—that they'd follow the sword and leave the Underground alone. Should've known better than to trust another thief, even one like Hawkness." A bitter edge tinged his voice. "*Look out for yourself.*"

"That's the spirit," a familiar tenor voice spoke beside Birdie, and George padded up to her, fur hanging in muddy clumps that clung to the leather collar and glass bead about his neck. "Sounds like you're finally mastering the concept."

By now the cat's sudden appearances and disappearances scarce surprised Birdie. He was always there one minute and gone the next, though how he continually managed to find them again was a mystery to her.

George began preening himself, speaking around licks. "You have to . . . fend for yourself . . . in this ruthless world of ours . . . because no one else will bother to look out for you."

In the face of Amos's sudden departure, George's words rang with the weight of truth, and Birdie almost believed him. But she couldn't deny that Amos had looked out for her in the past. He'd befriended her when she was a worthless drudge at the Sylvan Swan. He'd pursued her when she was a kidnapped orphan. So why abandon her now?

Thinking about it made her head ache and her throat swell, and she was still no closer to figuring out the answer. Tears pricked the corner of her eyes. She massaged her forehead with her fingertips. "Please, George, I'd rather not talk about it."

"Suit yourself." The cat shrugged. "I'm only trying to help."

"How do you do it?" Ky broke in. "Talk to the cat, I mean. How do you know what he's saying?"

Birdie narrowed her gaze at him, but she couldn't see any hint of mockery in his eyes. "I just do. The same way you and I are talking right now. You don't think I'm mad?"

"Not such a fool." Ky lifted his left hand and wiggled his fingers. "You healed my hand *and* all the wounded runners in the Underground. You made the river rise when you sang! Talking to animals is a mite tame in comparison."

"Tame?" George's fur puffed out, and his tone took on an air of injured pride. "My dear young two-legged sir, it is anything but."

The cat's voice called to mind a conversation Birdie had with him back when they traveled on the dwarves' wagon. He had told her she was special, that she could hear things others couldn't, but also that she wasn't the only one of her kind.

Birdie sat up straight and took a deep breath. If Amos truly had abandoned her, then she was on her own. There was no point in denying it. She couldn't just sit here waiting for him to return. She had to figure out what to do, where to go, *who to trust*. Starting with the cat . . .

"George, I need to—"

The black melody coiled around Birdie like the strands of an ever-tightening snare. Khelari. And they were close. She jumped to her feet and dragged her sword from its sheath.

"What is it?" Ky shot up beside her. "What's wrong?"

"Khelari. Nearby." Even as she spoke, she could hear the melody growing louder. The soldiers were approaching fast. Too fast. "Come on!" She snatched up her pack, tossed Amos's to Ky, and took off over the boggy moorland at a run. She didn't know where she was going, but anything was better than waiting for the Khelari to arrive.

George scurried to keep up. "My dear girl, I do believe you're overreacting. Surely there's no need to go dashing about helter-skelter!"

Birdie spun around, searching for a place to hide. Rising hills adorned with frosted heather and pocked with black boggy splotches surrounded them on all sides, but nothing offered concealment.

Ky grabbed her arm. "Look!"

A Khelari appeared over a rise to their left, jogging toward them, a sword in his hand. Birdie and Ky swung to the right. A hound and its keeper emerged from that direction, and another Khelari, mounted on a horse, raced up in front. Ky's sling whirred, and a stone felled the first Khelari, but more soldiers filled the empty space and advanced toward them, until they were surrounded by a ring of bristling weapons.

Birdie and Ky stood back to back, turning this way and that, trying to face all their enemies at once, while George darted about their feet chattering about death and doom and the end of all things. Fighting against such odds was hopeless, but Birdie wasn't ready to admit defeat.

Then Carhartan rode up, and all hope vanished.

The gray horse paced around the ring of Khelari and came to a stamping halt across from George. Carhartan's gaze rested on the cat, and he jerked his head, motioning the cat forward.

George glanced up at Birdie. "My apologies," he said, and then sauntered over until he stood directly beneath Carhartan's stirrup. "The Songkeeper, my lord. As promised."

The meaning of his words sank into Birdie like a dagger.

A suppressed sob constricted her chest. Was there no one she could trust? She couldn't recall any hint of the terrifying melody in George's song, unlike Carhartan and the other Khelari she had met, but she was too weary to try figuring out what that meant. Her head swam and her sword arm drooped. The soldiers pressed forward, and she allowed the sword to be wrenched from her grip.

Resistance offered no hope.

Carhartan had won, plain and simple.

Rough hands shoved a gag between her teeth, bound her hands with ropes behind her back, and dragged her to Carhartan.

He leaned forward in the saddle, and the teardrop red jewel swung forward on the chain about his neck. "What of Hawkness and the sword?"

"Not here." Ky glared up at Carhartan as if daring him to demand more information.

"I wasn't speaking to you, *boy*. Well, cat, what of Hawkness?"

It took Birdie a moment to realize that he had addressed the question to George and was actually awaiting a response. Carhartan could understand the cat—how was that possible?

"Missing, unfortunately," George said. "He left in the middle of the night and took the sword with him. He pursued a westerly course, but beyond that I cannot say, since I was unable to follow him *and* keep an eye on the Songkeeper at the same time."

Leather creaked as Carhartan dismounted, then his footsteps crunched toward Birdie, spurs jangling. He grasped her chin, forcing her head back until she looked up into his narrowed eyes.

"So, little Songkeeper, at last."

She pulled away from his gaze and spied George peeking around the side of Carhartan's leg. The cat's normally calm face wore a mask of terror, and he seemed to be trying to mouth something to her, but Carhartan jerked her back toward him, his grip tightening about her jaw.

"Wondering why your little friend betrayed you? Every creature has its price. He's been working for me since before you first met him."

Birdie's mind whirled as the implications of what she had just seen and heard registered. The cat had implied that the ability to communicate with animals was somehow bound to her role as Songkeeper, but how could that be if Carhartan could speak to them as well? Or had *everything* George said been a lie?

Carhartan chuckled. "Did you think your Song the only power in the world? My master possesses greater power than you can ever imagine. Power that you will soon witness firsthand."

He released her, and she fell back. Ky managed to steady her with his bound hands, but the soldiers yanked them apart.

Carhartan turned to mount his horse, but the yellow cat darted in his way.

"Our bargain?" George sat back on his haunches and pawed at Carhartan's legs. "My dear Lord Carhartan, surely you remember. I've delivered as we agreed. Now you must hold to your promise and release me from my bondage."

Carhartan lashed out with his boot, sending George skidding forward several feet. "Our *bargain* involves Hawkness and the sword as well. Without them, your task is not complete. So if you ever want to be free, beast, I suggest you find them."

29

Hooded and cloaked, Amos marched briskly across the Westmark, skirting bogs and ice patches with the care of a hunted man. He had a mission to accomplish before dawn, and he needed time to think. The cool night breezes served to clear his troubled mind.

Birdie's eyes haunted him. He could still envision her standing before him pleading for help, and the hurt that filled her eyes when he refused, smashing her hopes with all the sympathy and tact of a boulder. Why couldn't the lass see that everything he'd done had been to protect her? To keep her from Artair's fate.

Artair's sword dangled from his belt, carefully wrapped in a corner of his cloak to prevent it from touching his skin. He'd promised to see that the sword stayed out of the Takhran's hands, and he intended to do just that. Besides, if there was anything that could cause more trouble for his lass than simply being the Songkeeper, it was having the sword in her possession.

Since the River Adayn was neither wide nor deep enough to conceal the sword, the Great Sea would have to suffice. He was already drawing near to Bryllhyn and the coast, giving him plenty of time to dispose of the sword and head back to Birdie before dawn. Plenty of time to work through the problems besieging his mind.

With any luck, he'd be back before anyone realized he was gone.

Amos rounded a bog, his heels sinking into the mossy ground, and scaled a steep hillock. The Great Sea sprawled before him, a mass of black in the darkness. Pale moonlight crested the waves writhing upon the shore.

He breathed deeply of the salt air, and felt the tension drain from his muscles.

This was home.

He let his gaze wander to his left where the white stone cottages of Bryllhyn were scattered haphazardly here and there across the grassy hills and shore. A dismayed cry burst from his lips. The village burned with a dull orange glow. Shouts, so faint he almost missed them, fell on his ears, punctuated by the sharp clang of weapons.

Amos swiped the dirk from his sheath, and the familiar weight in his hand brought a sense of stability to his reeling thoughts.

The Khelari—were they responsible for this?

He spun back to face the way he'd come. Somewhere out there on the moor, Birdie and Ky slept in peaceful ignorance. After the collapse of the bridge, he'd thought they would be safe in the Westmark, at least for a short while. He should have known better than to underestimate the Khelari . . . and Oran.

A trailing scream drew his gaze back to the village. People—*his* people were dying. Waveryders he'd known since he was a lad. And his mother! Bloodwuthering blodknockers, she was in the village too. He couldn't leave her to be slain by the Takhran's cursed soldiers.

But what of Birdie?

He stood still a moment, torn, then his gaze drifted past the village to the shore and the dark outline of a sleek ship silhouetted against the firelight. That was no Waveryder vessel—the realization set his blood running cold. The attackers weren't Khelari. They were pirates.

Langorian pirates.

Amos dashed toward the village, sand flying beneath his feet. The orange glow grew brighter as he neared. Fire blazed among the Waveryder vessels beached in the sand, while smaller pockets of flame were scattered throughout the village. Pirates swarmed through the cottages, dragging half-awake villagers from their beds. Here and there, groups of Waveryders fell upon the pirates with swords, and dying screams assailed Amos's ears.

Straight through the center of the village he raced, heedless of the scenes of ruin and death, dodging past clusters of pirates and villagers, toward the smallest cottage at the far end where his mother lived.

A pirate lurched toward him from the side. Without slackening stride, Amos plunged his dirk into the man's side and shoved him to the ground.

Then he reached the cottage and raced up the shell-lined path to the sky-blue door. Bodies lay on the threshold atop a cushion of trailing white rock flowers. Two pirates and . . . his mother.

Amos dropped to his knees beside her and gently took her into his arms. Blood stained his hands and seeped into his shirt from the ragged wound in her chest. Her face was pale and pearl-like in the moonlight—peaceful—but her green eyes stared vacantly up at him. Empty. Dead.

A sob tore at his throat. Again, he was too late.

Someone spoke behind him—a strange voice uttering a harsh language. He clenched the pommel of his dirk, holding the blade flat against his arm so it wouldn't be visible, and raised his hands over his head. Slowly he turned around and inched to his feet.

Three dark figures stood at the end of the path. Gold flashed around their necks and arms, and they brandished short, heavy swords.

Amos flung his dirk at the middle pirate, and it buried up to the hilt in his chest. The pirate crumpled, and before the other two could recover, Amos charged. He ducked the first pirate's stroke, snagged the fallen pirate's sword and his dirk, slashed the throat of the second pirate, and swung back around to the first.

He cut at the pirate's head, but the man was already retreating, racing toward the village at top speed. Amos swore and leapt after him. He would not be cheated of revenge so easily. Holding his dirk by the tip, Amos focused on the pirate's broad back—an easy target. He let fly, and a moment later the dirk sprouted between the pirate's shoulder blades. He paused to retrieve his dirk from the body and looked up to find himself standing in the midst of a cluster of pirates.

Bilgewater.

Something slammed into him from behind, knocking him down and grinding his face into the sand. His gasp for breath inhaled a mouthful of dust instead. He lashed out with his dirk and struggled to rise.

Thud. A boot crashed into his side, followed by a kick to the chest, and then another and another. Blows poured down upon him. Beneath the crushing weight of pain, Amos was conscious of only one thing.

He had failed Birdie.

The home he'd promised her was gone. He'd dragged her out into the wilderness, left her alone, and who would protect her now when he did not return?

The blows stopped.

He was hauled to his feet, coughing and retching, and his hands were bound behind his back. His entire body throbbed. Blood tricked down his forehead and blurred his vision.

One of his captors knelt to pick a discarded sword out of the sand.

Amos's heart sank when he recognized the blade—Artair's sword. It must have slipped from his belt when he fell.

The pirate held the sword aloft so firelight glinted off the gold hilt and blued blade and then dropped it suddenly, cursing. He clutched his hand to his chest, and Amos could have sworn he saw steam arising from the man's blackened skin.

The sword was up to its old tricks again. Amos spat a glob of blood out of his mouth and grinned at the pirate. "Smarts, don't it?"

The pirate snarled at him and tore the cloak from Amos's neck, tossing it over the sword before he picked it up again. Then the other pirates closed around Amos and hustled him down the beach.

•   •   •

The ropes dug into Birdie's wrists. Her hands ached, but her fingers had long since gone numb. The gag chafed the corners of her mouth, and the foul taste of the cloth make her choke. Beside her, Ky was similarly trussed, but without the gag.

A quick glance at their surroundings exposed Carhartan's reasoning. Miles of bogs and barren hillocks revealed the lack of forthcoming help, and apparently he was only worried about *her* singing.

Several hours had passed since their capture, yet the Khelari had not moved from the spot. One lit a small fire, and the soldiers took turns roasting strips of meat over the flames and tossing scraps to the slavering hound straining against its chains. The smell set Birdie's stomach rumbling.

Carhartan sat on a hummock a few feet away, smoking a pipe with his elbows resting on his knees, eyes fixed on her. It was unnerving to think that the horrible man who had pursued her so relentlessly had once been a friend of Amos before betraying him and the other Songkeeper, Artair. But she didn't allow herself to dwell on it for long. Just thinking about Amos made her chest ache and her mind spin with questions all over again.

Soft footsteps pattered past, then George came into her line of vision, trotted to Carhartan, and sat at the soldier's feet.

Carhartan pulled the pipe from his mouth. "What information do you have for me?"

The cat licked his paws clean before replying. "Hawkness is in the next village, Bryllhyn. On the coast. But I'm afraid he's been captured by Langorians, led by the notorious Pirate Lord Rhudashka. They have the sword as well. It's caused quite a stir from what I heard."

Birdie exchanged a glance with Ky. Amos's capture was depressing news, but at the same time she couldn't help feeling the tiniest bit of relief. It left a chance—just the slightest—that maybe Amos hadn't chosen to abandon her.

George sidled past her feet, casting a quick glance up at her before scampering away. His eyes pleaded with her . . . for what? Reassurance that all was well? He had betrayed her and handed her over to her worst enemy. If reassurance was what he sought, he would wait long indeed.

"Time to move out." Carhartan tapped his pipe against the sole of his boot and stood, nodding toward Birdie and Ky. "Bring them."

A soldier with disheveled hair the color of dried dune grass hurried over and dragged Birdie to her feet. He turned to Ky next, but the boy had already scrambled up.

"You're Hendryk, aren't you?" Ky said.

Surprise flashed across the soldier's face. He rubbed the back of his head. "You were one of the thieves—"

"You killed my brother." Ky's voice lowered. "I'm going to kill you for that."

Hendryk shifted back a step and cast an uneasy glance around, then motioned one of the other soldiers forward. "Gag the boy, too."

Ky struggled, but the soldiers overpowered him and thrust a gag into his mouth. Birdie kept her gaze on the ground as the soldiers shoved her and Ky into line. Carhartan rode out in front with George trotting at his heels, while the hound and its keeper brought up the rear, sealing off any hope of escape.

30

Birdie hadn't expected to enter Bryllhyn like this—bound and gagged, marched along by a band of Khelari. This was to have been her home.

Sorrow flooded her at the sight of bodies lying in the open space between the cottages, sand stained crimson beneath them. The hound bayed at the scent of blood, and its keeper struggled to maintain control. A dead silence hung over the village. Shutters painted a variety of colors, once bright, now faded and peeling, swung in the breeze. Doors yawned open, but Birdie couldn't see anything through the twilight within.

Carhartan led his entourage through the village and down toward a blazing bonfire on the beach. A motley assortment of people milled around the fire, all clad in strange bright tunics and sagging breeches, arms and necks glittering with gold jewelry. They held overflowing tankards in their hands and were surrounded by a ring of broached casks.

Just off the shore, a long, low ship painted red and gold, with two masts and sails tightly furled, rocked on the washing tide. A massive iron prong stuck out from the prow like a giant spear. Three longboats were pulled up on the beach.

Birdie searched the beach for the prisoners. She finally spotted them manacled to a heavy chain that ran between two scrubby, salt-battered trees. Two pirates stood guard at the head of the line. The Waveryder captives were packed so close together that it was hard to tell how many there were—at least a hundred—but Amos's unruly shock of copper-colored hair instantly drew her gaze.

Carhartan ignored the gathering around the fire and rode straight toward the prisoners, halting and dismounting directly in front of Amos.

Amos raised his head. Dried blood streaked his face from a gash in his forehead. His eyes widened through a mottled mask of bruises as his gaze fell on Carhartan and then Birdie and Ky. "Lass!" He lurched to his knees, yanking on the running chain. The other captives cried out.

Birdie started forward, but the soldier behind her—Hendryk—seized her bound arms and held her in place. Carhartan set his boot in Amos's chest and shoved him back to the ground.

Heat flared down Birdie's neck. Suddenly it didn't matter that Amos had abandoned her, or that Amos couldn't care for her as the Songkeeper. That didn't change the fact that he had always been her friend.

Carhartan turned to the two guards. "This is the man. Release him to me."

The pirates exchanged narrow-eyed glances. Carhartan rattled off something in a harsh language that Birdie didn't understand. Then one of the pirates hurried across the beach toward the bonfire, returning a moment later with an enormous man who blazed with scarlet and gold in the sunlight.

"That's Lord Rhudashka," George said. The yellow cat sat primly in the sand beside her feet. Information, he'd once informed her, was currency. Apparently it was also his trade. But what made him think that she would care to benefit from his spying after he had betrayed her?

Rhudashka halted before Carhartan. A tangle of black hair hung past his jowls to mingle with his white-speckled beard. His eyes, mere slits beneath thick eyebrows, peered around him with such intense malice that Birdie's breath caught in her throat.

He was shadowed by a thin man clad in a blue tunic with a massive gold collar around his neck and jeweled bracelets on his arms. Dozens of dagger hilts stuck out from the broad black sash encircling his waist.

"That's Fjordair," George murmured. "Rhudashka's second in command."

Carhartan dipped his head in acknowledgement. "Lord Rhudashka."

"What is the meaning of this, Lord Carhartan?" Rhudashka's voice was a phlegmy rumble. He spoke the tongue of Leira slowly and with a thick accent. "Why are you here? These were not the terms of our *sahesk*, our arrangement, with the Takhran. Our tribute is not required before the death of the moon."

Like the onrush of a howling wind, the dark melody hammered into Birdie's skull. She braced herself against the impact, and a shiver skittered down her back. Surely this man was as evil as Carhartan.

"This is not about our arrangement. I hunt a fugitive." Carhartan nodded at Amos. "He has stolen something of importance, and my master wants it back."

"That is none of my—"

"I will take him and his weapons. The rest of the slaves are yours."

Rhudashka's eyes glittered. "And what of the tribute?"

"Forfeited."

Rhudashka turned to Fjordair and issued an abrupt command that sent him scurrying off across the beach. A moment later, Fjordair returned, bearing a long, cloth-bound bundle. He set it on the ground before Carhartan who knelt and undid the cloth—Amos's cloak—revealing the gold hilt and blue-white blade of Artair's sword.

"Release the prisoner and bring him to me," Carhartan said. He pulled Amos's dirk out of the bundle, wrapped the cloak back around Artair's sword, and then stuck both weapons through his belt.

Fjordair unlocked Amos's manacles from the running chain, and two Khelari dragged him forward and forced him to kneel in the sand.

Fear gripped Birdie. She glanced over at Ky and read the same terrible dread in his eyes. This—whatever Carhartan was doing here—would not end well. She struggled, trying to break free, but Hendryk tightened his grasp.

Amos glared up at Carhartan through hooded eyes. "I should have killed ye, Oran."

"You tried, remember?" Carhartan ran a gauntleted hand along the cloth-covered pommel of Artair's sword. "It would be fitting, would it not, to slay you with the Songkeeper's sword? You failed Artair and he was slain. Now his sword has been taken because you failed again. Were I to take this sword and drive it into your heart, it would be justice. Artair would be *avenged*."

Amos's ruddy face faded to a sickly gray, and his voice was quiet. "Ye know as well as I that it would not suffer yer touch."

"Then I suppose this will have to suffice." Carhartan pulled Amos's bronze capped dirk from his belt and spun it in the air, catching it by the hilt. "Even more fitting, don't you think, Hawkness?" He grabbed a handful of Amos's hair and yanked his head back, exposing his throat.

Birdie jerked against Hendryk's restraining grip, but he only squeezed her arms tighter. *Help us!* She wanted to scream the word, but all she could manage was a muffled grunt through the gag. She wasn't even sure who she was speaking to, or who she begged for help, but the Song sprang to life in her heart.

Energy raced through her. She smashed her heel into Hendryk's knee and wrenched free. With her shoulder, she tore the gag from her mouth, and the Song poured from her lips like a river of blazing fire.

Carhartan froze at the first note, and the dirk trembled in his hand. Lord Rhudashka's bloated face darkened in wrath. Loud and sweet and clear, the notes rose sparkling to the sky and then flashed down like diamond-tipped arrows toward her foes.

A wild, ringing bark cut through the melody. A scuffle broke out behind her, then cursing, and the frenzied baying of the hound.

"Lass, watch out!"

Birdie spun around. The hound streaked toward her, dragging a chain from its bristling iron collar. It coiled for the spring.

"A Waltham!"

With a screech, George sprang into the air and landed atop the hound's head, a whirlwind of ripping claws and flashing teeth. The hound growled and flipped over, and George vanished beneath the beast's furious attack. For a moment, Birdie could hear nothing more than the barrage of yowling, screeching, tearing, and biting.

Then the hound picked itself up, a torn bundle of red-soaked yellow in its mouth, flicked its massive head to the side, and flung the broken cat across the sand.

"No!" Birdie broke free from the shocked silence that had gripped her, dropped to the ground, and managed to work her legs through her arms so that her bound hands were before her. She struggled to her knees. "George!"

Blood dripping from its fangs, the hound twisted its hideous head around to stare at her. A growl rumbled in the depths of its cavernous maw. The beast took a step forward, then the dirk blossomed in its throat and the growl turned to a gurgling whimper.

The hound flopped down, dead.

Birdie looked up from the beast lying before her to Carhartan standing with his arm extended from throwing the dirk. She struggled to reconcile the rapid events of the last minute—George, her betrayer, leaping between her and death, and Carhartan, her captor, rescuing her.

Carhartan stalked over to retrieve the weapon. "My master doesn't want you killed, Songkeeper. You're far more useful alive."

An ear piercing screech came from somewhere high above. Then, like a bolt of lightning out of the deep blue, Gundhrold dropped out of the sky.

The griffin landed on the beach in front of Birdie, sand swirling around him with the force of his wings. A wild roar burst from his throat. Pirates and soldiers alike staggered back. Then his feathered wings closed about Birdie, sweeping her up onto his back, and he launched into the air.

31

"No!" Birdie beat her bound fists against Gundhrold's side, watching Amos and Ky and the Khelari dwindle below. "Take me back. I can't leave them!"

The griffin shuddered. The stroke of his wings faltered, and he dropped. Wind rushed past Birdie's head and her stomach threatened to rise, then the griffin caught himself and swooped down to the top of a rock-crowned hill behind the village, overlooking the beach. She scrambled off his back, but he leapt in her path before she could go anywhere.

"You must stay here, little Songkeeper. My wings can no longer bear even you for long, or I would fly you to—"

"What are you doing here? How did you find us?"

"I followed your trail from the forest. The Song summoned me. You must promise to stay here. I will return to help the others."

"I can't. I have to help—"

"If you wish to help your friends, you must sing, little Songkeeper." Gundhrold leapt into the air and flew back toward the beach with ragged strokes. "Sing!"

Bound hands clasped before her, Birdie stumbled to the crest of the hill. Confusion reigned on the beach. The griffin attacked, darting overhead, pouncing on both Langorian and Khelari, a whirlwind of death that knew no bounds. Gundhrold's arrival had bought Amos a few minutes at least—the prisoners were forgotten as Carhartan and Rhudashka scrambled to organize their men.

But she couldn't just sit here and watch. She had to do something. Her friends were in danger. She would not—no, *could* not—abandon them.

Sing, Songkeeper.

The words, a distant echo of the melody, blazed through her mind. Everything within her burned to rush down to the beach, weaponless if need be, and fight with every last ounce of her strength. But perhaps that was not what she was meant to do. The memory of the River Adayn crossing pricked her mind. And so she stood on the crest of the hill above the battle and sang.

Even now, the strength of the Song took her by surprise. It washed over her, warm and comforting, folding her in a loving embrace, until even the horror and chaos of the battle raging below faded. Brilliant light swept across her vision. Her wrists burned. She glanced down at the rope chaffing her skin. It was on fire? No, not burning. Glowing, a deep intense red like embers. Then the rope snapped and fell away.

She was free.

Birdie gasped, and the Song stopped as suddenly as a torch extinguished in a pool of water. Below, the chains fell from the captive Waveryders bound between the two trees, and Amos and Ky stood, free from their restraints. The captives stared at their hands in dumbfounded amazement. A few fled over the dunes or toward the village.

But Amos clutched a length of chain in his hand, and his shout rang out over the beach, carrying up the hill to Birdie. "Stand! Stand an' fight. Use the chains. Drive these cursed seaswoggling villains off our land an' out o' our seas."

The Waveryders stirred as if awakened from a dream, bent down, and grasped their broken manacles. Then Amos shouted the attack, and the captives charged toward the pirates and the Khelari.

The clamor of battle fell upon Birdie's ears as she raced down the slope toward the beach. She had sung. Now she was going to fight.

• • •

Amos swung the broken manacles around his head, batting aside the ineffectual sword strokes of a bumbling pirate. The fools had been drinking ever since capturing the village during the wee watches of the night. It was a wonder half of them could stand, let alone see straight enough to fight. And a mercy for the Waveryders. Chains left much to be desired as weapons.

His chain wrapped around the pirate's neck, and Amos dragged him close, delivered a thunderous left hook to the pirate's chin, and shoved him back. He snatched up the fallen pirate's short, heavy sword—a clumsy weapon—and swung back into the fight.

Overall, the battle seemed to progressing decently for their side. As decently as could be expected, leastways. The griffin wreaked havoc among the enemy, sowing confusion and terror wherever he went, like a physical manifestation of death. And the Waveryders fought well, considering.

But they weren't making any headway. The battle dragged on, and it would likely continue until both sides were so beaten and bloodied and battered that they retreated.

Or until the enemy lost one of their leaders . . .

Amos spun around, beating off another attack, and sought Carhartan in the crowd. He spied the dark figure and fought toward him through the press of the battle until it seemed a path opened before his feet, and his enemies fell away on all sides.

He tightened his grip on his weapons.

This time he would not fail.

At scarce five paces away, Carhartan's gaze fell upon him. The Khelari raised his red-tipped sword and beckoned him. "Shall we end this, Hawkness? You and I? It always was you and I, wasn't it?"

In answer, Amos set the chain whirling around his head, building up momentum, while holding the short sword out in front to ward off attacks. He swung the chain and it sparked against Carhartan's blade. He pressed forward with a series of lazy loops and then flicked his wrist, sending the manacle snaking toward Carhartan's helm. At the same time, he cut down at Carhartan's side with the short sword.

Carhartan parried and unleashed a progression of slashes and thrusts that were nigh impossible to block with the chain or clumsy short sword. Amos found himself retreating again and again before the attacks.

The red sword flashed past his guard and left a streaming cut on his cheek. A moment later, it flicked again and stung the inside of his forearm.

Amos swung high, as if he were going to bring the chain down on Carhartan's helmet. At the last moment, he altered course and whipped it around from the side. The manacle slammed into the side of Carhartan's helmet just above the ear. Carhartan staggered backward.

The thrill of victory beat a triumphant pulse in Amos's veins. He pressed forward, following the attack with a downward cut of the short sword.

But Carhartan darted into the stroke, and the short sword glanced off his armor. With a lightning backstroke, he batted the sword away. It tore free of Amos's grip. He stood with a hand full of air before his enemy, too close to use the chain. His hand flew to his belt, instinctively reaching for the hilt of his dirk.

But his sheath was empty.

Carhartan seized him by the shoulders and pulled him close—a brotherly hug. "Looking for this?"

A burning brand stabbed his side, tearing into his flesh. Carhartan released him, and he staggered back, tripping over his feet to the ground. He groped at the wound. Warm blood coated his fingers, and his hand settled around the hawk's head pommel of his own dirk.

Carhartan loomed over him, and the tip of the crimson sword dug into his throat. "I've waited almost thirty years for this, Hawkness. Thirty years a failure. Now it's your turn. And with you out of the way, there will be no one to stop me from bringing the Songkeeper and the sword to the Takhran."

Amos's gaze dropped to the gold hilt of Artair's sword stuck through Carhartan's belt. Despair swept over him. Always he failed. Every important task he had ever undertaken ended in disaster— first Artair, then the sword, and even his misguided attempt to keep Birdie from becoming the Songkeeper.

He had failed. He deserved to die and face Emhran's judgment.

A small hand reached around Carhartan and seized Artair's sword. Blue light flashed, and the blade leapt from Carhartan's belt and stabbed toward the unprotected patch visible beneath the Khelari's arm.

A quiet voice, like a whisper of music, spoke beside Carhartan. "You're wrong."

Ky whirled his sling around his head, loosing stone after stone into the mass of pirates as rapidly as he could. A slingstone bounced off a pirate's forehead, unleashing a fountain of blood. The pirate scrubbed at his face, screamed something Ky was grateful he couldn't understand, and charged. A second slingstone laid him flat in his tracks.

Shuffling steps approached from behind. Out of the corner of his eye, Ky caught a glimpse of a bright yellow tunic and a dark snarling face. He flicked his wrist, releasing a stone, and the pirate crumpled. Through the gap in the crowd left by the fallen pirate, he saw a flash of light-colored hair and black armor.

Hendryk.

The blood ran hot in his ears, and he charged through the battle, automatically reloading his sling. He had a score to settle.

Hendryk battled an old Waveryder, attacking with forceful swings that sent the man stumbling backward on quivering legs. But there was no mercy, no sympathy, in Hendryk's eyes. As Ky neared, Hendryk sliced through the old man's spear and stabbed him in the gut.

Ky stalled mid stride.

The Waveryder collapsed with a moan that Ky heard over the

clamor of the battle. For a moment he seemed to be standing again in the market place with Dizzier lying on the cobblestones at Hendryk's feet, life seeping from the wound in his side.

An axe swished past Ky's face, and he jerked back to the present. Anger simmered in his chest. He slung a stone at Hendryk. It missed, but served its purpose nonetheless, catching Hendryk's attention. He dropped another stone into the pouch and threw himself on the dark soldier, wielding his loaded sling like a hammer. Pounding . . . pounding . . . pounding.

Blood streamed down Hendryk's face, but Ky didn't let up. The soldier would be hampered by his nearness—one thing he recalled from battling Cade in the Ring. A sword was only an advantage if you had room to use it. But somehow, Hendryk managed to tuck his elbow back and bring his sword edge up to slice at Ky's side.

He threw himself back just in time.

Catching himself from a stumble, he tried to gather his wits and his strategy, but Hendryk advanced toward him, striking faster and faster, forcing him to dodge. And Ky knew he couldn't evade forever.

If he couldn't just disappear for a moment . . . regain the advantage of surprise and distance. Becoming invisible, that was the answer!

Ky lunged to the side and thwacked Hendryk's helmet with his loaded sling. Then he threw himself flat past the soldier, rolled, and came up on his feet behind a pirate battling a Waveryder. He turned heel and ran, disappearing into the chaos.

He could still see Hendryk, but from the way the dark soldier peered about him, it was clear Ky's ruse had worked. Guided by instincts gained through a life on the streets, he darted from cover to cover, the pattern playing through his mind: *forward two steps, swing left, back up one.*

He crept up behind Hendryk and tapped him on the shoulder. Hendryk spun around.

Thwack.

The sling hit Hendryk full in the nose. Blood gushed over his face, and water streamed from his eyes. Ky flung all his weight at the man, toppling him to the ground. He yanked the sword from Hendryk's hand, and kneeling on his chest, shoved the tip of the sword at his throat.

"You killed my brother. I told you I'd kill you for it."

A crooked grin spread across Hendryk's face, and his head rolled back as he uttered a derisive laugh. The sound turned Ky's blood to frost.

"I didn't kill him. He isn't dead."

Birdie pressed the tip of Artair's sword into Carhartan's side. The hilt turned to ice in her grip, and her hand seized involuntarily at the cold. The burning sensation spread up her arm and into her shoulder, but like a plunge into a cold spring on a hot summer day, it brought new life to her weary limbs.

"You're wrong," she repeated. "*I* will stop you."

At the first prick of her sword, Carhartan had jerked away from Amos. His sword now hovered over Amos's neck rather than resting with the tip piercing the peddler's skin, but it was still far too close for Birdie's comfort.

"Release him," she said. "And you can go free, unharmed."

Carhartan chuckled. "You are a fool, little Songkeeper. One little thrust is all it takes, and he will choke on his own blood. Whereas if you are too slow . . . if I act first . . . would you risk his life by trying to kill me before I slay him? Do you think I don't know you, little one? You are incapable of such a deed. You could not harm me if your life depended on it."

Birdie set her jaw. "No, I don't think you know me."

She had fought and killed in the Underground, and she would do it again if she had to. If it would save Amos. More troubling though, was Carhartan's assertion that she couldn't stop him before he cut Amos's throat. Who was to say that even if she did stab Carhartan, he wouldn't still be able to harm Amos?

Carhartan tensed.

"Wait!" Birdie licked her dry lips. "Don't do this. Let Amos go . . . I'll . . . I'll come with you." She nearly choked on the words. What was she saying? She *couldn't* go with him. Yet looking down at the peddler sprawled helpless before Carhartan, she knew that she could, and she must.

"Lass, don't even think it!" Amos groaned. "Ye can't. I won't permit it."

Carhartan's dark gaze turned upon her, considering her a moment in silence. Then slowly, he pulled the sword away from Amos's throat.

Now, a voice within her cried, and her sword arm shook with the desire of it. *Stab him and be done with it*. She could be safe. No longer hunted. Free. In the whispered voice, she heard echoed the poisonous strains of the dark melody.

And in that moment, her decision was made.

She lowered Artair's sword.

A smile spread across Carhartan's face, and he drew his arm back to thrust at Amos.

Before his action had even fully registered in her brain, Birdie's sword arm was moving. She stabbed straight up into the gap beneath Carhartan's arm where the two halves of his breastplate came together. The sword pierced flesh—a sickening feeling—and Carhartan's scream filled her ears. He staggered back and collapsed in a clatter of armor.

Birdie trembled, watching the red drops congeal on the blue-white blade, then she dropped the sword and flung herself beside Amos. Blood soaked his shirt around the dirk protruding from his side. "Amos? Are you all right? Oh please, please, tell me you're all right."

"Aye, lass. Just grand," he said, but his voice sounded feeble. "Help me up, would ye?"

She bent over him and tried to get her hands under his arms, but someone grabbed her from behind and dragged her backward.

"Birdie!" Amos clutched at her, but he was too far away.

The edge of a blade stung her throat, and Carhartan's voice hissed in her ear. "We made a bargain, little Songkeeper. Now let's forget about Hawkness, because you and I are going to take that sword back to the Takhran. And don't even think about trying to escape, or I will slit your throat."

Sing, little Songkeeper.

Without pausing to think, she opened her mouth, and the first notes poured out. Then Carhartan's hand settled around her throat, choking her, and the melody died. He spun her around to face him, and she quailed at the hatred in his eyes.

And suddenly she knew. Carhartan *couldn't* kill her, or he would have done it long before. He'd said it himself earlier. The Takhran wanted her alive, and she could only imagine the sort of horrible punishment he would inflict on the one who deprived him of his prize. Carhartan didn't dare harm her.

A muffled groan drew her attention to the side where Amos lay. The peddler was struggling to rise, but Carhartan, so intent on her, didn't appear to have noticed.

If she could just stall him long enough, perhaps Amos would be able to do something.

Carhartan's fingers dug into her throat. She tried to speak, and his grip loosened just enough that she could choke out a few words.

"You and I . . . both know . . . you . . . can't . . . kill me," she gasped.

His scowl deepened, but he said nothing. His hold relaxed a little more.

"A dead Songkeeper isn't worth anything to the Takhran."

She didn't dare look at Amos now, for fear Carhartan would discern her plan. She could only hope that Amos would see the opportunity and take advantage of it.

"We both know the sword is just an empty threat, so you might as well put it away and then we can sit down and talk it over like reasonable people." She continued talking, scarce knowing what she was saying, just speaking the first words that came into her mind. "Who knows, if you have a good enough argument, I might be convinced to go with you. Or you might be convinced to forget about the whole thing. What's so important about it any—"

His hand constricted about her throat. She could no longer speak . . . could no longer breathe. Gray tinged the edges of her vision. Panic seized her limbs. Carhartan might not be able to kill her, but he could choke her into unconsciousness.

Then Amos's deep brogue spoke beside her. "I swore t' kill ye if ye harmed my lass, Oran."

Something whipped past Birdie's head and struck Carhartan in the neck. Convulsions shook his body, tearing his hands away from her throat. She tumbled to the ground, heaving for breath.

Carhartan toppled at her feet, a look of horror on his face, hands clutched around Amos's dirk in his throat.

Dead.

32

Birdie could scarce believe it. Carhartan lay at her feet, lifeless and empty. The noise of the battle faded, and she sat in stunned silence, massaging her aching throat. For so long, she had been running. Hunted. Afraid. Now with the passing of Carhartan, she felt free.

A breath of wind trickled toward her, lifting the hair from her sticky forehead. She flung her head back and closed her eyes, reveling in peace in the midst of ruin.

"Lass? Are ye all right?" Amos dropped beside her and gathered her into his arms. She laid her head on his chest, content to simply be held. "Oh lass, I'm so sorry. Sorry for denyin' ye were the Songkeeper, for lyin' t' ye, for everythin'. Can ye ever forgive me?"

Hearing those words from Amos warmed her through and through. Tears welled in her eyes and rolled down her cheeks. She tried to speak, but no sound came out.

"Hush, lass, don't try t' speak. Everythin' will be all right now. Just wait . . . wait an' . . . see . . ." Amos's voice slurred and his body went limp, sinking back to the ground.

"Amos!" The word came out as a gasping croak. Birdie started to her knees beside the peddler and reached out to touch him, then froze at the sight of blood covering her arm where it had rested against Amos's side.

The peddler moaned and his eyelids fluttered.

She fought against the panic constricting her throat. She had to think, *do* something, anything! If she could just stop the bleeding . . .

Her roving gaze caught on Amos's cloak laying where she had dropped it when she drew Artair's sword. Skirting Carhartan's corpse, she snatched up the cloak and brought it back to Amos. She pressed it to the wound in his side and held it in place, but didn't know what to do after that. Amos needed better help than she could offer.

In the Underground, the Song had healed the injured runners. Perhaps it could do the same for Amos. But try as she might, she could not coax a single note from her throat, and the melody itself was strangely distant.

A tear slipped down her cheek as she turned to survey the battlefield. All around her, the cries of the wounded and dying rose to the sky. During the confrontation with Carhartan, the battle had drifted shoreward of them, leaving them in between the main fight and the sea. As she watched, the pirates retreated, streaming back toward their ship, past her and Amos. She hunched over the peddler's still form and hoped she would go unnoticed.

But scarce a dozen pirates had raced by before a hand gripped her shoulder and flung her onto her back in the sand. She looked up into Fjordair's blade-like visage. He fingered the hilt of one of the many daggers in his belt, then looked over his shoulder and reeled off a long sentence in Langorian.

Lord Rhudashka lumbered past Fjordair, his red robe shimmering as if covered in blood. His bulbous eyes narrowed at the sight of her. "The little Songkeeper . . ." He spoke the tongue of Leira deliberately, as if each word was completely unrelated and uncomfortable on his tongue. "Bring her."

Birdie opened her mouth to cry for help, but could only manage a little croaking yelp, like the meow of a kitten. Fjordair pounced, stifling her cries, stuffed a kerchief in her mouth, and tied it behind her head. With the fury of despair, she kicked and hit, trying to fend him off, but he outweighed her by far too much. In a few moments, she found herself bound hand and foot yet again.

Tears streamed down Birdie's face. She searched the beach for Ky, the griffin, anyone who might help. But the griffin was locked in battle with four Khelari, and she saw no sign of Ky. She was captured . . . again . . . and there was no one to save her.

But this time, Amos needed her. Without aid, he would bleed to death.

She crawled toward him and gripped his hand in both of hers, silently begging him to wake and be well. Then Fjordair yanked her up and dragged her after the retreating pirates to the longboats beached on the shore.

Hendryk's words sank into Ky's brain like one of his slingstones. He knelt on the man's chest, keeping the dark soldier from rising with the tip of his sword. "What do you mean he isn't dead?" He tightened his grip on the weapon. "What happened to him?"

"Same thing that happens to all criminals arrested by the Khelari. Sent to a slave camp to be employed in good honest labor advancing the Takhran's might." Hendryk slowly raised his hands. "And if you kill me, you'll never find out where."

If Dizzier was truly alive, then Ky was glad. Glad that Dizzier's life had not been sacrificed for his, and yet Dizzier *had* fought to save him. But if Hendryk told the truth, then Dizzier was a slave, and wasn't slavery a fate worse than death?

"Where is he?"

The soldier shook his head. "First give me your word that you won't harm me. Your brother's not dead—there's no reason to kill me."

A bitter taste flooded Ky's mouth. He wouldn't slay anyone in cold blood, yet here he sat listening to a man bargain for his life. This was something Cade might do—maybe even Dizzier—but not Ky. This wasn't who he was. He was sick of the charade.

He eyed the sword with distaste and stood, removing his weight from Hendryk's chest. "Tell me what I need to know."

Hendryk stared at him in silence, and then scrambled to his feet. He cast a fleeting glance over his shoulder as if he were going to run for it.

Ky's sling dangled from his sword hand, a stone already in the pouch. He slipped his fingers in between the strands, ready to drop the sword—if necessary—and send a stone after the dark soldier. He might not murder a man in cold blood, but a man reneging on a deal for information? That fellow might just be better off after receiving one of his slingstones.

But Hendryk didn't run. He leaned in until his shoulder brushed Ky's and spoke in a whisper. "Dacheren. He's in Dacheren."

The name was unfamiliar. "What's—"

But Hendryk was already gone, dashing away across the battlefield, leaving his sword in Ky's hand. Ky fingered his sling and considered sending a shot or two flying after Hendryk, just to teach him a lesson.

Better not to waste the stones. Though the battle did seem to be drawing to a close, and the beach was littered with the dead and dying. The flying beast—Ky had never before seen the like, half bird and half lion—had made short work of the pirates, and the rest were retreating past Ky to their longboats pursued by a horde of victorious Waveryders.

He fell into line with the others and scanned the beach for Birdie and Amos and the sword. So far his plan to drag the cursed weapon all over Leira in the hopes of drawing the black soldiers after him seemed to be working. Almost working *too* well.

Scores of Waveryders surrounded the pirates clustered around the longboats, attacking them with fist and chain as they tried to embark. In the midst of the confusion, a small figure tore away from the pirates.

Dark hair, a ragged blue dress—Ky's heart thumped—it was Birdie.

A pirate seized her by the waist, dragged her back to the longboat, and shoved her aboard. In another moment, the longboat would set out for the pirates' ship, and once it left land, there wouldn't be anything he could do to save her.

He had to act fast.

If he was going to act at all.

Look out for yourself.

Even as the hated words whispered in the back of his mind, Ky despised himself for thinking them. He could no more stand by while Birdie was captured than he could have ignored Meli's plight on her first apple-bobbing run.

If there was one good thing he'd learned from Dizzier, it was that at the worst times, the best plan was often no plan. And Ky excelled at coming up with no plan.

Dozens of pirates grasped the sides of the longboat, hauling it across the shore toward the sea, beyond the reach of their pursuers. Ky shouted, drawing their attention. Ignoring the cold dread in the pit of his stomach, he dashed toward the longboat with Hendryk's sword in his left hand and the familiar *whirr-whirring* and *thrum-thrumming* of his sling filling his ears.

The snap of the leather and the crack of the stones steadied him as the pirates closed in from all sides until they were so near that the sling was useless. But he could hear the echo of its humming even as a blow knocked the sword from his grip, and a fist hammered his back, and the edge of a knife stung his throat, bringing his charge to a halt.

Into the longboat he tumbled with his hands bound behind his back, landing with an aching thud at the feet of the crimson-clad pirate lord.

33

His lassie was gone. The thought seeped into Amos's mind and consumed him, like the keening wail of the night moths. Taken by the pirates along with the lad, Ky, while he lay unconscious in the sand.

A failure to the end.

He slumped on the shore amidst the ashes of the Waveryder vessels with the waves hissing toward his toes, Artair's sword bundled in his lap, his feathered cap resting on his knee. With hesitant hands, he fingered the heavy bandages on his side as he watched the Langorian ship scudding away, bearing his lass far from him, and there was naught he could do to stop it.

The ache of his wound paled in comparison to the pain of that knowledge.

Heavy footsteps padded toward him, then Gundhrold sat at his side. The griffin looked to have had a hard time of it during the fight. Numerous gashes along his sides leaked blood, matting his tawny fur and revealing the gaunt frame of a beast past his prime. One wing was broken and hung cockeyed from his back.

Only such an injury, Amos suspected, could keep the griffin land-bound while the Songkeeper was taken into captivity.

Gundhrold shaded his eyes with an unharmed wing tip. "The pirates follow a southern course. It appears they may be returning to Langoria."

To Amos's eyes, the pirate ship had already dwindled to a smudge on the horizon. "*May be* doesn't tell us much, now does it?"

A growl rumbled in the beast's throat. "What do you intend to do, *Hawkness*? Sit here contemplating your many failures—"

"Don't lecture me, beastie. I've sworn t' protect the wee lass, an' I intend t' do just that."

"How?"

That was the question that haunted Amos—had been haunting him ever since he caught sight of the crimson and gold ship sailing away and heard from the Waveryders that his lass and the lad had been seen aboard one of the longboats. He permitted his gaze to wander across the battle-scarred beach and the pockets of Waveryders picking their way through the bodies sprawled in the sand, tending to the wounded . . . and the dead.

"Ye say the pirates are headed south, back to their homeland?" He coughed to clear his throat and put as much force into the words as he could contrive. "Then we go south as well—overland—through the desert of Vituain. Cut them off before they reach Langoria. Rescue Birdie."

The griffin nodded. "Indeed, we must."

A jaunt through the desert was no small undertaking, yet the griffin accepted it without argument. Amos might just grow to tolerate the beast.

"And yet," Gundhrold met his gaze, "we cannot hope to accomplish such a task on our own, Hawkness. We must seek aid."

Should have boggswoggling known there would be *something*. "Who would help us?"

"The resistance is strong in the south. There are many among the desert dwellers—especially the Saari—who would be glad to fight for the Songkeeper and have the Songkeeper and Hawkness fight for them in turn."

Resistance fighters . . . like Nisus and Jirkar.

Amos stood, ignoring the flare of pain, and jerked his cap on his head. "Right. It's settled. We'll seek the boggswoggled fools and charm them into helping us rescue Birdie."

"Best leave the charming up to me. Hawkness was never renowned for the gentleness of his tongue." With a stiff nod, the griffin padded up the beach.

Charming or not, Amos had a mission now, and he would do whatever was necessary to accomplish it, whether that meant working with the curmudgeonly old griffin or storming the walls of Serrin Vroi. Anything to bring his wee lass back.

He started to follow the griffin and then stopped, glancing from Artair's sword in his hand to the fathomless depths of the Great Sea.

The muscles along his jaw tightened.

Then he spun on his heels and hurried across the beach to overtake the griffin, sliding the sword into his belt as he went. He wrapped his hand around the hilt. Cold seeped into his fingers through the cloth, spreading into his hand and up his arm until it settled in his chest.

Vibrating.

Amos halted, stock still, head cocked to listen. He could have sworn that he heard *something*, deep in the sword's vibrations. A tremulous note, the beginnings of a whisper.

Of a melody.

He released the sword and clutched his hand to his chest, allowing the warmth of his beating heart to drive the chill from his skin. Back over his shoulder he glanced, to the sea and the ship that had taken his lass away, and he whispered a promise.

The hatch clanged shut, leaving Birdie in the pitch black of the hold. Manacles scraped her wrists, chafing the rope burns she'd received while a prisoner of the Khelari. The chains attached to the deck, allowing her only a few feet of crawl room, but she was free of the gag.

Movement rustled to her right.

"Ky?" Her voice was still a hoarse whisper.

Groping fingers brushed against her arm. "Shh, listen."

In the darkness beyond them, chains clinked, echoing hollowly through the hold, and shuffling feet scraped the floor. A hacking cough. Muttered voices. Stifled weeping.

Her breath caught in her throat, and Ky's grim voice confirmed her fears.

"We're not the only ones here."

She slid back until her shoulders rested against the frame of the ship, sitting side by side with Ky, swaying with the motion of the sea, weary with despair.

The creaking of the wooden timbers, the hum of the rigging far overhead, and the groan of the masts blended and formed a melody. Deep below, the ocean depths sang in answer, and the Song coursed through Birdie's veins.

Throbbing. Vast. Unfathomed.

Her eyes slipped shut, and a different hum filled her ears. Shriller, colder, more metallic. It beckoned to her and she followed it in her mind, unraveling the tangled strand of melody. Bright blue light flashed across her vision, and she bolted upright, gasping.

Her ears rang with the rumble of a familiar voice.

"Don't worry, lass. We're comin' for ye."

ACKNOWLEDGMENTS

Writing a fantasy novel is an epic adventure in and of itself, and I've had enough encouragement, support, and assistance along every step of the journey to make any character jealous! So a *special* thank you goes to my incredible parents who suffered through the meandering first drafts and offered invaluable advice; my siblings who vowed not to read the book until it was published—giving me extra incentive to see it completed; writing mentors Jill Williamson and Stephanie Morrill who both helped chip this novel out of the rock; and my incredible agent, Amanda Luedeke, for brainstorming ideas, offering brilliant suggestions, and answering every single one of my gazillion questions!

I also want to thank the gracious folks who stopped after my accident this summer and rescued my laptop (and the latest version of *Orphan's Song*) from the flames; John W. Otte who supplied the extra bit of encouragement I needed to enter my first pitching session with confidence; and my writing conference buddies, Emileigh Latham and Claire Talbott, who are a big part of my inspiration for writing! And thanks to you, dear reader, for picking this book off the shelf. I hoped you enjoyed reading it as much as I enjoyed writing it!

ABOUT THE AUTHOR

Gillian Bronte Adams is a sword-wielding, horse-riding, coffee-loving author from the great state of Texas. During the day she manages the equine program at a Christian youth camp, but at night, she kicks off her boots and spurs and transforms into a novelist. Her love of epic stories and a desire to present truth in a new way drew her to the realm of fantasy.

Visit her web site: www.GillianBronteAdams.com

 Facebook: GillianBronteAdams

 Twitter: @theSongkeeper

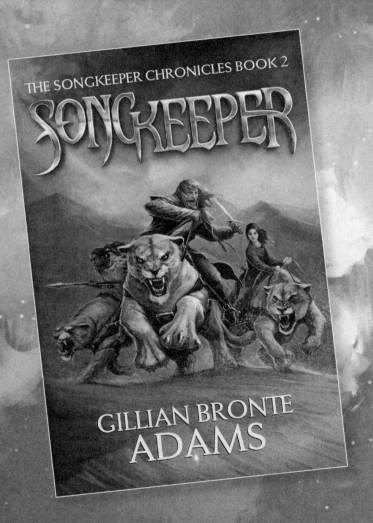